P9-APL-675

GRANT MICHAELS —
EITHER YOU WERE HIS FRIEND
OR YOU WERE DEAD

It started as a tiny red dot, a flicker in the cavity of his chest that spread steadily as he eyed the snickering faces in the crowd. It grew like a flash fire eating away at old ragweed and dead grass, yet this flame was fueled by human emotion.

It grew within him to immense proportions, until the raging flames burned through his chest and licked at his mind. Then suddenly the flame seized control of the mechanism in him that operated his arms and legs, as the little boy in charge bailed out. The raging fire within was now in command. . . .

Other Leisure books by Sal Conte:

CHILD'S PLAY

THE POWER

SAL CONTE

LEISURE BOOKS ❧ NEW YORK CITY

For Dad, who nurtured my mind,
and engendered my spirit.

A LEISURE BOOK

February 1989

Published by

Dorchester Publishing Co., Inc.
276 Fifth Avenue
New York, NY 10001

Copyright © 1989 by Sal Conte

All rights reserved. No part of this book may be reproduced or
transmitted in any form or by any electronic or mechanical
means, including photocopying, recording, or by any
information storage and retrieval system, without the written
permission of the Publisher, except where permitted by law.

Printed in the United States of America

BOOK
ONE

CHAPTER
1

It wasn't the dogs he hated most. It was the town—a shambling relic of a town, left over from some forgotten past.

Its streets were heaped with red clay that had been cracked dry from the drought and trampled to dust. The sidewalks were wooden planks, stretched out like dead men before the doddering shops that lined the street.

It wasn't the place for a man who had come so far, and he resented his presence there.

He stepped from the doorway of the Tambien Hotel onto the wooden sidewalk. He was wearing a wide-brimmed straw hat over dark hair, the hat having been purchased several days earlier to shield his eyes and head from the baking sun.

A thick hand now moved to the brim, pulling the hat down until his eyes were nearly covered, and he had to raise his head to see where he was going.

He began walking. Heels from shiny black boots echoed from the wooden sidewalk, and the dogs started to bark.

Rafael hated dogs. The dogs of this town—Tambien, Mexico—he hated most. They called attention to his presence. When unfamiliar footsteps rapped upon the wooden sidewalk, the dogs, once quiet in their masters' yards or lying beneath cars to escape the heat, began to bark. Rafael couldn't make a move in the town without the dogs marking it.

Purposefully he walked to the town saloon at the end of the street, feeling the town's eyes boring into him, while the dogs continued their incessant yapping. As he entered, a wave of hot air nearly chased him back outside. The saloon wasn't air-conditioned, and the old wooden structure held onto the heat. Already he could feel his shirt sticking to his back.

The large room was empty, as it always was during the day, and Rafael took a seat at the table to the far left, facing the door.

He also hated the saloon, which sold watered down tequila that he suspected wasn't tequila at all but homemade corn whiskey.

"Tequila again today, señor?" the mustachioed saloon keeper said. He had dashed from behind the bar and now hovered over Rafael like a beggar.

The town, the dogs, the saloon, the saloon keeper—Rafael hated them all. They churned up memories of small towns and migrant farm workers, of families with too many sisters and brothers, of many hours in the groves picking fruit until his fingers cramped into the grip of an orange or a mango. Things he thought he had forgotten.

The saloon keeper brought him a clean glass and a bottle, then scurried away.

Today will be the day, Rafael thought. If he doesn't come today he is not coming. He told himself that yesterday and the day before, yet each day he returned to the saloon. This was the seventh day, and Rafael had promised himself there would not be an eighth. Then the dogs began to bark.

When the saloon keeper looked up, Rafael heard the footsteps on the wooden sidewalk and knew his wait was over.

A second later the man walked in. An American man of Spanish descent, he was short and stocky, with thinning brown hair and tiny beads of moisture flecked over his piglike features. He wore a lightweight American suit, the kind that could be put in

3

the washer and hung out to dry. With a scowl he surveyed the room, then quickly moved to join Rafael.

"Is this seat taken?" he asked in Spanish. It was Castilian Spanish, the kind taught in American schools.

Rafael ignored the question, pouring a shot of tequila and salting the back of his hand.

"Anyone sitting here, señor?"

"This seat is for my friend, José," Rafael answered.

The scowl on the man's face vanished, replaced by an ear to ear grin. He sat down with a heavy plop.

"I'm Sanchez," he said. "Your contact."

"What kept you so long?"

"A precaution. We had to make sure you were not followed or being watched."

"And am I clear?" Rafael snapped.

Sanchez looked over his shoulder at the saloon keeper, who eyed them from behind the bar. "Yes."

Rafael stood. "You insult my professionalism," he charged, now speaking in English. "Your man has watched me every day for seven days. Did you think I would not know he was working with you?" Accusing eyes penetrated the saloon keeper. "You are the ones who are clumsy. I can't afford that. Good day, sir."

"Wait!" Sanchez said before Rafael could take a step. "We were deliberately clumsy, to see if you were truly Rafael. We knew the real Rafael would notice such things. Excuse our feeble test, but while your reputation precedes you, your face is not known by many."

Rafael stood in place.

"Please try to understand our position, señor. The delicate nature of our mission demands an extreme amount of caution."

Still Rafael did not move.

Sanchez went on. "To be quite honest with you, if you do not join in our mission, we will probably abandon the project. You are the only one, we believe, who can carry it out."

Rafael sat.

"Thank you," Sanchez said.

"It is the unique nature of your project that intrigues me," Rafael went on in Spanish. "It could quite possibly be the greatest terrorist victory in the history of the world." He savored each word as he spoke it.

"Then you will join us?"

Rafael's pale blue eyes clouded with anger. "I am here, aren't I?"

"Yes."

Rafael threw down a shot of tequila and sucked the salt. "How will I get into the United States?"

"A chartered cargo plane."

They sat for the next hour, conversing in Spanish and mapping out a plan of action.

Finally Rafael stood, handing Sanchez a slip of paper. "You will deposit fifty thousand American dollars in the Swiss bank account with this number. When I hear that the money is there I will be ready to leave."

Sanchez took the slip of paper, and Rafael walked from the saloon. The dogs were barking.

Carefully Sanchez read the numbers from the paper, committing them to memory. Then placing the paper in an ashtray, he lit a flame to it, watching it change to ashes. He then turned and faced the saloon keeper who smiled and turned thumbs up. Sanchez nodded.

"The thing is set in motion," he said. "From here there is no turning back."

CHAPTER 2

The nose of the Bird Dog lifted gently into the breeze, as the small plane caught the up-draft on the windward side of the mountains.

Charlie Sachs understood the winds and knew that if he continued paralleling the ridges this way, not only would he save fuel, but he'd also be in Mexico sooner than expected.

"The sooner there, the sooner back," he mumbled as he began counting his percentage of $100,000.

He checked his altitude, 8000 feet MSL, and held steady. The trip was as smooth as a baby's ass, Charlie thought, and that's the way he meant to keep it.

The weather was good, and his thoughts began to wander as he glanced down at a small patch of clouds that appeared as angel cushions, resting in the heavens.

He was a seasoned pilot, logging over 4000 miles since 1966, the year he began flying. Flying was now second nature to him, and often he found his mind drifting to other things, as it did today.

He'd learned to fly in the air force, joining at 17, just out of high school. During his tour in Nam he'd flown over 20 missions, all in Bird Dogs for Uncle Sam.

God, he loved the small cargo craft. So when the opportunity to purchase one came three years ago, quite naturally he jumped at the chance.

Of course Doris balked at the idea of his becoming a charter pilot. He knew she would. The plane was expensive and needed work, and there was no real guarantee that once they poured in their life savings, the plane would pay for itself. Then there was the safety factor. Doris feared flying, and the thought of Charlie going up everyday unnerved her.

"She was right, damn her!" Charlie mumbled out loud, as he banked the plane sharply to the right. He smiled, thinking of how often she'd been right about things. She was just too reasonable. "Damn her!" he repeated.

The charter business had been a failure. Last year they both had to take jobs, just to support the Bird Dog. Doris knew how he loved the plane, and although she thought they'd be better off without it, she bit her tongue.

He smiled again as thoughts of his pretty lady began to form. He pictured how she looked when he left her that morning. Lying naked in bed, her pale body was still smooth and firm, not ravaged by time, her dark hair tusseled on the pillow.

She was a good woman. The best!

He'd realized this before, but when he thought of the sacrifices she had made he realized it even more.

The small plane began its descent.

Several months ago things suddenly broke for them and Charlie still couldn't believe it. Doris was wrong about something.

They met a man who could make them rich. His name was Sanchez, and he said he would pay Charlie $10,000 per drop, just for flying into Mexico and bringing back loads of marijuana.

"It's dangerous," Doris insisted.

"Shit! For ten thousand dollars it ought to be."

"We don't need the money."

"Huh? Come again? This is Charlie-boy you're talking to, babe. Remember? I live with you. I know how you break your ass everyday so I can keep that friggin' plane. It's about time it started paying for itself."

"You shouldn't do it."

She dropped it at that, knowing of course that he had already made up his mind.

The plane now came in for a landing, touching down gently in a narrow field. Charlie was a whiz at maneuvering the craft, able to take off and land almost anywhere. Still, he was a careful flyer. The only real danger he felt was in being caught, and that was unlikely.

A few more of these trips and Sanchez could find himself a new boy. He had told Doris this and was now repeating it to himself. Five missions in two months, he thought, and $50,000 in less than three. That was nothing to sneeze at. But now that the plane was totally paid for, and they had a tidy nest egg to boot, his thoughts turned to getting out.

Charlie unbuckled his seat belt and peered through the windshield. The familiar clearing was covered with dead grass that Charlie surmised had been the victim of drought. A thicket of trees sprang up several hundred yards to each side of the clearing, and Charlie fully expected to see someone approaching from the right.

He checked his watch and saw he was 13 minutes early. "I've been early before, but someone's always been here. Maybe something's gone wrong."

A twinge of fear rode through his gut, but he laughed it off.

"You're too old to get spooked, Charlie-boy. They're just a little late, that's all. Probably been smokin' too much of that dope themselves." He laughed again and felt some of the tension drain off. Then he settled back for the wait.

Five minutes later he checked his watch again. "He did say Thursday, didn't he?" Slow beads of perspiration now trickled along his forehead. Was it getting warm in the cockpit, or was he beginning to panic? It was warm, of course. I'm not scared, he told himself.

He threw open the cabin door and a spring breeze drifted in. "There, that's better."

When he checked his watch again the 13 minutes had passed, but still no one approached.

Hell! Maybe they *did* get busted!

"Shit!" he groaned. If no one came in five minutes he would get out and survey the area—carefully, of course, and making damn sure he didn't wander too far from the plane. He hadn't gotten this far in life by taking foolish chances, and he wasn't going to start now.

The thought of getting out unsettled him, but he couldn't return without making at least an attempt at getting the dope.

"What do you mean you left? My people

11

*inform me they had a flat tire not ten kilo-
meters from the pickup point."*

"But I didn't see anyone!"

"Did you get out and check?"

"No."

*"And for this you want ten thousand
dollars? You have wasted my time and
money. You have caused me an important
sale. I'm sorry, Mr. Sachs, but this is not
charity. I'm not giving ten thousand dollars
away. I'm afraid your services will no longer
be required."*

That will never do, thought Charlie. I
have to make every attempt at bringing the
marijuana back.

"What do you mean you left?"

*"Shit man, I waited nearly half an hour. I
got out and checked the area, and there was
absolutely, positively no one there! I even
hiked up the road, just to make sure they
didn't have car trouble nearby."*

*"You have done more than was required,
Mr. Sachs. You are truly an asset to me, and
I'm sorry for the inconvenience."*

"That's all right."

*"No, it isn't. As a token of my gratitude I
will pay you for the trip despite your returning empty-handed. After all, it wasn't
your fault."*

"Thank you, Mr. Sanchez."

There, that was better. If he had to come
back without the dope, that was the image
Charlie wanted to project when he returned

to California.

He was thinking just this when someone stepped from the clearing to his right. It was a tall, slender man, wearing jeans and a light blue cotton shirt, with a wide brimmed straw hat atop his head and dark glasses covering his eyes.

He didn't look like the previous ones, all field hands in work clothes. But as he approached, Charlie saw the package he was carrying and climbed out of the plane to give him a hand.

As Charlie neared, the man broke into a wide grin, and Charlie noticed the perfect teeth.

Charlie was almost on top of the man now and realized that the package in the man's hand was a parachute.

"Buenos dias, señor. Mas vale tarde que nunca!" Rafael said, his perfect smile widening.

"Huh? No habla."

"Oh, excuse me. I said better late than never."

Charlie was taken aback by the man's perfect English. "Where's the pot?" he asked, eyeing the stranger cautiously.

"Do not worry. I have it."

"Where?" Charlie insisted. He had stopped and was now standing a few feet before the man. Up close the stranger appeared to be a businessman, neatly dressed and clean shaven. A narc? He was not the type one expected to find in the hills of Mexico.

"Patience, my friend," Rafael replied. He glanced over Charlie's shoulder. "A beautiful plane. An L-19 Bird Dog, is it not?"

"Yes."

"I have been in many single prop planes, but the L-19 is my absolute favorite. She is in wonderful shape. How old is she?"

Charlie smiled, turning to face the plane. She was indeed in great shape. "She's close to twenty years old now," he said, "but she's as chipper as the day she was born." Suddenly he wheeled on the stranger. "Where's the dope?" he snapped.

"In here," Rafael replied, holding up the parachute. "A most clever disguise, eh?"

"Yeah," Charlie said, breaking into a grin of his own. There couldn't have been enough marijuana in that bundle to pay him a paltry $1,000 to pick it up, but it's not my money, he thought.

"My orders are to see it safely to the plane. Allow me to load it and you can be on your way," Rafael said.

"Suit yourself," Charlie replied.

Together they started for the plane.

"A four cylinder engine, am I correct? Gets about 180 horsepower?"

"You know an awful lot about Bird Dogs," Charlie said.

"I went to school in America, where I learned English and how to fly. The Bird

Dog is my absolute favorite," Rafael repeated, "and yours is a beauty. Tell me about her."

The compliment wasn't wasted on Charlie. He had found someone who shared his interest in the thing he knew best—Bird Dogs. Information spilled from him like rain from an open sky.

"The engine is a Continental, C-470, re-worked. And actually she gets about 213 horse, with maximum speed of 151 miles per hour."

Charlie was like a computer stocked with information on the plane. Entranced, facts on the Bird Dog rolled from his lips. He didn't even notice the stranger lagging behind.

"I flew Bird Dogs for Uncle Sam over in Nam. What a great observation plane," he said.

Suddenly realizing the stranger was no longer by his side, Charlie stopped and turned. At once he felt as if an ice cube had been lodged in his heart.

The parachute was on the ground, the stranger's hand on Charlie's chest. That was odd! And when Charlie saw the slender blade emerge, covered in crimson, it took him almost a full minute to realize that the blood he saw was his own.

He reached for the knife, but his hands were moving slowly, too slowly.

The second blow caught him in the

throat, rupturing his larynx. Pain soared into his head, exploding into thousands of tiny fragments. He listened to the gurgly sounds coming from the gash in his neck.

He wanted to ask why, but the words were stifled by his severed vocal cords.

Again he tried reaching for the knife, but his arms were now thousand pound weights, too heavy to budge, the mere exertion of energy causing him to collapse to his knees.

Rafael smiled down at him, baring his perfect teeth. Then dropping the stiletto onto the dead grass, he picked up the parachute and headed for the plane.

Charlie Sachs lay dying on the open field, unable to move, life rapidly flowing from his body. He realized that it was all over, and he didn't even know why.

At that moment images of Doris fired through his consciousness. He saw her as he'd left her that morning, lying naked with a pout on her lips, and realized that she had been right after all.

She was right again, damn her, right about everything!

CHAPTER 3

"SAYS-NAAAH!"

Allen and Eve Michaels were arguing when they heard the scream. It was Grant. Allen reached the room first.

When he pushed open the door, he found his son lying on the floor, panic dancing behind the child's eyes.

"What's goin' on in here?" the boy's father demanded. He was a beefy man of medium height, with a booming voice and choleric disposition.

His wife arrived seconds behind him.

"That's no way to talk to him," she said reaching for her son, who lay staring silently up at his father. "Can't you see something's scared him?" Kneeling, she cradled the child's head in her lap, gently stroking his smooth, brown hair. "What's the matter, Granty?"

"*Granty*! Haven't you heard a word I've been saying?"

"I've been listening to you since you walked through the door this evening," Eve snapped.

"And doesn't what I say mean anything around here?"

"Only when you make sense!"

"Now listen here, Eve, that's just the type of thing I've been talking about." Allen moved in closer, and now loomed over his wife and child. "Stop that!" he demanded. His wife's stroking hand immediately came to rest. "What's been goin' on here, boy?"

Silently the child stared up at him. The obvious fear on the boy's face sickened him, and he reached down, grabbing his son by the arm and yanking him to his feet.

"Allen!" Eve protested.

"Shut up!" His attention was once again on the boy. "All right, Mr. Michaels, I'm gonna ask you just one more time. What the hell's been goin' on here?"

"Nuthin'," the boy whispered.

"What?"

"Nuthin'."

"Then would you mind telling me what that screaming was all about?"

"I got scared, that's all."

"Scared!" the boy's father bellowed, incredulous laughter leaping from his throat. "How old are you?"

"Nine."

"And are you a baby?"

"No."

"You a big boy?"

"Yes."

"Well, would you mind telling your loving dad just what is it that could scare a big boy like you?"

Allen's face contorted into a grimace, and Grant found it easier to stare at the floor. Just looking his dad in the face was scary, and he was already scared enough.

"Well?" his father prompted.

"Please, Allen, you're intimidating the boy."

"Me?" Allen said innocently. "I'm not intimidating you, am I, son?"

"No."

"Huh?"

"No, sir."

"There, you see," he said, his eyes slashing into his wife. "Now son, just what is it that you're afraid of?"

"The bad thoughts."

"What?"

"I had bad thoughts."

Both parents were intrigued by the answer.

"What kind of thoughts, Granty?" Eve asked.

"*I'm* talking to the boy," Allen said, once again glaring at his wife. He noticed his son staring at the floor. "Look at me!" Slowly the boy's head came up. "What kind of thoughts?"

"I thought someone was going to die."

"Who?"

"A man."

"And do you know this man?"

"No, I don't think so."

"And how is this man supposed to die?"

"In a crash. A airplane crash."

Allen and Eve glanced at each other.

"He must have had a bad dream," Eve said.

"Dream? He's supposed to be up here studying. Not playing or dreaming, but studying. The only way to get ahead in this world . . ." Once again Allen's attention turned to the boy. "What are you doin' up here?"

"Studyin'."

"You tellin' me the truth, 'cause you know how I feel about lying?"

"Yes, sir. I've been studyin'."

"Good. You'll make me proud of you one day. Right?"

Grant nodded.

"All right. Get back to work. And no more bad thoughts. You hear me?"

"Yes, sir."

"Eve, I wanna see *you* downstairs."

Grant's parents walked to the door. Then

suddenly his mother turned.

"What was that I heard you scream, Granty?"

Allen rolled his eyes.

"Huh? I didn't scream nuthin'."

"Yes, you did. It sounded like 'says no.'"

"I don't remember."

"Okay, baby. Daddy and I will be downstairs. Now give Mommy a big smile."

Grudgingly, the smile appeared on Grant's face, but he made sure it was only for his mother. In a moment they were gone, and already he could hear the argument starting afresh as they walked away.

He didn't want to be left alone, not with them arguing this way. That was how the bad thoughts came in the first place, and he feared their return.

What was that I screamed? Says-nah.

The arguing continued down the stairs.

I will not go away, Grant told himself. I will stay right here and listen.

He moved to his desk and looked at the special homework his father had left for him. He decided he would concentrate on the columns of numbers that lined the page. He would concentrate real hard. He would look at the numbers and not think of or hear anything.

His parents' voices drifted up to him.

"Add up those numbers, Mr. Grant Michaels," he said out loud, hoping his own voice would drown out those of his parents.

"Add up this first column, and do it right now. And screw being scared!"

He sat, squinting at the numbers, trying to close out everything but what he was supposed to be doing.

"It's your fault," he heard his father say.

"The first number is six, and carry the three," Grant said, now looking down at the second column of numbers.

"I know what's good for him," his father insisted.

"No, you don't," Grant stammered. "I'm sorry. I wasn't trying to listen. Really! Please, God . . . The second number is . . ." But the number wouldn't come. "Screw it!"

He'd lost his train of thought, and now his parents' voices came in loud and clear, as clear as if they were sitting across the room.

Then he thought of going away.

No! I won't go!

When he was away he didn't hear the arguments, didn't have to know they were talking about him. When he was away the things that happened in the house didn't matter. He wasn't aware of them. It was so peaceful.

"But I'm never going away again. Never!" Grant insisted as he tried tackling the arithmetic problems.

"The first number is six, carry the three and . . ."

Images of the airplane sputtered into his

thoughts. He remembered seeing and hearing it crash into the side of the mountain, the explosion, the fire, the sizzling of the man's flesh as it fried on his bones—and the smell, the sickeningly sweet odor of burning flesh.

"No!" he screamed. "No! No!"

He was not going away again. He was never going away again. He was going to stay right here and listen. No matter what happened he was going to stay right here. Then suddenly the door to his room burst open, and Mommy and Daddy were back.

Dinner was finished, and the family was seated in front of the TV, watching the evening news. Grant fidgeted in his seat.

"Sit still," his father, sprawled in a high-back leather recliner, demanded.

Eve, who sat next to her son on the sofa, patted the boy's hand.

"And quit babying him!"

"I'm not babying him," she snapped. "Something scared him this afternoon. He's not one to just cry out."

"That's true," Allen had to admit. "You all right, son?"

"Yeah," Grant replied.

"I don't mean to be so hard on you. I just want you to get ahead in this world. It's tough out there. You know that?"

"Yeah."

The national report came on.

"This is the kind of stuff you need to watch, son. Cartoons don't get you anywhere. This is important."

"Allen, I'm concerned about what scared him," Eve prompted.

"Yeah, so am I. All right, son. Could you tell us more about it?"

'There's nuthin' to tell."

"A man dies in an airplane accident, and you weren't asleep?" Allen asked.

"No, I was studyin'." He couldn't tell them that he'd gone away. They wouldn't understand.

"Can you tell us anything more about it?" Eve asked, squeezing his hand.

"L-one-nine. That number keeps poppin' in my head. Maybe it has something to do with arithmetic. But everytime I think of the crash that number pops in."

"I'm gonna get a beer," Allen said, "and when I come back let's put an end to this thing. He just imagined it, that's all. The kid has a vivid imagination. Maybe he can use that imagination to make us all rich." He chuckled as he left the room.

"Why do you think you had the bad thoughts?" Eve went on.

"I don't know."

"Do you want someone to die? Me or maybe . . ." She allowed her sentence to trail off.

"No, Mom, it wasn't like a make-believe crash. It was awful."

Allen returned. "Enough of this for one night."

As he stood in the doorway, a news bulletin flashed on the TV screen.

Just after six this evening, a Cessna L-19, traveling from Mexico en route to Riverside Municipal Airport, crashed somewhere in the Santa Ana Mountains. Details at this time are sketchy. Stay tuned to this network for further developments.

There was a short silence in the Michaels' living room, broken by the sound of a beer can hitting the floor.

CHAPTER
4

This time things were more to his liking. He was stuck in a crowd on busy Alvarado Street in Los Angeles and blended easily with the mostly Mexican-American traffic. Drifting past the restaurant, he spotted Sanchez pacing nervously out front.

He sticks out like a sore thumb, Rafael thought, continuing to the corner. He doubled back, walking slowly and enjoying the power of obscurity.

He looked at Sanchez again. He'd have a conniption if he had to wait another ten minutes, Rafael mused. Seven days. He'll pay for that.

Rafael was now ten feet from Sanchez.

The man turned and looked right through him.

He moved in closer.

Now he was practically on top of his contact. He could have killed him easily with a small hand gun or the stilleto, a weapon he favored for its silence.

Power surged through him as he contemplated Sanchez's death. Of course he wouldn't kill him—not today—but it was a good feeling. At that moment Rafael realized he was getting a hard-on.

He touched Sanchez gently on the back of the neck.

"Huh?" The fat man spun around. "What are you doing?" he snapped in Spanish.

Rafael smiled and removed his dark glasses. Something in his eyes, the cool arrogance, told Sanchez it was him.

Anger bubbled up inside the fat man. "A clever disguise," he snapped, changing to English.

Rafael was no longer the man he'd met in Tambien, Mexico. The change was startling. The smooth, dark hair that had been covered by a straw hat was now unruly and flecked with gray. His face was covered by a heavy salt and pepper beard. The perfect teeth were gone with the removal of a few caps. And he wore filthy jeans and a U.S. army fatigue coat. The eyes were the only distinguishing characteristic he could find.

"Shall we step inside?" Rafael asked.

"What kept you?"

"A precaution," Rafael said with a wry grin. "I had to make sure you were not followed."

They entered the Mexican restaurant and chose a back booth. Ordering coffee, they spoke in guarded English.

"That was a good man you killed," Sanchez said angrily.

"He was in love with the airplane. Now they are together."

Sanchez pounded his fist into the table. "Listen, Rafael, he will be difficult to replace. There was no reason to kill him."

"I will be the judge of that."

"No!" the fat man blurted. "I will not have you killing everyone I put you in contact with. You will kill no one else without orders from me. Do you understand?"

Rafael's right hand darted across the table, closing around his contact's throat. A grin slithered across his lips as he slowly increased the pressure on the man's windpipe. Both of Sanchez's hands worked on the viselike grasp, but removing it was impossible.

As his wind supply was gradually stifled, his face reddened and he gagged.

"I take orders from no one," Rafael said, bringing his face close to that of the fat man's. "I kill because it is necessary. I kill to stay alive. I killed your man because he saw me."

"Please!" Sanchez gasped. His face had turned a deep purple.

"I take orders from you for one thing. Do *you* understand?"

"Yes," Sanchez croaked.

Rafael released him. Sanchez sat back, sucking in sweet fresh air. His fingers moved to the bruise on his neck.

"When?" Rafael asked.

Sanchez sipped his coffee and spoke in a whisper. "The first phase of our mission does not begin for another few weeks. Until then you must . . . I would prefer that you stay where I can reach you."

"No, that is too dangerous. I will be moving often until you need me. But I will walk past this restaurant a week from Monday. If you need to tell me anything be here then. If I do not see you here I will wait another week. If I do not see you on the third consecutive week, I will consider the mission scrapped."

"But what if something . . ."

"Be here then."

Sanchez sighed. "All right. What time?"

"I am not sure, but to prevent missing me get here at six A.M. and do not leave until I arrive." Rafael smiled into the fat man's eyes.

Her name was Angel. It was just a name.

Sanchez parked the old Mercedes across from the luxury apartment building in North Hollywood. Getting out, he attempted to smooth wrinkles from his rumpled suit. He ran a hand through his thinning hair and looked up at the building.

Her terrace drapes were drawn. Asleep? Sanchez wondered, checking his watch. 12:40 P.M. No, not sleeping. Working.

He thought of killing time for the next hour or so, but changed his mind. This is important. Whoever's getting his rocks off can wait. I wonder if she gives rain checks, he thought, grinning.

When his third knock was louder and more insistent than the previous two, he finally heard stirring within. He knocked again.

"Relax, will ya?" Angel called out.

A few minutes later the door opened a crack, and Angel's tiny head peeked out. She was lovelier than Sanchez had remembered.

"You! Shit! You know better than to come banging on my door without an appointment!"

Her elfin nose turned up slightly, and there was fire in her blue eyes. She was even more lovely when angry.

"Please excuse my most untimely intrusion, but it is . . ."

"Fuck off!"

The door slammed in his face.

"Bitch!" Sanchez mumbled. Hot blood rose into his head and fists clenched as he fought the urge to kick the door in.

"Miss, Angel, there is a considerable amount of money involved."

No reply.

"Please, look at this."

He opened his wallet and removed five, crisp $100 bills.

"This is just for listening," he said, sliding the money under the door. "Much more if you'll give me a week of your time."

He stood silently for a moment and heard her pick up the money.

The door swung open wide on Angel's smiling face.

"You sure know the way to a girl's heart."

The apartment was as elegant as he remembered and even more immaculate. They sat on a beige sectional sofa, sipping white wine from Baccarat crystal. They talked briefly of forgotten times before getting down to business.

"Let me get this straight. You'll pay me three thousand dollars just to know where this guy is for a week, and a two thousand dollar bonus for keeping him out of trouble?"

"That's correct."

Angel was truly a heavenly vision—smooth blond hair ending at her shoulders, flawless white skin, gently carved lips. A pearl white negligee highlighted the blue of her eyes and the blush on her cheeks. Sanchez found himself wondering who was in the bedroom, who had been enjoying this exciting creature.

Angel sipped her wine. "This guy must be worth a mint to you."

"You could say that."

"Does he like girls?" she asked. "He ain't no weirdo or nothin'?"

"He seems normal."

She grinned. "Well, if he is I'll keep him out of trouble all right, and if you want to find him, he'll be right here in bed. And I'll take my five G's in cash."

There was a stirring in the bedroom. Sanchez looked up to see a naked, large busted woman stepping into the living room, her pendulous breasts surging as she moved.

The fat man's gaping eyes fixed on her perfect body. A woman! He tried hiding his disbelief.

"You comin' back?" the girl said to Angel.

"Soon, baby."

"Yeah, well, if I had known this was going to be like family reunion day at Getty Square I coulda gone to school, you know."

Her eyes locked on Sanchez, and for the first time he realized how young she was, not more than 16.

"Hurry it up. All right?" she said to him.

There was no answer, just the incredulous stare.

"Shit! Whatsa matter with this guy?" she squealed, her eyes flashing to Angel, then back to Sanchez. "Hey," she said, locking gazes with the man on the sofa, "I don't mean to be presumptuous, but ain't you never seen tits before?"

"The kid's a goddamned psychic!"

Allen Michaels sat in the tiny office of Harold Carmody, station manager for tiny KDOJ radio in Hollywood.

Carmody, a youngish 35, with soft, brown eyes and a nose that he considered "Irish," sat behind an aluminum desk shaking his head.

"You always did want fame, Allen. That's what I most remember about you in high school. The man who wanted fame and fortune."

"It's true," Allen barked. "I saw it with my own eyes."

Carmody clucked. "A kids grows up in your home for nine years, and he's an average schmucko. Hell, maybe even below average. Then one night—boom! He's the great messiah. Excuse me if I don't buy it, okay, Allen?"

Carmody remembered things about Allen, many of them not good.

"But . . ."

Carmody cut in. "Look, you called in a

favor, so here you are. We'll tape my afternoon talk show with the boy, and that'll be that. But don't go asking me to believe any of this psychic bullshit. I've seen my share of psychics at this station, and I'll tell you something. They're all phony—as phony as three dollar bills," Carmody said, his fingers drumming on the desk. "I'll tell you something else. You manage to get the kid some publicity, and then what? Everyone'll know he's a fake in no time. Think of the embarrassment you'll cause the kid. Is it worth that for your own personal glory? Because if it is, you're one helluva dad!"

"What the hell are you talkin' about? It's true," Allen insisted. "The kid's a goddamned psychic!"

"Yeah, and Skippy is a cockroach." He looked at his watch. "We begin in ten minutes. Get the kid and meet me in the studio—second door on the left—and remember, this is pay back. Consider us even."

When Carmody put his head down and began rifling some papers, Allen knew the man was dismissing him.

The son of a bitch, he thought, rising. What the hell does he know!

Allen Michaels retreated from the office to the reception area, where his son, Grant, sat engrossed in a near ancient issue of *Motor Trend* magazine.

"How are ya, son?" Allen asked sliding in

next to the boy.

"I'm okay. We still gonna be on the radio?"

Grant looked up quizzically, and Allen noticed the fiery green eyes. Actually there wasn't much fire in them, not like his own, not yet. But they were green like his, and he was sure the boy was going to be a regular firecracker, despite what his mother was doing to him.

"Yeah, we're going to be on the radio," he replied, a little boy's grin appearing on his face. "That'll be real exciting, huh?"

"I guess so," Grant said.

"Son, I know we've been through this before, but I want to ask you this question just one more time. All right?" His grin disappeared.

"Sure."

Allen removed the magazine from his son's lap and placed it back on the rack.

"You ain't playin' a joke on your old man, are you?" he said suddenly, the words coming in a rush. "I mean, you didn't hear this airplane thing on the radio, and then make up the bit about seeing the airplane crash, did you?" He tried not to look desperate, but when his face twisted into a grimace, Grant looked away.

"Oh, no, Dad," the boy said.

"Look at me, boy!" Allen grabbed his son by the chin, jerking his head around. "This is important to me, about as important as anything I can remember. If you didn't see this thing, tell me now, because if I find out later I'm going to be very angry."

"It's real, Dad."

Allen sighed. "I knew it, son. I really did, but I had to check." A playful hand mussed Grant's hair. "I'm proud of you."

Grant perked up. "You are?"

"Yes. Very proud. This is a wonderful gift you have."

"Really?" A smile unfolded on Grant's lips.

"Son, with this wonderful gift of yours, you could help me and your mom quite a bit. Why, we might never have to worry about money again."

"Because people are going to pay us for what I know about the airplane crash?"

"Not exactly. People won't pay us just for that." He swallowed hard. "I mean, that's just the beginning. The money comes when you do it again. When you predict all sorts of things."

Allen Michaels saw the shock registering on his son's face and stopped abruptly. "Do you think you can do it again?"

There, it was out. The question had gnawed at him since he realized the potential behind what his son had done. It had kept him lying awake every night since the accident and had paraded through his thoughts while he worked.

Can he do it again? Of course he could.

He did it once, and common sense told you anything you did once you could do again. Right? But it was only an assumption, a question he had been afraid to ask, afraid to see his dream of a life without struggle dashed so soon. So he had continued to dream of a life of opulence, while not pursuing the question—until now.

"Come on, Allen. You guys should be in the studio already." It was Carmody.

"Can you, son?" he asked again. He had to know—now!

"No. I don't think so."

"Allen, if you want this amazing psychic of yours on the air, get into that studio *toot sweet!*" Carmody called.

"Come on, son," Allen said, rising.

Grant Michaels noted the pain scrawled across his father's face as they met Mr. Carmody.

"How are ya, kid?" Harold Carmody asked. There was a broad smile on his lips.

"Okay," Grant said. He looked around the room. "This is the studio?"

"I'm afraid so. Not what you were expecting, huh? It was a disappointment for me the first time, too."

"Oh, I'm not disappointed," Grant said. But Carmody saw it in his eyes.

In the middle of the room was a small table. Two microphones sat atop the table, and Grant realized he'd be talking into one of those mikes. Harold Carmody brought in three wooden chairs, then went out again and returned with a pitcher of water.

"Just in case someone turns up dry," he said with a short laugh.

"I always thought there was a glass you could look through from the outside, and a room with an engineer and records and stuff."

"Yeah, I know the picture. Bigger stations have that sort of stuff. Actually we have a room similar to that, but this one is just for taping interviews. Maybe when we're finished I'll show it to you."

"If you want," Grant said.

"Yeah, well, we'll see."

Carmody set up the chairs, seating Allen and Grant opposite his. He set the microphones in place, then moved to the tape recorder by the far wall.

"This machine is going to record everything we say," Carmody said to the boy.

"Oh."

"You nervous, kid?"

"Oh no. I don't have any reason to be nervous. I'm telling the truth, and when you tell the truth you don't have to be nervous. Right?" Grant looked to his father for confirmation but received none. Allen Michaels was trying to grow accustomed to losing his dream.

Carmody looked at the boy and then his father. "Yeah, well, here goes something," he said, depressing the button that started the tape to roll.

The interview began.

"He said the calls started soon after you left."

Eve Michaels stood in the kitchen of their tiny home, fussing over a pot on the stove. Allen was seated at the table sipping a beer.

"I was right. The kid was goddamned beautiful on the radio. I knew people would be interested, plenty interested, damnit!" He slammed his fist into the table.

"What's the matter? I thought you'd be pleased."

"Pleased? I'm as pleased as a pig in shit. Too pleased. The kid was goddamned terrific, Eve. We got a call to do another radio show, and now people are callin' from all over, just to talk to the kid."

"Allen, what's the matter?"

"The matter? Did I say something was the matter?"

"No."

"He can't do it again!" Allen roared. "Once and that's it. A freak thing, maybe. Who knows." When he gazed into his wife's eyes, she saw the pain. "Eve, I asked Grant could he do it again, you know, predict things. He said he couldn't. On the way home in the car, he told me he didn't even know how it happened in the first place." Allen looked down and saw that he had crushed the empty beer can.

"Is that so bad?"

"Huh? Eve, sometimes I wonder if we're living on the same planet," Allen remarked. "Of course it's bad. Radio was just the beginning. People were getting interested. One local show and they were interested already. After would come television, personal appearances, books. I'm talkin' about a future for all of us. Eve, baby, we could have been rich."

"I'm glad he can't do it again," Eve finally said.

"What? Am I hearing you right? Does my wife love poverty?"

"Allen, he's not a circus freak, he's our son. I don't want my boy treated like sideshow entertainment, like one of your other get-rich-quick enterprises that always fails."

Allen's eyes widened. "We could be rich!"

"I don't care. It's not worth it."

"I'll decide if it's worth it or not!" Again his fist rammed the table. "It could have been good for all of us. Not just the money, but Grant's being special. And no, not like a sideshow freak, but maybe like . . . God."

The pot cover Eve Michaels held went crashing to the floor. She regarded her husband for a long moment, mouth agape. Carefully she chose her words.

"But he can't do it again," she said grimly. "So whatever you had planned doesn't matter. It's over."

Allen Michaels stared off into thin air. Defeat licked at his heels. What could he say? She was right.

He heard the voices.

Grant Michaels sat on the floor of his room, playing with the Rambo and Mr. T figures he'd borrowed from Jimmy Buckley and listening to his parents' voices. Mommy and Daddy hadn't yelled or talked loud since he'd seen the airplane crash. Now they were doing it again, and he knew they were talking about him.

Grant pulled the figure of Rambo up to eye level. "No, Rambo, I'm not going away!" He brought up the figure of Mr. T. "I'm never going away again," he said.

He thought of the pain on his father's face when he told him he couldn't do it again.

"Well, I can't!"

He brought the figure of Mr. T before his lips. "But Daddy said he would be proud of you," he said in a gutteral voice. "Don't you want Daddy to be proud?"

"Yes," Grant said in his own voice.

"Then go away."

"No, I'll never go away again!" His hand darted out, sending Mr. T flying across the room.

He heard the voices.

"I don't want Mommy and Daddy to argue," he said to Rambo.

Grisly images of his last trip returned,

softened by thoughts of his father mussing his hair at the radio station.

"Rambo?" he asked. "If I go away again, will it be good?"

He regarded Rambo for a moment, then brought the figure to his lips.

"It will be good."

"Promise?"

"I promise. And Mommy and Daddy will be proud, and they will never argue again."

Grant Michaels sat in the middle of the floor looking at Rambo and thinking about going away. But the bad images returned. The last time was just too frightening, too terrifying.

"I can't do it."

Mommy and Daddy will just have to be proud of my school work. It's getting better, he thought.

He got up and moved across the room to fetch Mr. T.

He heard his parents' voices.

CHAPTER 5

Thick, black clouds played cautiously overhead.

Sanchez glanced up at the threatening sky and checked his watch. 9:40 A.M.

The man in the dark business suit and grey fedora watched him from the front of the Bank of America branch, down the block and across the street. A lonely raindrop spattered one of the man's shiny, wing-tipped shoes. He smiled, then switching his briefcase to his left hand, he turned and headed inside the bank.

By the time he was finished the rain would have begun, but Sanchez would still be waiting.

Rafael proceeded to the service area. He thought he looked more like a Secret Service agent than a businessman. In fact he'd used a similar disguise when impersonating an S.S. agent in Washington D.C. He was operating with the F.A.L.N. at the time, plotting to blow up the Lincoln Memorial.

Of course, Rafael realized it was more than how he looked that mattered. It was how he carried himself that convinced people. I am a businessman, he thought. That is the role I am playing.

"May I help you?" a secretary asked as Rafael approached the platform.

"Yes. I'd like to talk to someone about a loan." He flashed his perfect smile and pulled a business card from his breast pocket.

"All right, Mr. Arroyo. Have a seat, and someone will be with you shortly."

Rafael sat on a cushioned bench. He glanced out of the plate glass window and noted the beginnings of the storm. The power surging through him at that moment was immense, and he fought off the urge to laugh out loud.

"Mr. Arroyo?"

Rafael looked up, and a thin man with wire-rimmed glasses and a sedate smile approached. His skin appeared bleached, and Rafael wondered if he'd ever spent any time in the sun.

"I'm Art Barber, your loan counselor. Step this way." He squeezed Rafael's hand gently and led the way to his desk. "Mr. Arroyo, I see from your card you're in the electronics business."

"Yes," Rafael replied. He was seated in a soft-backed chair. "I own a factory that makes printed circuit boards for use in televisions and radios."

"That sounds exciting," Barber said, his head down as he filled in a loan form. "How much would you like to borrow?"

"Twenty-five thousand, roughly."

"Good. Twenty-five is a fair amount. What's the purpose of this loan?"

"Renovations. The roof leaks in spots, and it's about time the whole building got a face lift." Rafael felt the power rushing through him. He was getting to the exciting part.

"Renovations. That sounds like a wonderful idea, Mr. Arroyo. How's business?"

"Could be better," Rafael said with a grin. "But I can't complain. How's business with you?"

"Just fine."

"Making lots of money for Bank of America, huh?"

"Well . . . I'm serving the people and the bank at the same time, aiding customers in receiving loans everyday. I'm working on both sides, so to speak. I'm in an enviable position."

"Yes, you are," Rafael said dryly. "An enviable position."

"Mr. Arroyo, getting back to the business at hand, do you have any loans presently outstanding?" And if so, with whom?" Barber was writing again.

Rafael leaned closer, looking into the man's downcast eyes. "Yes, Mr. Barber, I do."

"With whom?"

"Bank of America." It was coming. Rafael watched his eyes.

Barber looked up. "That's a good sign, Mr. Arroyo. We prefer to do business with loyal customers. A loyal customer is rarely turned away."

Rafael snorted.

"Is there something wrong?"

"No, Mr. Barber, there isn't. I was just wondering how lenient you were with defaulters?"

"You aren't planning on defaulting, are you, Mr. Arroyo?" Barber said with a chuckle.

"It's not this loan I'm concerned with. It's the last one."

"Oh?"

There! Distrust flickered behind his eyes.

"Mr. Barber, I borrowed sixty thousand dollars from this bank a few years ago, and

I'm afraid I have not paid a penny of it back," Rafael said.

The expression in Barber's eyes changed. The look on his face was the same, the sedate smile, but his eyes gave him away.

Barber laughed again. "Mr. Arroyo, you're pulling my leg." It seemed a question.

"No, Mr. Barber, I am not. Still, I want the new loan. I'll pay it back."

"But why haven't you paid back the original loan? Illness?"

"No, I just haven't paid it. But I will pay this one."

"Oh, you will!" Barber snapped. "Mr. Arroyo, I don't know what kind of a joke this is, but you have some nerve . . ."

"Does that mean I can't have the money?"

Barber became animated. "Mr. Arroyo, no one is going to give you money after you've defaulted. It's a bad risk!"

"Do you wish to take a chance?"

"No, Mr. Arroyo, I do not. And I don't believe any other bank in California will either. Now, if there is nothing more, good day!"

Rafael knew that the moment he left Barber would be checking the computer for the name Philipe Arroyo. Of course he wouldn't find anything, but Rafael had what he needed to go on.

He stepped out into the rain.

It was a steady, saturating downpour, and he immediately began searching for Sanchez. He saw the knot of a man huddled in the doorway of the restaurant.

"Poor, baby," Rafael mumbled. He started across.

A rain drenched Sanchez dripped into his coffee as he spoke.

"I have good news for you," he said in hushed English. "Things are going well. A little slow perhaps, but we will be ready for phase one within the week."

Raphael nodded and sipped his coffee. "I do not appreciate your operating so slowly, Mr. Sanchez. I wonder how competent your friends are."

"Oh, very competent."

"I am thinking that this mission is not for me."

"*Qué?*" Sanchez's voice rose an octave. "You can't quit now!"

"I may quit whenever I choose."

"The thing is in motion. We will be ready for you within days. There is much invested in this mission. Many people are depending on you."

It was as if Sanchez had said nothing. Rafael sat, his gaze cautiously surveying the room. The golden haired woman disturbed him.

She had come in a few minutes after they were seated and had chosen a booth that kept them in her line of vision. Although Rafael had never looked directly at her, peripherally he was aware that she was watching him.

"We will be forced to abort if you drop out now," Sanchez went on.

"The lack of haste on the part of your organization annoys me. You should not have brought me in if you were not ready. I wish to spend as little time in America as possible."

A growing hatred for the arrogant Rafael blanketed Sanchez.

"I assure you we will begin very shortly, and once begun, things will move quickly. We need you." The final sentence was the hardest to say. He was not a nursemaid and detested feeding Rafael's ego. He consoled himself with the knowledge that all would be made up to him in time.

"Be here, Monday," Rafael said.

"Be reasonable!" Sanchez blurted.

"Monday!"

"All right. Is it possible that you could arrive a little earlier?"

"Monday," Rafael said again, rising.

"Suppose I need to get in touch with you before then?" Sanchez asked. "We have to tighten up on our communications now. The moment is at hand."

Rafael sat. "Thursday," he said. "Meet me in the lobby of the Boneventure Hotel at noon."

"What?"

"At noon. I will be there. If you are there, I will find you. If not, Monday."

"Yes," Sanchez said with a sigh.

Again Rafael rose and turned, his eyes falling on the golden haired woman. She was smiling at him.

She was very pretty, a young American with sky blue eyes and an interesting smile. Rafael donned his perfect smile and went over.

"Good morning," he said.

"Hi. I was wondering what a girl had to do to get a man's attention around here."

"You did the right thing." Rafael sat opposite her.

"Did I? I tried everything short of sending up smoke signals. What caught your attention? Tell me so I'll know what my most potent weapon is. A lady needs to know these things."

"I understand," Rafael said with a short laugh. "It was your smile."

"Well, lordy me, the next time I want to meet a guy I'm gonna smile like a mad-woman."

"Hey, give me a chance!" Rafael said. "Who knows? There might not be a next time."

CHAPTER 6

I'm goin' to be on television!

It wasn't a dream. Grant Michaels sat in a big, comfortable leather chair in the waiting room at the CBS station in Los Angeles. He pinched himself for the third time that morning.

"Ouch!"

"What's wrong?" his father asked.

"Nuthin'," he said, smiling secretly.

When he'd told Jimmy Buckley and all the guys that he was going to be on TV, they had laughed.

"Liar, liar, pants on fire!"

"It's true," Grant had said. "I was on the radio twice, and the second time a man asked my father could I be on TV."

"Aww, bull! Why would anyone want you to be on TV? You a movie star or somethin?" Again laughter from his friends.

"No, but I saw somethin' really neat."

"Yeah, like what?"

He couldn't tell them about going away. He knew they'd never believe him.

"Somethin'. That's all."

"Yeah, sure. Liar!"

Screw 'em! They'll see. Grant looked over at his father and smiled.

"You nervous, Grant?" Allen Michaels, dressed in his tan three-piece suit, sat alongside his son.

"Nope."

"Good," his father said and mussed his hair.

Grant held onto his secret smile. He was happy. The yelling at home had stopped, and his father hadn't again mentioned predicting things.

He'd been on the radio a second time, and still his father never mentioned doing what he had done. He realized that after a while people weren't going to want to hear about the airplane crash, but that was all right. The bite had been taken out of his father's bark, and he was happy.

The door to the waiting room opened, and a young woman was escorted in.

"Ms. Doris Sachs, this is Allen and Grant

Michaels," the escort said before retreating. "They're also going to be talking with Mr. Reed."

The woman flashed a curt smile and sat down.

She's pretty, Allen Michaels thought, about 35 and in great shape. Wonder what she does? he mused, glancing around the room.

A reporter type? Suddenly dread filled him.

No, not a reporter. Allen had seen the Phil Reed show many times. Often when Phil spoke with someone of questionable reputation there was an antagonist, a shill brought in to expose the phony.

That's her purpose, Allen thought. She's here to prove that my son isn't a psychic—and he's not!

Allen Michaels became more and more convinced of this daily, as he waited for his son to predict something—anything! He hadn't coaxed the boy. He remembered the look on Grant's face when he mentioned doing it again. The boy just needed time.

He did it once, right?

He had to do it again. Had to.

"Excuse me, but you *are* the boy who predicted the airplane crash a month ago?"

The woman was talking to Grant, and Allen felt a tightening in his throat.

"Yes."

"Who are you?" Allen snapped. "A

reporter of some kind?"

"No, I'm . . ."

"I suppose you don't believe in psychics?" Allen's voice was rising. "I bet you're here to make fools out of us. Well, you're not going to do it," he blurted. "My son saw what he saw, and he can do it again!"

"He can?"

"You bet your sweet . . . bippy he can. And if you try to make fools out of us, you'll wind up embarrassing yourself on national television."

"Please, Mr. Michaels, that's not why I'm here. I believe in your son."

"You do?" Allen asked, suspicion in his voice.

"My husband, Charlie Sachs, was flying the plane that went down."

"The man who died in the crash?"

"Yes."

Allen Michael's face flushed with embarrassment. "I'm sorry. I didn't know. I mean . . ."

"Is it true?" the woman asked, directing her attention to Grant. "*Can* you do it again?"

The child looked at his father and saw the pain slowly waxing across his face. "Yes," he said softly. "I can."

Lazy plumes of smoke drifted toward the ceiling. Angel sat up in bed, puffing on a cigarette and luxuriating in the warm tingle that seemed to engulf her.

"He's a good man," she murmured, releasing a tiny cloud. "Better than I could have ever imagined."

For nearly a week she had been under the spell of the mysterious man who called himself Joe. He was a quiet man, yet she saw in him a will of steel. He could not be dominated or swayed. His presence there was his own desire, and not because of any manipulating she might have done.

Angel looked towards the closed bedroom door. Wisps of light streamed under. Joe—and she knew that wasn't his real name—was a strange one. Often, after they'd made exquisite love, he would retreat to the living room to sit alone in the darkness. At first she thought it was out of fear, the fear of intimacy she herself had felt in the past. But with Joe she knew it was something else, something more primitive and deeply rooted. Recently, she had finally persuaded him to turn on a light.

What does he do out there?

She would never ask. She had asked something too personal once before, and the fire in his eyes had warned her off.

He's the best, she thought, embracing memories of the passion they'd shared a few minutes earlier. I'll keep him as long as I can.

She reached for the bedside phone and

punched up the number.

"Yes?" a distant voice crackled.

"Everything is fine," she whispered. "Going according to plan."

"Is he there?"

"Yes. In the living room."

"This is a risky call."

"No, it's all right. He'll be out there for another ten minutes or so."

"Are you enjoying the job?" Sanchez cackled.

"It's a job," she replied flatly. "When will I be paid?"

"Monday. Call if there are any changes. And stay close to home."

"All right," she said, and in a moment the line was dead. Gently she recradled the phone.

She sat for a few moments, her thoughts a blur, recollections of the week that had fled so quickly.

It wasn't just a job; something special was happening. Something inside was being torn open, and out spilled her pent up emotions.

It's not love.

She had loved a man once when she was 17 and he a year older. He had told her one day to wait for him.

"What do you mean, wait?" she demanded.

"I'm going away, and I want you to wait. Don't give yourself to anyone. I'll be back."

He explained that he had done something wrong and swore his undying love. "It'll only be a few years." And it was.

At first the time went slowly, dragging through like the endless cold of winter. In time she learned to warm her heart with memories—fond memories and plans. Their future was to be bright and lovely, but after his release he didn't come home. After nearly a year of grievous searching, she discovered he'd married a pen pal and moved to Albuquerque.

But this is different, she thought. It isn't love, not yet, but whatever it is it feels good.

She knew he felt it too. It showed on his face mornings over breakfast and was in his every animal-like thrust when he made love to her. Whatever it was, it was shared.

The bedroom door opened and light poured into the room.

What does he do out there?

He was back, standing in the doorway, silhouetted against the harsh light. She saw the perfect smile, and then her eyes fixed on his rising penis.

He moved towards her, eyes locked onto hers, but she didn't see; her gaze was transfixed by his erection.

Sitting on the bed, he pulled the covers back with his left hand. As she sat up, white light spilled across alabaster breasts.

"Come," he whispered.

She slid over and pulled him in with a

long, inviting kiss. Her eyes shut, and she felt her passions rising. He, too, was excited. His nerve endings tingled with raw sensual pleasure, the most since he'd known her.

Rafael crushed her against him with his powerful left arm, while his tongue explored the wonders between her lips. Her body, fraught with expectation, seemed to vibrate in his hold.

Slowly his right hand came into play.

Angel never noticed the glint of gleaming steel, as the stiletto made its way into position. Six inches from her back he drove home the blade with monstrous force.

She jumped, shuddering in his arms for a full minute before sagging against him. The flood of his own emotions soared as he ejaculated onto her already cooling leg.

He pulled her away from himself, saw the surprise registered on her face, and lay her gently on the bed. Then he removed the blade, wiped it on the sheet and went into the bathroom, where he luxuriated in a steaming shower.

He was dreaming he was king of the world, or something damned close to it, when the phone rang.

"Shit," Sanchez grumbled. He looked over at the clock on the night table. A digital 2:45 winked up at him. "Shit!" he squawked, louder this time, sitting up and shaking off the grog that had settled over his mind. He answered on the fifth ring.

"Hello." Silence. "Hello?"

"Do I detect a bit of annoyance in your voice? Ah, but it is two forty-five in the morning."

"Who is this?" Sanchez growled. The annoyance in his voice was rampant.

"You will be pleased to know that I passed still another of your feeble tests."

The fat man's eyes widened. "Is this . . . ?" He dared not say the name over the phone.

"I grow tired of your games. No more tests, do you understand?" There was no wait for a reply, just a click.

The receiver lay in Sanchez's hand like some small dead thing. Gingerly he replaced it. Rafael, he thought. Then Sanchez thought of Angel.

Hurriedly he moved to switch on the lamp on the nightstand. When he fumbled for the phone, it went tumbling to the floor with a loud twang. Sanchez snatched up the receiver. Leaning over the edge of the bed he dialed Angel's number, pressing the receiver to his ear as if that would make some grave difference. Pick up, he thought. Pick up, dammit!

He allowed the phone to ring 14 times, the monotonous chime of the bell falling against his ear, a grotesque death march. Reluctantly he hung up, his fingers lingering on the lifeless instrument. He sat slumped in remorse, thinking of Angel, her soft, supple skin and her beautiful smile. This time it wasn't anger that rose in him but horror, as he finally realized the kind of monster with which he was dealing.

Angel was dead. There was no doubt in his mind about it. She was dead all right. Slowly he rose from the bed, fatigue gripping him and hunching him over like the old codger he was destined to become. The incident had sapped his strength and aged him suddenly. But he couldn't rest—not now. He had to make sure there was nothing left in Angel's apartment that could lead the authorities to him. Slowly, methodically, he began to dress.

Perhaps using Rafael was a mistake. Ah, Julio Sanchez, master of 20-20 hindsight! Of course he knew it was too late for hindsight. The thing was in motion, and Rafael's methods were something they were just going to have to live with—hopefully.

"And now ladies and gentlemen, Phil Reed."

Mild applause rang out from the throng of spectators crammed into the tiny studio. A smiling, bouncy Phil Reed came out and took his seat on the beige, semicircular sectional sofa.

Grant watched on the monitor in the waiting room where he sat with his father and Doris Sachs. His father fingered his blue blazer. Earlier a man had come in and told his father he could not wear the jacket to his tan three-piece suit on television.

"Why not?" Allen Michaels asked.

"That thing'll strobe like crazy," the man said.

"Strobe?"

"Under the lights, pal, that jacket of yours'll go off like a Christmas tree." And before Allen could say another word the man hustled out of the room and returned with a blue blazer. Grudgingly Allen removed his jacket.

Now Grant watched as Phil Reed addressed the audience and told them their guest today was a child phenomenon. While Grant didn't know what it meant, he knew it was something good. Phil Reed smiled when he said it and looked very impressed. Then the man who brought the jacket was back, this time carrying a clipboard.

"You got three minutes," he said. "Follow me. You go on right after the opening commercial."

Exactly three minutes later Grant Michaels was on television. He still couldn't believe it, although he wasn't going to pinch himself, not here on TV. He hoped all the guys were watching, especially that big-mouthed Jimmy Buckley.

Grant looked around. The lights were bright, much brighter than he thought they would be, so bright they hurt his eyes. And it was hot. He wondered how Phil in a dark grey suit could seem so cool. He could see the beads of perspiration already flecked along his father's forehead, and he himself felt that a nice, cold lemonade would do just right about now.

"Well, Grant, would you please tell our audience about the incident that occurred on March 15th of this year," Phil Reed said. He was a handsome man with a pleasant moonlike face and rusty brown hair. He wasn't as tall as he appeared on TV, but then Grant noticed that nothing was as it appeared on TV. The living room that seemed so large and luxurious was actually a tiny set, just large enough for Phil and a few guests to squeeze on without appearing cramped. The furnishings were cheap, plastic and phony. Grant was unimpressed. Still, I'm on TV, he thought.

"Son, the man's talking to you," his father prompted.

Grant looked over at his dad and saw the look in his eyes. *Don't blow this one for me, son—please!* He thought of the yelling that had stopped at home.

"I was in my room studyin'," he said softly. A camera swung in front of his face, and an overhead microphone dropped to just above his head. Grant swallowed hard.

"You say you were studying?" Phil asked.

"Yeah."

"Well, folks, it seems our little friend isn't very talkative this morning," Phil said grinning into the camera. A soft titter rose from the crowd. Then he turned his attention to Allen. "Perhaps you could enlighten us."

"Sure," Allen Michaels said, jumping on the statement. And he did. He told everything, from the moment he rushed into Grant's room right up to the point where he dropped his beer. "I don't know where the power comes from, but it's damned creepy. The kid can just plain predict things," he added, ending his monologue.

"It's indeed amazing," Phil said, "but there have been other cases of predicting air disasters on record. Are you aware of that?"

"No," Allen said, worry lines furrowing his brow.

"There was a man in Cincinnati back in 1976 who predicted America's worst air disaster to date. Two hundred and seventy-two people died."

"Really," Allen said in mock amazement. But he was worried, too worried about his own ass to care about the deaths of two hundred and seventy-two people. He'd never heard of anything like that before, anyway. Was it for real? Or was this son of a bitch trying to sell short his son's talent?

"Of course, in all documented cases the person predicting the accident got his information while asleep." Phil turned his attention to Grant. "Were you asleep when you saw the airplane crash?"

"Oh, no," Grant said, searching his father's face. "I was studyin'."

"How could you possibly see an airplane accident wide awake, sitting in your bedroom studying?"

"I don't know," Grant said, his eyes diving for his shoes, "but I saw it." He couldn't tell them about going away. He was sure if he did they'd ask him to do it again.

I'll never go away again!

"Of course you did," Phil said, shooting the boy a benign smile. Then to the camera he added, "And when we return we'll meet Doris Sachs. Her husband, Charlie Sachs, was the pilot of the plane Grant saw go down. We'll be right back."

Phil continued staring into the camera until a man yelled "Clear!", then people began rushing around. Someone came up and wiped Allen's forehead, then dabbed on a fresh coat of makeup. The man with the clipboard came out and began talking with Phil, while Allen and Grant sat by, totally ignored.

"You okay, son?" Allen asked. Grant looked up and saw the perspiration waxing fresh along his father's forehead. He nodded, and his father mussed his hair.

A minute later the people were gone, the

show started again, and Phil introduced Doris Sachs. Slowly Phil and Doris eased into a conversation. They both praised Grant's "amazing power," and the worry lines on Allen Michaels forehead began smoothing over, like tiny ripples slowly folding into a pond.

Things are looking good, Allen thought. He really likes the kid. Allen Michaels sat back, relaxed and smiled, wondering how much they'd get for their next TV appearance. That's when the trouble started.

"I hear you can do it again," Phil said. Once again he turned to Grant. The child nodded. Allen Michaels squirmed in his seat. "*Can* you do it again? Predict air disasters?" Phil implored.

"Yeah," he softly answered.

"Would you mind speaking up for our audience?"

"Yes."

"Just like that? No special preparation? How do you do it? Gaze into your crystal ball?" A slight twitter rose from the audience.

"No."

"Then how?" Phil Reed pushed his face towards Grant's. "Do you look up at the ceiling? Don't tell me you have x-ray vision? You're not Superboy, are you?" This time there was definite laughter from the crowd. "Can you predict train wrecks or automobile accidents? Can you locate the lost

69

SAL CONTE

mines of Solomon?"

"Hey, what goes?" Allen blurted. "You don't believe the kid or somethin'?"

"Do you? Oh, but of course you do. *You're* his father. Mr. Michaels, did you put your son up to this?"

"Are you callin' me a liar?" Allen squawked. And as quickly as it had vanished, the fear came rushing back, returning in one gigantic tidal wave that washed over him, engulfing his entire being. Quickly he doused the fear with a layer of anger. "The kid's a goddamned psychic!"

"Oh, really? Mr. Michaels, the only *real* proof we have that your son did this is *your* word."

"You're callin' me a liar," Allen Michaels said again. The worry lines were back, as the anger dissipated quickly and fear seeped into his words.

"Mr. Michaels, what line of work are you in?"

"What?"

"Come on, Mr. Michaels, isn't it true you're just doing this for the money?"

"The kid's a psychic, I tell ya! He can do it again!" His voice filled with panic.

"I believe him," Doris Sachs said suddenly. She had been sitting quietly, her hands folded on her lap in front of her. "There are powers in this world we just don't understand," she went on.

"True. True," the host conceded. "But the world is also filled with charlatans, crackpots, fortune seekers and phonies." Then to the camera, he added, "Ladies and gentlemen, which is Grant Michaels? You decide. We'll be right back."

Another commercial began to roll. As soon as they were clear Allen Michaels began to scream.

"What the hell are you tryin' to pull?" Rising, he attempted to smooth wrinkles from his pants, but the perspiration that now skated over his entire body had steamed them in. There were salt streaked stains in the armpits of the borrowed blazer.

Phil Reed appeared calm. "The question, Mr. Michaels, is what are *you* trying to pull?"

"I got a mind to walk out right now!"

The host's pasted-on smile widened. "Good. That will prove my point all the way around, won't it?"

Allen's argument died on his lips. He hadn't thought of that. Walking off now would defeat his reason for being there. He'd be running away, and he didn't have anything to run from. The kid really did predict the airplane crash. Even if he couldn't do it again, the first one was for real. What did this Phil Reed asshole know anyway?

Allen Michaels sat down and waited for

the commercial to be over.

Grant saw the confusion on his father's face and looked away, but the image had already burnished its way into his memory, and no matter where he looked—even into the lights—he saw his father. They don't believe us, he thought. But it's true. It's true! Of course the only way anyone would know for sure was if he did it again.

I'll never go away again!

As soon as the commercial break was over, Phil Reed started his attack anew. "Come on, level with me, son. Did you really see a plane crash? No one's going to punish you if you tell me the truth. Right, Dad?" Accusing eyes penetrated Allen.

"Damn right," the boy's father said. "Go on, son. Tell him the truth."

"Yes," Grant said. "I did see a plane crash." He stared into unbelieving eyes.

"Could you describe it for our audience?"

"It was awful."

"Awful? Awful, did you say? Don't kids enjoy wrecks, accidents, crashes? Don't you watch Knight Rider or the A-Team?" His voice dropped an octave and came out soft and confiding. "Isn't a good car crash exciting?" Grant nodded. "Then what made this so awful?"

"The man," Grant said. "He . . . He . . ." And suddenly his nostrils filled with the odor of burning flesh. His stomach churned as hot bile rose into his throat. He forced it back down. His vision clouded, and his head began to swim.

"He knows something about my husband," Doris Sachs said suddenly. "He knows something about my Charlie. Is it a message for me?" She jumped up filled with emotion, and took a halting step towards the boy.

"It's a cheap trick!" Phil Reed charged.

"No!" the woman cried, taking still another step. "It's a miracle."

She clasped her hands together as if in prayer, and suddenly the whole thing turned into a circus—a gala three ring job replete with clowns, a fortune teller, and a man being shot from a cannon.

Hurry, hurry, step right up and see the amazing two-faced boy!

Through the whirling haze that had seized his mind, Grant glanced over at his father now nearly drenched in sweat, the perspiration running in tiny rivulets down the side of his face. His shoulders were hunched forward, and like a flag on a windless day he hung limp on the edge of his seat.

Grant's gaze spun to Doris who had become a figure in comic animation, stumbling over and falling to her knees in front of him. "Please, boy, what did you see? Is there a message from my Charlie?"

Phil Reed said, "Ladies and gentlemen, we have evidence that Allen Michaels has attempted several get-rich-quick schemes in the past. Perhaps, this, is another in a string of attempts at financial security."

"No!" Allen bleated as the words slammed into his soul. "Show 'em, son. Show 'em!" he said, pleading for his boy to do what he knew he couldn't.

"Yes! Show us!" the host challenged.

"Please!" begged Doris Sachs.

Audience voices surged up at Grant, as the crowd hooted and challenged. Camera men and technicians rushed everywhere trying to get a better angle, a better shot. Then suddenly Doris Sachs did the strangest thing. She keeled over, her head falling into Grant's lap.

"She's fainted!" someone shouted. "Give her air!"

Seeing the lady lying there, feeling her dead weight pressing against his thighs, Grant was reminded of the man in the airplane. Is she dead, too? The noise, the fear, his hazy merry-go-round vision and his father's pleas weighed on him like an elephant's paw. He opened his mouth, gasping for air, but his lungs clogged with confusion. That's when he thought of going away.

"Please, son, show 'em! Please!"

I will not go away.

"For me, son. For your mom!"

I will not . . .

"For all of us!"

. . . go away!

And suddenly he couldn't take it any-more. He had to be somplace peaceful and quiet. Rambo said it would be all right. And then without any warning Grant Michaels broke his promise to himself. He went away.

It was an eerie feeling at first, as it always was. It was as if he were dreaming. He was overcome by a feeling of weightless-ness that started in the tips of his toes and slowly coursed upward. Then he began tumbling towards the sky, away from his body, leaving it amidst the confusion in the studio below.

Over and over, head over heels, he tumbled. He watched as quickly the studio disappeared, dissolving into a milky melange, while breathtaking clouds un-folded around him. Then the tumbling stopped, and he was floating in the heavens, faraway from the problems on earth. All was at peace. Nothing mattered, until he noticed a Douglas DC-9 moving towards him—a shining razor, knifing its way through the ice blue sky.

CHAPTER 7

"Son, you all right?"

Grant Michaels slowly opened his eyes. As the fog drifted from his mind muted shapes began forming around him. His vision cleared, and he realized he was lying with his head on his father's lap. He was back.

"Grant," his father said softly. Grant was surprised by the concern that shaped his words and looked up.

They were alone, back in the waiting room. The TV monitor was still on, and Phil Reed's voice droned in the background. Grant noticed relief inching across his father's face.

"You had me worried," his father said.

"I'm sorry." Grant tried sitting up, but his father pushed him back down.

"Don't be sorry," he said. "Rest."

Then Grant remembered going away.

"Dad, I saw another one."

There was a long silence, pointed by the tightening of every muscle in Allen Michael's face. "Another what?" he said rather matter-of-factly, trying unsuccessfully to mask the hope that crept into his voice.

"Another plane. This one didn't exactly crash. An engine started smoking, and it had to do a belly-flop on a field."

The next several minutes were minutes Grant would never forget. His father smiled at him like he'd never smiled before. His entire being seemed to change right before the boy's eyes; joy, relief and gratitude alternately washed over him. The steadily warming smile that cracked his lips appeared as rays of searing sunlight, slowly parting storm clouds that had lingered far too long. But that wasn't what Grant noticed most. It was the look in his eyes—genuine pride, not spoken but heart-felt.

"It was an Eastern Airlines jetliner," Grant went on.

"Thank you, son," Allen Michaels said softly and mussed the boy's hair.

He's proud of me! My daddy's proud of me! Rambo was right.

He thought he saw a tear forming in the corner of his father's eye. He'd never know for sure. All at once his father rose and dashed from the room. Grant looked over at the monitor. Phil Reed was looking to his left, off camera. "Let him on," he said. There was a slight commotion, and in the next instant Grant's father was on television, telling everyone about the crash landing.

Grant lay back. Resting his head against the arm of the sofa, he stared at the ceiling.

He's proud of me!

Grant basked in this pride, feeling it was over him. Like an incoming tide, he was soon covered in it's warm, soothing waters, as it lapped at him, inviting him out into an ocean of proud smiles and fingers mussing hair.

He smiled his secret smile. Now that he'd done it again it wasn't so bad after all. He thought of how happy they would all be—no more yelling—but in doing this he allowed something very important to slip just below his level of consciousness. The thought had emerged and lingered on the precipice of memory for a moment, before tumbling into the recesses of his mind. It was something about the plane crash being different this time—and no, not because this one had done a belly-flop on a field somewhere, and that most of the passengers were all right. No. This was something very, very scary.

CHAPTER 8

The games were over. Today was the day. History was about to happen, and every nerve ending in Rafael's fingers and toes tingled in anticipation.

The sheer magnitude of the thing had a power coursing through him the likes of which he'd never felt. It had yanked him out of bed that morning, dragged him through breakfast, dressed and propelled him to the restaurant where he was to meet Sanchez.

Today is the day!

How long he had waited. But the wait was finally over, and the name Rafael was about to be etched into the annals of history forever.

Rafael stood patiently in front of the familiar restaurant, the straw hat and dark glasses masking his features. Thoughts of greatness paraded through his mind, and he wondered how many he would have to kill to get the thing he desired. Of course Sanchez was a dead man, but that was personal.

"Good morning," Sanchez said. Rafael spun around. He had been so absorbed in his thoughts he had not noticed the fat man's approach.

"Buenas dias," Rafael said. He was glad the dark glasses covered his surprise. It had been a long time since he'd been caught off guard. The last time had been a near disaster. This hanging around had dulled his senses and made him soft, like a woman. He would have to be more careful. He was about to go back to work and would need to be as sharp as ever.

"I am ready," he said in Spanish.

"Good, good," Sanchez replied. He stared at Rafael for a long time. "Why did you kill her?" he finally asked. "She was a lovely girl." Emotion crept into his voice.

"A spy!" Rafael charged. "Besides, she saw my face. I couldn't afford to let her live. You should have considered this before you sent her to spy on me."

"I too, have seen your face," Sanchez fumed. "Will you kill me also?" His eyes challenged, and Rafael removed his glasses, returning the stare while displaying his perfect smile. "I don't like you," Sanchez went on flatly.

"The games are over. I do not need your friendship. I am hated by many, feared by most. Perhaps you are on both lists?" Their eyes continued to do battle.

"We mustn't be late," Sanchez said, breaking the gaze first, and Rafael knew that the fat man had not only lost the hand but the game as well.

He followed Sanchez to the car. "Where are we going?" he asked. There was no reply. Sanchez climbed in behind the wheel and pushed open the passenger door. Rafael got in.

They began their journey. Traveling in utter silence they moved out of the Hispanic neighborhood and into a predominantly black one.

The colors of the skin around them changed, but the poverty was the same, as were the looks of hopelessness in the eyes of the elderly, contempt in those of the youthful, and hope in the children. These people and the Hispanics were all the same, yet separated by language, style of dress and skin color the two groups would never unite. We are in this together, Rafael thought, but he realized that few felt as he did.

The car pulled into the driveway of a rundown single family dwelling on Naomi

Street. There was no grass in the front yard, and the fruit trees had long since turned barren. The soil that they clung to was a forgotten shade of gray. Nothing could grow there; nothing would want to.

The two men climbed from the car in silence, mounted the dusty porch and entered the house. The place was as dark as a tomb. Rafael removed his shades, and the two men stood in the doorway allowing their eyes to adjust to the gloom. Rafael immediately became aware of the fetid atmosphere of the place. It was the odor of despair.

They proceeded down a short corridor that emptied into a tiny living room. There, seated at a long wooden table in the dimly lit room, was The Coalition, five men of Mexican descent. Their eyes immediately fell upon him, eyes filled with respect, wonder and mistrust. Their clothes matched the bleakness of the neighborhood, but Rafael knew that in this room there was real power. And it was *he* they were waiting for.

A fat man (fatter than Sanchez) rose from the group with great expanse and prepared to speak. He leaned against the table, clearing his throat. His eyes touched those of each of the men before him before coming to rest on Rafael's.

"You may call me Rodriguez," he said in a voice that commanded respect. Rafael sensed he was a man used to giving orders. "In fact, you may call all of us Rodriguez," he went on. "Our names are unimportant. What is important is the task we are about to undertake." He paused for effect and again eyed the faces of the men at the table. "Gentlemen. Rafael." His right arm arched in a flourish towards the terrorist.

There was a brief, awesome silence in which the power again shot through Rafael. These were important men, but not as important as he was.

A thin man with watery eyes and slivers of gray slicing through his black hair broke Rafael's train of thought.

"Excuse me, señor, but how do we know that you are truly Rafael?" he asked. He spoke in guarded tones and possessed the beady eyes of a man who has built his career in mistrust.

"Gentlemen, we have been over this," Sanchez said. "I have taken the proper precautions." The annoyance in his voice was obvious.

"What precautions?" the thin man asked. He wore a floral print shirt, the kind any small-town midwesterner might bring back from his first trip to Hawaii. He appeared idiotic and insignificant, but Rafael knew this couldn't be farther from the truth.

"Amigos," Sanchez said, "I thought you trusted my judgment, my ability to bring you Rafael. Questions like these offend me greatly. Are you suddenly questioning my ability to bring you the right man?" Ignoring his adversary, Sanchez's eyes moved to Rodriguez.

"Yes," the floral shirt growled. "There is too much at stake here. Our lives, our fortunes, our futures. I cannot see myself putting these precious things on the line just because someone claims to be Rafael."

"You should have thought of that before you gave me full responsibility," Sanchez snapped.

"Believe me, it wasn't my idea!"

Finally Rodgriguez chimed in. "Amigos, please, we have a guest in our presence." There was a softness to his voice, yet immediate silence fell over the room. The power he exercised over these men was obvious.

"Have I not passed the tests?" Rafael said suddenly. His eyes moved mockingly to Sanchez.

"Tests?" Rodriguez asked. "What tests?"

"There were precautions," Sanchez replied and began to fidget.

"Did Sanchez not tell you?" Rafael went on with a smirk. "The wait. The woman."

"It is not for you to know," Sanchez said.

"We demand to know," the floral print said. "All of our asses are on the line here. The least we can know is what you did to assure you brought us the right man."

Sanchez began to squirm. He looked to

Rodriguez for assistance but saw only un-flagging contempt lurking behind the man's eyes. Thoughts of Angel crept into his consciousness, and he suddenly found it difficult to stand. His legs felt as though they were turning to jelly. "There was a girl," he said helplessly. "A prostitute."

"Enough!" Rodriguez finally said. "Why are we suddenly at one another's throats?" he asked, pushing his contempt aside for the moment. Yet he knew there was a score to be settled with Sanchez. "For the first time since the plan has been hatched our objective is in sight. Our coalition has been built on trust. Do we choose now to begin mistrusting one another?" Confident eyes challenged the faces around him. "We do not need to know, Señor Sanchez." And to Rafael he added, "Welcome to our little family." He extended his hand and smiled.

"Welcome," the others said, all except the man in the floral shirt, who sat eyeing Rafael contemptuously.

A moment later they were all sitting, as slowly Rodriguez began to outline what was to be done.

"So you're the big TV star."

It was recess at the Sixth Street Elementary School. Grant had come running out, as he always did, into the yard, lining up at the fountain for a drink. He'd reached the front and was about to take his turn when there was a tap on his shoulder. He turned and stared into the smirking face of the new kid in the fifth grade—Bert Reynolds.

"I'm no TV star," Grant said, his eyes dropping quickly to the ground. Grant had heard about the new kid. He was ten, a full year older than Grant.

"I'm no TV star," the new kid repeated in a nasal singsong. Mean eyes peered at Grant with contempt. "Doggone right you ain't," he said. "I'm the only star in this school. My name's Bert Reynolds. Bert with a *e*. I'm named for a movie star." Grant nodded. "You're not a TV star at all. Know what you are?" Grant shook his head. "You're nuthin' but a hunk of shit," he said with a grin. He looked to the faces around him for approval.

"Shit," the new kid repeated with a loud chuckle. Smiles appeared on each of the faces his eyes challenged. Then he looked at the fountain.

"Go on, get your drink," he said in a voice that reeked false sincerity.

Grant glanced quickly at the scattering of kids. They too had heard of the new boy and had come to see him in action. Jimmy Buckley was among them. Grant was glad to see a friend's face among the greedy-eyed kids.

"I'm not thirsty no more," Grant said, his confidence beginning to soar as he contemplated a way out. "Hey, Jimmy, let's go play some kickball," he called to his friend, hoping to make a clean getaway.

"Uh-uh," Jimmy said softly. Grant couldn't hide his surprise.

"But . . ."

"Jimmy says you think you're a big TV star," Bert Reynolds said.

Grant looked at his friend and saw the betrayal scrawled across his face and the envy in his eyes.

"TV stars go first around here. Even if they are only shit," Bert said. He paused, then added menacingly, "You gonna drink, or am I gonna havta make you?"

Frantically Grant's eyes scanned the yard, searching for a teacher, any teacher, but they were all somewhere else, supervising play.

"Drink!" Bert Reynolds commanded.

And Grant did. Slowly he brought his head down to the fountain and started to drink. He knew what was going to happen, but he was too scared to do anything about it. The cool water slid by his lips, entered his mouth and began its soothing trip down his throat. He really was thirsty.

Then a hand was on the back of his head, pushing him closer until his entire face was bathed in the flow. Water skittered up his nostrils, dripping down the front of his shirt. Abruptly the hand pulled him up.

"I'm drinkin' first," the new kid said.

"Man before beast!" He laughed again,
eyeing the growing crowd for support.

Grant blushed with humiliation, as water
slid from his chin, splattering his shoes. He
again looked at the crowd and saw that
Jimmy Buckley actually was enjoying it.

Bert Reynolds started his drink. Grant
watched, the humiliation of it all building
inside of him. It started as a tiny red dot, a
flicker in the cavity of his chest that spread
steadily as he eyed the snickering faces in
the crowd. It grew like a flash fire eating
away at old ragweed and dead grass, yet
this flame was fueled by human emotion.

It grew within him to immense proportions, until the raging flames burned
through his chest and licked at his mind.
Then suddenly the flame seized control of
the mechanism in him that operated his
arms and legs, as the little boy in charge
bailed out. The raging fire within was now
in command.

The next few seconds went quickly, yet to
Grant they seemed frozen like a fossil in the
sediment of suspended animation. His
hand, seized by the monster within, darted
out and went to the back of the new kid's
head, pushing down—hard!

The *thunk* of the boy's tooth hitting the
steel spigot reverberated through him, and
he jerked back in revulsion.

Now the kid was standing, facing him.
Tears were in his eyes, but a nasty grin was

slithering across his lips. When they parted Grant saw his mouth was filling with blood that spurted freely from a gash in his gums.

"S . . . sorry," Grant said.

"Not half as sorry as you're gonna be," Bert stammered angrily. Then he started to swing.

The initial blow caught Grant in the eye, and he actually saw a star, big and bright, just like he might see when one of his favorite cartoon characters got clobbered. The pain went singing through his head, reminding him this was no cartoon.

Then the new kid was on him, forcing him to the ground with a flurry of misguided punches, as the ring of specators knotted around them.

And just as quickly, it was over. Mrs. Redmond pulled the new kid off and was shaking him like a dust rag.

The bell rang, ending recess. Slowly the kids headed back to class. They'd gotten what they'd come for.

Grant peered at them through a rapidly closing eye, hurting like hell all over. He realized that Jimmy Buckley hadn't moved. He stood motionless, staring at Grant, delight waltzing behind his eyes. Grant couldn't understand what had gotten into him.

A flicker of a smile passed across Jimmy's lips, then he too ran for class. And at that moment the flame of humiliation that raged so recently inside of Grant was doused by an emotion he'd never felt before. It wasn't a new emotion. It was something old and base, something that stank from ages of violence, culled from centuries of hate and locked into his genes. As Grant watched Jimmy running for class, he wanted to kill him.

The dog was barking.

Rodriguez was lying poolside, basking in the warmth of an orange evening sun, when Ginger's distant call came to him.

"Coming, baby," he called back. Rising, he pulled on his beige wrapper and stepped into his thongs. "Coming," he called again, doubting whether the dog could hear him. Her kennel was clear around the other side of the house, facing the road.

When he'd moved into the large, ranch-style home nearly a year ago, he deliberately had the kennel installed on the front of the property, facing the road. Ginger, his golden retriever, had always loved to bark at cars. He knew how miserable she'd be if her living quarters were to the rear, away from all possible contact with automobiles. It was bad enough that very few cars found their way down his secluded stretch of road as it was, but he knew that Ginger waited patiently, and when each car passed, his ears were rewarded by the sheer joy of her calling to the interloping hunks of metal.

Rodriguez rounded the house enroute to the front of the property. His was a beautiful home, with dogwood and Aspen trees to the rear, and flowering beech and gardenia to the front. It was the perfect home for Ginger.

The dog's bark changed in pitch, and he knew she sensed his coming nearer. He was sorry he had to lock her up today. He normally allowed her to roam free when they were at home alone, but today he was expecting a guest, and he didn't want Ginger to frighten him—or harm him, he thought and smiled. Rafael was important to them. He didn't want Ginger scaring him off.

He reached the kennel and unlocked the gate. Ginger's cries changed to good-natured yelps as he approached. She leaped at him, her flagging tongue lashing his face with loving swipes. He reached in the pocket of his wrapper for a dog yummy.

The big dog gobbled up the treat, licking his fingers. He ran a hand over her glossy, sandy colored coat. The dog strained at the chain that bound her to the house and let out a whine of despair.

"Sorry, baby, I can't."

She barked as if she understood, then pulled against the chain again. "Sorry," he repeated, running a soothing hand through her hair. Slowly her agitation abated, and she lay down panting at his feet.

She's a beautiful dog, he thought. He'd had her since she was a pup, six years earlier. During that time his business had grown. His small investment firm had become a factor in the marketplace, but it took hard work and long hours.

Often he worked 12 hour days, seven days a week to build his success, but his ambition had taken its toll on his family life. His relationship with his wife had turned to dust.

I gave her everything, he mused, and she left me for another man. Yet during that time Ginger's unfailing love remained, as each evening when he returned home she was waiting for him with a warm tongue and love.

They'd been through a lot together—success, separation, divorce—the dog's constant loyalty a beacon of support, guiding him over the rocky shoals of difficulty.

"I'll release you soon," he cooed. "As soon as Rafael is gone."

His thoughts turned to the famed terrorist. He had been concerned over Sanchez's sudden revelation: "Perhaps we've chosen the wrong man." He repeated Sanchez's words. The dog's ears pricked up. "Perhaps the wrong man is among us," he said, "but it is not Rafael." He thought with contempt of the fat man trembling before The Coalition.

Ginger began to growl.

"What is it, baby?" Suddenly she was up, barking angrily. Rodriguez looked towards the gate.

Someone was standing hunched by the entrance. He appeared to be an aging derelict, a beggar, but Rodriguez knew better. He smiled, and a soothing hand glided over Ginger's head.

"Relax, baby," he said. "This is the man we've been waiting for, the man who will help make us wealthy beyond our wildest dreams."

He stroked her head again, then left the kennel, walking towards the gate.

The dog was still barking.

The house was quiet and still, with an interminable peace that rankled rather than relaxed, like the quiet before the storm or like a tomb.

Grant lay in his bed. The lights were out but he wasn't sleeping. He shifted his head slightly, searching for comfort, and the dull throbbing in his eye increased momentarily. The new kid had blackened it.

"That's one helluva shiner you got there," his dad had said with a short laugh. He seemed proud that Grant had been in his first fight.

Is this the kind of acceptance I really want? Grant asked himself. Yes, came the answer, though none of this was in cohesive thought. His little boy's mind wasn't sophisticated enough for that. All it understood was that any attention was better than none at all.

Things had been different since his appearance on TV, but not better. The offers were pouring in, and the house was still, but there was something wrong. His mother rarely smiled anymore, and when she addressed his father it was in monosyllables and terse phrases. What Grant had wanted was no more yelling, but not this. This silence was cold and inhuman like stone, with an icy grip whose tentacles ensnared them all. There was no escaping it. Even with the TV blaring it was there, waiting to resume its hold over all of them.

Going away hadn't solved anything. His father went out every evening, returning quite late, and from the looks of his eyes in the mornings Grant thought he might be drinking. Hitting the bottle again is what they said about uncle Harry whenever he looked that way.

His mother had changed, too. Roaming around like a zombie, she executed her dance macabre through a life she seemingly wanted no part of.

Grant shifted again. The pain in his head screamed, then gradually softened to a banshee-like wail. He closed his eyes to sleep, to paint over the problem with an ink blot of dark, tangled dreams, but sleep would not come. The house was quiet, so quiet he wanted to scream.

While Grant was lying wide-eyed waiting for sleep, Ginger was staring up at the sky. From where she lay in front of her dog house she had a full view of the huge, pale sphere drifting through the heavens. It had seemed years since a car had gone by, and she was considering howling at the moon.

She remembered the tone in her master's voice the last time she howled, and she knew she shouldn't. However, if she did howl her master would come out, and no matter what his tone, it was good when he was around.

The truth, however, was that she had no choice. This decision had been made for her eons ago, its residue now stored in each of her canine chromosomes. When Ginger looked at the moon it touched something within, something that dragged up the fear and loneliness of centuries of leading a dog's life. When Ginger looked up at the moon something reached down into the hollowness of her soul, and she was compelled to call to her ancestors.

She stood, and a low, baying moan started deep in her throat.

"Wooooooo."

The loneliness and fear would not go away, so she threw back her head and yowled.

"Yowoooooeee!"

Her voice went from low to high, covering the spectrum and then back again.

Crack.

What was that? The howl died instantly in the large dog's throat. She looked around. Something was out there, perhaps a skunk or a rat. If only her master had come out to undo her chain or open the gate. Then she could catch the thing, maybe even kill it. That would please him.

A large, shadowy figure dashed from behind a tree near the front of the grounds, heading for one closer to the kennel. It ducked into a shadow. This time she heard nothing, but she saw.

The moon totally forgotten, a ferocious growl lulled in her chest. She sniffed at the air, catching the odor of the shadowy creature. Man.

Ginger began to bark, shattering the night silence. These were not the good-natured, fun barks she reserved for cars. These were cries of warning. If her master came out now he would be pleased with her.

The dark figure was moving again. Boldly he stepped from behind the tree and approached the kennel. Good. If he was foolish enough to get too close she would go for his throat.

The man, dressed all in black, stopped at

the gate. He displayed his perfect teeth for the dog, and a flurry of questions—impulses, really—exploded in her mind. Who is this stranger? What is he doing here? She realized of course the answer didn't matter. If he came too close she would kill him.

A low, gutteral groan came from somewhere deep in her chest. She strained against the chain that bound her to her house, every muscle intent on snapping the steel links.

The stranger removed something from his pocket and began working on the lock. A few minutes later something clicked and the lock fell open, like a whore yielding up her secrets for something cheap and gaudy.

The man was staring at her now, smiling, and suddenly Ginger was afraid. The fear tore into her like a shot in the dark, ripping her instincts to tatters. She looked into the man's eyes and in them saw the hollow emptiness of the moon.

He entered, the thing in his hand now concealed behind his back.

"Good doggie," he cooed.

Ginger hauled back the loose flesh around her mouth, showing her teeth. Spit slicked incisors glistened in the moonlight.

The stranger came nearer.

Ginger crouched, her belly brushing against the hard, brown earth, each sinewy muscle wound tight as piano wire.

He was now just six paces from her.

Their eyes locked. A steady rumbling drifted from her throat. She waited for her time.

Now!

The large dog sprung at the man with all the nimbleness of a bear. Launched in flight, her gleaming teeth zeroed in on her target.

Then at once, almost dreamlike, the man sidestepped her, and 75 pounds of dog went sailing clumsily in the wrong direction.

As she drifted past him her mind was already working on the second strike, and the third, if need be. It was then that the man's hand swung from behind his back. The dog didn't see the knife as it moved towards her with blazing speed.

Wham!

The blade slammed into her midsection with monstrous force, passing through flesh and fiber like a hot spoon through a pound of butter. Ginger let out a terrific yelp as the pain throttled her belly.

She thudded against the ground, the wind flying out of her, as the ground pushed the hot thing deep into her intestines.

She rolled onto her back and looked up. This stranger, had tricked her. He loomed over her, and she let out a cry of mercy, hoping he would remove the hot thing from her aching guts, yet from the malevolence that danced in his eyes she knew he would not.

Her leathery tongue lashed out, hoping to lick his boots, as her breath came hot and raspy. He was the victor, the king. Now if only he would remove the hot thing, she would be his forever. She screamed, the anguish in her cries calling to whatever mercy was buried in his soul.

As he kneeled over her, she offered him her throat, a symbolic gesture of her conqueror. He reached for the knife.

Puppylike cries now drifted from her lips as he rested his hand on the butt of the knife. Then suddenly the night silence was destroyed by a grief-stricken scream. It started in the depths of her bowels and flew from her lips on the wings of the pale dove of death. His powerful hand had yanked the knife upward, towards her rib cage, sliting the dog up the middle. He turned her onto her side, and her guts came slithering out.

No longer strong enough to cry, Ginger lay on the ground, her tongue lolling from her mouth. She stared at the stranger, tried to lick his boots, to apologize, but her strength, along with her life, went spilling to the earth, and all she could do was stare. She wanted his forgivness, wanted to be his friend, but she'd never be able to tell him.

Ginger died, her tongue resting against the smooth leather of his boot, her eyes pointing skyward, glinting at the pale loneliness of the moon.

Rafael stood. The animal had been large

and powerful, and it had taken much of his strength to subdue her. He stared down at the carcass. A steamy smoke rose from the gash in the animal's belly. The odor of blood and the dog's internal gasses wafted up to him.

He bent, wiping his hand on Ginger's cooling coat. Then turning, he stole away from the kennel, darting behind trees, only to be swallowed whole by shadows in the night.

CHAPTER
9

"Hey, babe," Allen Michaels called as he strolled through the door. "Still up?"

Eve didn't answer. She looked at the clock—3:15 A.M.—then balefully at her husband.

"Whatsa matter?" he said a little too loudly. He moved towards her on the sofa, banging his knee on the coffee table. "Damn," he muttered as he stumbled and fell into his recliner.

He pulled up his pants leg and eyed the reddish bruise on his shin. Then lowering it again he looked at Eve. "Whatsa matter with you lately? Got a bug up your ass or something?"

No answer.

"You should be grinning from ear to ear, not going around like the grim reaper."

Still no reply.

"Don't you wanna be rich?"

Eve's mouth dropped open, her reply coming in a gush. She strangled the words on her lips, only emitting a quick, soft sigh.

"What the hell's the matter with you?" Allen charged.

She eyed him gravely, choosing her words carefully. "What's the matter with you?" she said softly.

Allen started to say something, but the look Eve shot him stopped him.

"Is this the kind of life you've talked about all these years? Is this what you want?" Her eyes bore into him. He wasn't used to seeing his wife so commanding and sat mesmerized. "Yes," she finally said, "I suppose it is." She stood before continuing and peered sadly down at her husband. "It's my fault, you know? I should have stopped you years ago."

"Stopped me? Why?"

"Because it's wrong. I tried to fool myself into believing that what you wanted you wanted for all of us. I told myself 'he's just thinking of his family,' but I knew it wasn't true. You've never thought of us."

"What?" Allen blurted. "It was true! It is!"

"No." She shook her head sadly. "It's for

you, just for you. It's some crazy need to prove yourself you've probably had since you were a kid."

"That's crazy," he said.

"You don't care about me or Grant." She said this with realization coming only the moment the words hit her lips. "You're using your son as a tool."

"Now, listen here, Eve . . ." Allen was regaining his old composure. He said the words he'd spoken many times, but this time when he looked into his wife's eyes he saw a challenge that hadn't been there before. The fight tumbled out of him.

"Look at you," she said, her voice steady and controlled. "You've been drinking again."

"Celebrating," he said. Realizing he was slumping in the chair, he straightened. "Nothing wrong with a few drinks, is there?"

"No. But you've never been a drinking man before, and now . . . every night." She paused. "You're drunk."

"No . . ." He started to say more, but realized it was useless. "Okay. I had a few too many."

"And today, when Grant came home with the black eye, you seemed almost proud."

A flicker of a smile blossomed on his lips. He killed it, but not before Eve had a chance to see it there.

"I'm ashamed of you," she said. Her

words thudded against his ears.

"I *should* be proud of my son," he said half-heartedly.

"Not for fighting. And why have you started to drink?"

He looked at his wife and did not see the woman he married so many years ago. Young and frightened, she then was more girl than woman. Who this person was he didn't know. He had no answers for her.

"I asked myself this question every night," Eve went on. "Why? I had the answer all along, but I kept dismissing it. But I can't anymore. I can't avoid the truth, Allen."

"What truth?" he asked.

"This elusive thing you've searched for all your life is dropped in your lap, and you don't know what to do. You're scared."

"Me, scared?" He let out a short, nervous laugh. "That's ridiculous."

"Oh? Then tell me, what's wrong?"

"Nothing. Everything is fine. Honey, it's for all of us. Really!"

"Now you just listen here, Allen Michaels, 'cause I'm only going to say this once. He's my son, too, and I can stop this whenever I'm ready."

"You wouldn't do that," he said. It was more a question than a statement.

Eve continued staring down at her husband for a long moment. Then without another word she moved to the staircase, shooting a final, baleful glance over her shoulder before climbing the stairs to bed.

The dreams finally came—clingy black things with a mortician's grip on his mind. In them Grant was going away.

It was night, inky and moonless, and the sky was filled with an unseen terror. Grant tumbled out of himself into the heavens. A lone, sparkling rocket sped through the gloom.

When Grant drifted over and peered into the window, the pilot, Bert Reynolds, grinned out at him like a Cheshire cat.

"I kicked your ass," he said. "I kicked your ass good, faggot."

If it had been daylight and Grant had been in the schoolyard he would have been scared. But it was night, and they were in the sky. The sky was his domain.

"Don't mess with me," he said with the new kid.

"Aw, shut up, faggot!" He tried to speed the rocket away, but it couldn't travel faster than Grant's thoughts. His thoughts were powerful, and he knew it.

"Apologize," he told the boy.

"Fuck off!"

"Apologize!" he commanded.

"Make me, shithead." The gun metal sky was filled with the laughter of a thousand kids.

"If you don't apologize I'll crash your

plane."

The new kid laughed.

"I'll crash the plane. I will!" Grant said, remembering the last time he went away.

"Fuck you," the new kid said. The voices were laughing all around him, unseen voices that filled him with humiliation.

"I don't want to crash the plane," he said. "I don't want to do it!" He could feel the perspiration beginning in his armpits. "But I will if I have to," he added. The laughter around him increased, his father's bellowing guffaws joining in. "Apologize," he said helplessly.

"Beat it!" the new kid said, banking the rocket sharply to the right. But escaping him was impossible.

The laughter was now so loud it banged around inside his head, the humiliation in him bubbling up until he thought his reddened face would burst. "I warned you!"

The power leaped out of him. He didn't want to do it. He had warned them all, but they just wouldn't listen.

The force traveled from him like a bolt of lightning, smiting the rocket like a fly. Suddenly the rocket was in a swift, helpless swan dive, and there was nothing anyone could do about it.

He again peered into the window. Bert Reynolds looked scared. Good! He looked into the passenger section and saw Jimmy

Buckley and all the smirking kids. Grant smiled.

Then suddenly he looked into the last row, and there sat his mom and dad.

"Granty, stop the plane!" his mother screamed. "Please!"

He wanted to stop it, or at least slow it down so they could jump out, but it was already too late. "I can't!" he cried. "Jump!"

They never had a chance. The rocket slammed into the ground. There was a thunderous explosion that sent a spray of molten cinder splashing the black canvas of night with blotches of violent reds and yellows.

"No!" Grant screamed. "Mommy, Daddy! No!" He pitched and turned in bed, and the fire jumped into his eye.

Grant bolted upright, the nightmare still alive in his mind. The pain in his eye from the fight that afternoon was a bitter reminder that his reality was almost as bad as the dream.

Slowly he took in the familiar sights of his room, and the terror subsided. He sat for a full minute reliving the final moments of the dream. Throughout the encounter he felt as if someone had been watching.

After a while he lay back down, attempting to recapture sleep, yet afraid of what he might find. So he lay, his eyes wide open. When finally he did close them a clear image of dark hair and a perfect smile invaded his thoughts. Grant Michaels began to shake.

CHAPTER 10

Allen Michaels was in the grips of a fitful sleep of his own. He fidgeted restlessly in the highback recliner while Johnny Carson's voice wove its way into the fabric of his dreams.

Allen was guest host on the Tonight Show, subbing for Johnny. Phil Reed was in the audience, heckling.

"Fake!" Phil Reed screamed. "Phony!"

"I told you he could do it," Allen said, trying to remain calm, but the entire audience was laughing at him. Hundreds of laughing voices attacked him. "He can predict air disasters," Allen said.

"No, I can't. I'm a fake." It was Grant.

"Don't play, son," Allen said nervously. "Tell them the truth."

"I *am* telling the truth, don't you remember? I told you I couldn't do it again."

The crowd was no longer laughing. Led by Phil Reed they suddenly turned into angry hecklers, filing out into the aisles and heading for the stage. Venom was in their eyes.

"I'm a fake," Grant said.

"A phony," Phil Reed called. He was now walking onto the stage and the audience like zombies followed, mimicking his cry in echoed tones. *Phony . . . phony . . . phony . . . phony . . .*

Allen Michaels rose. "It's true!" Phil and the audience surrounded him.

"You knew he couldn't do it again," Phil Reed said. "He told you."

Like a hangman's noose the ring of zombies knotted around him, their fingers reaching for his throat.

"It's the truth," Allen said. He tried to run, but everywhere he turned hungry fingers reached out.

They fell on him.

"Noooo."

"Dad."

"Tell them, son! Tell them you can do it again!" Viselike talons began wringing the life from him.

"Dad."

"Please, son. Tell them!"

Allen Michaels' eyes flew open like a window shade with a faulty spring. "Dad, you okay?" It was Grant.

Allen looked around. He was seated in his recliner in front of the TV. It had all been some horrible dream.

"Dad?"

"Yeah, son, I'm all right. I had a bit of a nightmare. Dreamt we were hosting the Carson show. Fans were so excited they were mobbin' us." He smiled at Grant. "We'll probably get a chance to host for Carson one night. Just you wait and see."

"I had a bad dream, too, Dad." There was a soft seriousness in Grant's eyes.

"Oh, yeah?" Allen changed the subject. "Say, you got any other exciting news to share with the world. You know, maybe another plane crash or something?"

"No, Dad, but . . ."

"Good. Save it. We're going to be on *That's Incredible Special Edition* next week. I think you should have your next revelation on national, prime time TV. How 'bout that, son?"

"Dad, about the dream, I . . ."

"Surprise me, son," Allen said with a short laugh. "Surprise me along with the rest of the world. This way I won't have to fake it."

"Dad, there was something about the plane crash, the first one that . . ."

"Yeah, you really surprised me with that one."

". . . the man, Charlie Sachs, he died . . ."

"Yeah. Tough way to go. Hey, maybe we could save somebody next time, you know. Kinda predict a broken wing or somethin', before he takes off."

"*Dad!*" Grant was surprised by his own outburst. He stood silent for a full minute, trying to make sure it was really him.

Allen Michaels sat upright, staring at his son. There'd been a lot of changes in the boy lately, all to the good. "Grant, was that you?" He'd been waiting for the boy to show a little fire, and it was finally coming.

"Dad, the man in the airplane. There's somethin' I gotta tell you," Grant said. His father looked questioningly into his eyes. "I don't think he died in the crash."

"Huh? Come again? He's dead, son, deader than a doornail. Fried to a crisp."

The odor of burning flesh again invaded Grant's nostrils, but he forced it away. The image of the incident rather than fading in his thoughts had become more vivid as time passed. Each night as he lay in his bed the image became clearer, until finally he realized he'd seen more than he thought. "Dad, he was dead before the plane hit. Someone killed him."

Allen slowly digested what Grant had just told him. "Come here, son," he said softly. Grant drifted over. His father grabbed him firmly by the wrist. "Are you sure?"

"Not really, but . . ."

"Listen to me, son." Allen's grip tightened. "This is none of our business. He's dead, and there's nothing either of us can do about it. Besides, you're not sure anyway. Right?" Grant nodded. "Then let's keep this just between us. Okay, pal?"

Grant stared silently into his father's eyes. He was sorry he had spoken. "Okay," he said.

The grip loosened on his wrist. "Hey, now what about predicting something that could save lives? You know, maybe prevent an accident before it happens."

"I can't do it," Grant said softly.

"Sure you can. You did it twice already. And son, the second time was beautiful, just beautiful. I still can't get over the look on that Reed jerk's face when they verified what happened. Just like you said."

Grant looked away. "I can't do it again. And even if I could, I don't want to."

Allen Michaels exploded. "What the hell are you talking about? Now see here, Grant, it ain't up to you to decide if you want to do it again. I'm your father, and you *will* do it again." Allen jmped up and nervously began pacing. "I took out a second mortgage on this home just so I didn't have to work, so I could be around to manage you and make sure no one took advantage of this wonderful talent of yours. Don't you love us?"

"Yes." Grant's eyes were misting over. He didn't want to cry, but he couldn't help it. Confusion tangled his thoughts.

"Well, you couldn't prove it by your attitude, could you? Me and your mom bust our humps to give you everything, and this is our payback? Well, thanks a lot, son!"

"Dad, you don't understand. I can't sleep . . ."

"Oh, I understand, all right." Allen gripped his son by the shoulders, bringing his face inches from Grant's. Grant tried to look away, but no matter how hard he tried his father's eyes bore into him. "Listen here. Next week we're going on *That's Incredible*, and you're gonna predict something wonderful and fantastic. And this is the last time I want to hear about not doing it again. You better do it again, or you're in big trouble. You got me? Big trouble!"

Allen Michaels released his son. Grant, his eyes filled with tears, ran into the kitchen.

A lazy fly drifted aimlessly around the room, and Grant's gaze locked on the fly as he remembered his father's words. "Big trouble!" He had come downstairs to confide in him, to tell his father of the trouble he was having, but he wouldn't listen.

I can't go away. I can't!

Anger coursed through him as he remembered all the things that had gone wrong, all because he had gone away. And now his father was insisting he do it again.

"I hate you, Daddy! I hate you!" A shout in his mind fell from his lips as a vile whisper. The energy and anger were still somewhere inside, expanding like hot air, filling his brain and searching for a way out. But he wouldn't scream; he couldn't. He continued holding onto his anger.

Then without warning something inside him jumped. A force he never felt before leaped from his mind with the fury of a thousand megaton lightning bolt. He was staring at the fly when the thing jumped out of him.

Splat!

The fly exploded, miniscule bits of dead insect hanging in the air before dropping to the floor. The force retreated, back inside Grant's mind.

Grant stood motionless for endless minutes, his mouth hanging open, his eyes staring into nothingness. "Oh, shit," he said, horror creeping into his vacant stare. "Holy shit!"

CHAPTER 11

Rafael threw down a shot of tequila and salted the back of his hand. He was seated on the bed in front of the TV, in a tiny hotel room he had called home for the past few days.

Idiots, he thought, rich, pompous idiots. All of them. His mind was on The Coalition as his eyes clouded in anger. They knew nothing of working in the groves 12 hours a day, or tattered clothes and debts you could never hope to repay. They did not, could not, understand terrorism. They were rich, from an elite class. They were the ones upon whom acts of terror should be perpetrated.

Rafael eyed the TV as he mapped out a plan. Now that he knew all of the details he no longer needed The Coalition. They were a luxury he could ill afford; those money hungry capitalists were just using him to get richer. He spat on the floor.

"Their kind never has enough," he said to the TV. On the other hand, he was not in this for monetary gain. He was in this for the sake of terrorism, a noble cause.

Rafael grabbed the bottle atop the bureau and poured himself another shot. Memories of his boyhood lapped at his thoughts, but he quickly blotted them out. These memories left a bitter taste in his mouth, a taste he wanted to obliterate once and for all.

Rafael threw down tequila and sucked salt.

This had been a special mission right from the beginning. It was time to set things straight and to punish the world for the injustices heaped upon his family. Still, he could not allow himself to be swayed by emotion. There was no room for emotion in terrorism.

Rafael poured another shot, salting the back of his hand. That's when he heard the noise. He set the shot glass down quietly on the carpet and listened. The drone of a silly man's voice on the TV was the only discernible sound.

Reaching under his pillow Rafael

clutched the stiletto. It's reassuring coolness sent a wave of confidence riding
through him. With catlike quickness he was
at the door, listening. Yes, there was someone out there. He could hear the breathing
—one man, alone.

Fools, Rafael thought. Yet he was also beginning to wonder about his own careless-
ness.

There was movement, directly opposite
the door.

Rafael's left hand caressed the doorknob as the stiletto slipped open. His
muscles tightened into hard little knots.
Quickly he swung the door wide, leaping
into the corridor, the stiletto rapidly
moving into place opposite the man's
throat. Then with the knife inches from its
target he stopped cold, looked dumbly at
his victim.

A drunken sailor stood fumbling with the
door across the hall, just a boy, not more
than 20. Reflexes slowed by drunkeness,
the sailor didn't turn fully around until the
blade was out of sight.

"Shh," he said in a loud whisper, placing
a finger to his lips for demonstrative
emphasis. "Don't wake Susiecue." Close
cropped blond hair peeked from beneath a
white sailor's cap. His eyes were a raging
river of red. "Susiecue's my wife. Just
married," he added with a drunken smile.
"This is my wedding night."

Rafael donned his perfect smile. "You look a little too . . . how you say, inebriated to enjoy it."

"Oh, no," said the sailor. "Now I'm just right." He glanced around the corridor as if he and Rafael were hatching a conspiracy. He stepped closer. "See, I never did it before." Rafael caught the odor of cheap wine on his breath, as he draped an arm around Rafael's shoulder. "Hell, Susiecue's the only real woman I ever seen naked—'cept for Mom." He gave a short, embarrassed laugh. "I'm no pervert or nothing. You know how things are?"

"Yes," Rafael said.

"Anyhow, how could I tell her, you know, me bein' a sailor and all? How could I tell her the truth? She kind of expected . . . Hell, one of us ought to have some experience. Right?"

"Go in and tell her the truth," Rafael said.

"Hey, that's easy for you to say. I bet you're a real lady-killer, right?"

Rafael's smile faded.

"She's asleep now," the sailor went on. "I'm shipping out in the morning. She'll be pissed, of course. Think I been with another woman. Hell, that's better than believing I'm less than a man. Right?"

Rafael didn't answer. He removed the man's arm from his shoulder, also relieving himself of the sailor's dead weight, and helped him over to the door.

"Talk to her," he said softly. He helped the man open the door and shoved him in. "Just talk."

"Yeah. Okay," the sailor replied.

Rafael returned to his room. The silly TV program droned on. He plopped down on the bed, listened momentarily, then punched the TV to black. Bedtime, he thought. Things were starting to heat up. He would need his rest.

Friday afternoon at 2:30 is a special time for a kid. When that final school bell of the week rings, announcing the beginning of the weekend, a fog seems to lift over school houses across America.

What on Monday morning had seemed an evil queen, a harbinger of foreboding doom, by Friday afternoon somehow became a dear old friend. And while you've hated her all week, by the time that final bell goes off, she's slowly snuck into your heart, and you can't help but have a speck of remorse for her as you leave her protective arms and head for home. No kid ever admits this, of course, not even to a friend. Saying you miss the old school house is like saying you miss the measles or the chicken pox or liver.

At 2:32 Friday afternoon, Grant Michaels stepped to the sidewalk in front of the Sixth Street Elementary School and breathed a sigh of relief. Over, he thought. The week was finally over.

He lingered briefly on the steps of the old building before beginning the lonely trek homeward, his mind flirting with his choice of Saturday morning cartoons. Since he'd predicted the crashes his father had given him the privilege of watching whatever he wanted.

Grant slowly headed up Sixth Street towards Sycamore. He hated walking alone, but what else could he do? If Mom ever found out he no longer walked home with Jimmy Buckley she'd insist on picking him up—and that would happen over his dead body. After all, he was in the fifth grade. He wasn't a kid anymore. Besides, if Bert Reynolds saw his mom picking him up it would just make things worse, and things were already bad enough.

Crossing Sycamore he continued up the block towards Magnolia. It was a nice walk, even if he was doing it all by himself. Most of the kids went in a different direction, and the few who traveled his way were sixth graders, who wanted nothing to do with him. But that was all right. Grant could get lost in his thoughts.

Grant turned left on Magnolia and started down the block. This was his favorite block to walk through. Here he could look at the beautiful homes with their flower gardens. Grant liked flowers, and no, he wasn't no sissy. He liked them for his mother. She always wanted a nice flower garden. Maybe with the money from TV they could buy a new house like the ones on Magnolia.

I will not go away again!

Walking home seemed to be the only time Grant could escape from the thing that gnawed at his thoughts. Walking, he thought of Mom and pretty homes and flowers and cartoons.

"Hey, Grant, wait up." It was Jimmy's voice.

Grant turned with wonder and delight. Maybe Jimmy had come to his senses.

"Hey, wait for us," Jimmy called. Grant saw he wasn't alone. Bert Reynolds and Albert Weinmeiller were with him.

Grant wanted to run. He could tell from the mischief in their eyes that it was his turn again, but if he ran they'd catch him for sure. Besides, you couldn't run forever. If they didn't catch him today they'd catch him Monday or maybe Tuesday. No, running was out. If he got his ass kicked at least they'd know Grant Michaels was no fag.

"Hi, Grant old pal," Bert said as they approached. "Jimmy tells me you're going on TV again. *That's Incredible.*" The boys stopped, automatically encircling him in a triangle. Bert Reynolds was smirking.

"Yeah," Grant said, looking Bert in the eye, "I am."

"I hear you can predict airplane crashes."

"Uh-huh."

"Go on. Predict one." Bert's lips curled into a challenging sneer. "Go on!"

Grant looked into six disbelieving eyes. "I can't right now," he said.

"I can't right now," came Bert's singsong voice. "Never could. Liar!"

Grant didn't answer. He was wondering why Jimmy would go around with a creep like Bert Reynolds, and how bad the beating would hurt.

"I knew you couldn't do it," Jimmy said. "You just wanna be a big shot. You and your old man."

"I gotta go home," Grant said. "My mom's waiting to take me to the dentist."

"Oh, Mommy's waiting," Bert said.

"I meant my dad," Grant said.

"My father says your father's an uppity so and so," Jimmy said. He eyed Grant, the green flames of envy flickering behind his pupils. "And you're phony, too."

"Jimmy, what's the matter with you?" Grant found himself asking. "You're my best friend."

Fury blazed across Bert's face. He turned to Jimmy, his face a mask of questioning contempt.

"Liar, liar, pants on fire," Jimmy said. "I ain't never been your friend."

"Yes," Grant said boldly.

"You let him lie on you like that?" Bert asked Jimmy. "If it was me I'd fix him good."

Now the ball was in Jimmy's court. "You take that back," he said to Grant. His voice lacked conviction.

"You loaned me your Rambo and Mr. T., remember?" A flicker of a smile flashed across Grant's lips. It was a pleasure watching Jimmy squirm.

"You stole them!" Jimmy charged. He turned to the others. "He stole them!"

"Hit him," Bert said coolly.

Jimmy turned back to Grant. He stared into his eyes, and Grant noticed he was trembling. "Crapola breath!" he said and shoved Grant into Albert.

"Crapola breath," Albert called with a grin, getting the gist of the game. He shoved.

Grant went caroming into Jimmy, then catching his balance he stood staring at his old friend for a long moment. Years of friendship passed between them, and suddenly the friendship was over—forever. Jimmy slammed Grant into Bert, Bert into Albert, Albert into Jimmy.

Grant bounced from one to the other like a pinball, barely catching his balance before being shoved again. But Bert was getting bored, so he knocked Grant in the back of the head, then kicked him onto someone's lawn. Grant stumbled and tripped, then landed in a bed of geraniums. He sat sprawled in the flower garden, his face a rash of humiliation. A bee buzzed by his head, then realizing he was no flower, the insect flitted off. That's when the laughter started.

Bert was first, his laughter long and loud, as the malice he felt towards Grant came spilling from his lips, a richly high pitched overture of what was to come. Then Albert joined in, and finally Jimmy, their voices joining Bert's rat-tat-tat, a crescendo that assaulted Grant's ears.

Grant sat, staring up at the boys and hating them, but this hatred was different than the last time. It was no longer hot but instead icy cold and deadly. He hated them with a cold, calculating hate that oozed from his pores, slipping over his entire being, a sticky web waiting to ensnare its victims. At that moment Grant wanted to hurt. The pain inflicted upon himself no longer mattered. All that mattered was hurting the boys—badly.

"Spit on him," Bert said. The laughter ended abruptly.

"Huh?" asked Jimmy.

"He lied on you, man. Spit on him."

"But . . ."

"Spit on him. You scared or sumphin'?"

"No." Jimmy latched onto every bit of malevolence he'd ever felt towards anyone and aimed it at Grant. "You lied on me!"

His words filled the air with contempt. "I'll teach you!" *Phloom.*

Suddenly the thing again leaped from Grant's mind. It beaded on the glob of phlegm, making it turn an impossible arc. The spit landed—*splat*—in Bert Reynold's face.

"Stupid!" Bert screamed, wiping his face with his shirt-sleeve. "Can't you even spit?"

"I did," Jimmy stammered. "He did it. He did it." He was pointing at Grant.

"Yeah," Bert said. The smirk was back. "He did, didn't he? Let's fix him good."

The boys stepped towards Grant, and for the first time he realized there was something important happenng inside of him. For one thing, he wasn't scared. In fact, he felt powerful—powerful and mean.

"Don't come any closer," he said. His voice, no longer weak and wispy, dripped new found confidence.

The boys kept coming.

"I'm warning you," he said. Bert Reynolds smirked, just like he did in the dream. "Stop!" The word exploded from his lips, freezing the boys in their tracks.

The power seemed to grow with every step Bert took. And while the other boys had stopped and were now eyeing Grant with new found caution, there was no caution in Bert. He was a living reflex action, a Neanderthal, living from impulsive moment to impulsive moment.

Grant knew what he had to do. He realized he'd known it all along. The power in him now was enormous, booming around inside his head and wanting out. Grant looked around the yard. Flowers were all around him, and so were the bees.

Bert stepped closer.

"Please, stop," Grant called, but he knew his warnings were hopeless.

Bert took another step. *Thwap!* A bee went zinging across the yard, banging its stinger into Bert's abdomen.

"Shit!" he screamed. *Thwap. Thwap.* The second slammed into his arm, and the third his shoulder. He saw the fourth coming and knocked the bee out of the air.

"Bert, something funny's going on here," Albert said. He was looking around the yard and was scared. Bees were seemingly being yanked from flowers and flung in the boy's direction. The angry bees must have been calling for reinforcements, for as Albert stared dumbly on, the yard was filling with the singing hum of bumblebees.

He turned to run. *Thwap, thwap, thwap.* Two bees caught him in the shoulder, one in the side of the neck. "Ow!," he bawled, his flailing hands trying to ward off the assault.

Now all three boys were running—or at least trying to—but the bees were on them. When Jimmy Buckley opened his mouth to scream for help, a bee flew in, banging its stinger into the back of his tongue.

Bert's face was a mass of red blotches, his eyes swollen from the barrage of stingers. None of the boys could see, and they scattered, running helter-skelter, not going anywhere, just trying to find refuge from the onslaught of angry bees.

Grant sat silently watching it all, a spectator at a live horror film festival. A slight smile teased at the corners of his lips. The boys were crying and begging. Good. Teach them to mess with me. The bees did not come near him. He was in control, and he knew it.

Grant was watching, enjoying, and then suddenly without any warning, the power thing retreated, slowly folding itself into a tiny pocket somewhere deep in his mind. The attack was over.

Grant rose slowly and powerfully, brushing himself off, as the boys, crying and hobbling, no longer united, staggered away. He watched them go, then stepping from the lawn he picked up his books. He glanced for a moment in the direction of the old school house. Then turning, quietly and happily, he resumed his walk home.

CHAPTER 12

Raphael was dreaming.

The man with the handlebar mustache stood on his porch staring down at the boy. From the boy's vantage point, the mustache appeared thick, black and shiny. Along with his close-set eyes this made the man appear sinister, almost monsterish.

"Qué pasa, mi amigo?" the man said. He wasn't particularly tall, about five foot eight or nine, but to the boy, way up there on the porch, he seemed a giant, dressed all in black. A black Gaucho hat rested atop his head.

"My father has sent me," the boy said in a

soft Spanish. "My mother is not well. She needs a doctor."

The man regarded the boy questioningly for a long moment. He was a small, frail child. His clothing was cheap, thin and tattered, definitely not suited for the coolness of the weather. The toes of his bare feet curled against the earth, a sign that he was cold.

"There are no doctors here in the groves," the man said. "Tell your father if she is too ill to work you will all have to leave."

Rafael didn't move.

"Did you hear me, boy?" the foreman said.

"Yes."

"And tell your father I do not appreciate being disturbed with personal problems. I have enough to worry about, what with the harvest coming so late this year. If the weather turns any colder, we could lose some of the crops." He turned a knowing gaze on Rafael. "These things are important. If things do not go right many families will be out of work. You see what I mean?"

Rafael nodded. He knew that if things did not go right it was the foreman who would be out of work, but he said nothing.

"Your mother, is she dying?" The foreman appeared concerned.

"No."

"There you see," he said, smiling. "Don't

trouble me with such trivial matters. Your mother will be all right in the morning. And now if you will excuse me." The foreman turned and went back into the house.

Rafael stood staring up at the door for a full minute. He wanted to rush up onto the porch and kick it in. Of course, he knew that if he did his father would have to pay for it, and next year the foreman would not give them work. No. Causing any kind of commotion would only make things worse.

He didn't know if his mother was dying or not. Her cough was hacking and thick with phlegm. She'd lost much weight since they'd come to the farm and seemed to be wasting away. Rafael had seen it before—the coughing, as if one's guts were coming undone; the weight loss and fatigue, so gripping that many had to be carried from the groves, until they were carried for the last time. Was this his mother?

Rafael finally turned and headed back towards the small community of makeshift huts thrown together to house the workers. The wind slapped at his face, and he felt cold tears dripping down his cheeks. He told himself he was not crying. The wind had caused his eyes to tear.

The odor of citrus and soil rose around him as he headed down the dirt path for the community. It was at least a quarter of a mile away, and he was cold, but the weather was nothing compared to the health of his mother. He couldn't tell the foreman that he suspected the worst. Death in the groves gave the farm a bad name. Had the foreman suspected that his mother was dying, he would have had Rafael's family evicted in the morning.

The odor of bonfires now touched the air, and he knew he was nearing the community. The fires were for warmth, the only amenity provided by the huts being shelter.

When Rafael approached the familiar hut, his senses were assailed by a new odor—death. He entered.

His father, three sisters and younger brother were huddled around the pallet on the floor. The family attempted to blot out the wind, hoping their bodies would generate enough heat to supply warmth. As he entered all eyes turned to Rafael, but their expressions held no hope. Rafael shook his head. It was as they had expected.

"Rafael," his mother's feeble voice called.

His father stood aside. "She has been calling for you," he said.

As Rafael stepped up, a skeletal hand reached out for him. He caressed it in his own. The coolness of his mother's flesh sent goose bumps rising along his arm.

"Son," his mother said. He knelt, his ear practically pressing against her lips to hear. "You have brought hope, yes?" his mother said.

"Yes," Rafael replied. He forced a smile, but an uncontrollable tear fell from his chin onto his mother's face.

"Then why do you cry?"

"The wind makes my eyes tear."

She smiled a knowing smile. "Don't worry. It is not my time yet. You are a good son, yes?"

"Yes," Rafael said again.

Just then his mother was wracked with a coughing spell that left her gasping for air. Rafael rose. This was no life for humans. God could not have planned it this way. He moved to the door, opened it and stepped outside. It was not her time—not yet—but the pall of death surrounded him, and he knew it was someone's time tonight, and his mother's could not be long away. . . .

Rafael bolted upright in bed from the horrible, childhood dream. Sweat streaked his forehead, and the sheets were drenched. He could force the thoughts out while he was awake, but when he was asleep they came creeping back.

He rose, switched on the lamp on the nightstand and moved to the TV. He punched it on and sat on the edge of the bed, his eyes searching the screen, his thoughts miles away. He hoped he could arrest the dreams once and for all. Once the thing was done Rafael hoped he would once again find childhood peace in his sleep.

Grant Michaels sat in his bedroom, staring at his homework and feeling very pleased with himself. He had licked the bullies. All by himself, he had licked them.

He looked down at the reading assignment lying on the desk in front of him. His eyes passed over the words, but nothing seemed to penetrate. Something was wrong. No, not wrong but rather different. Something was different about him today. It had nothing to do with licking the bullies, or with his inability to concentrate. He guessed it had been happening for a long time, but only now did he realize what it was. I'm no longer a kid, Grant thought. I'm almost a man. He smiled secretly, deliciously, deluding himself as boys had done and would continue to do throughout eternity. As their voices turned from cracking sopranos to smooth melodious baritones, as they watched themselves shoot up like corn stalks, as their muscles took on the hard lines of definition, as the sight of girls caused a stirring within that wasn't there a year ago, they knew something was happening, and they were fooled into believing that they were fast becoming men.

"They better not mess with me," Grant whispered, the sneaky smile spreading across his face. He closed the book, allowing his thoughts to move to worlds only he could conquer alone. "No one better mess with me, ever again."

BOOK
TWO

CHAPTER 13

Epps opened the dosier that that wise-ass son of a bitch, Patches, had given him and began reading.

"Shit," he grumbled as he peered down at the first page. The words "The Coalition" stared back in bold face near the top. Beneath were the names of several men, possible members of this Coalition, and beneath that a list of possible activities. "Mickey Mouse," Epps grumbled as he went over the list. "Mickey-fucking-Mouse."

He turned the page and looked over the information on Julio Sanchez. "Crap," he muttered. This was not Epps' type of

assignment, and that wise-ass Patches knew
it. He was coming down on Epps because he
was pissed at everyone since the Philippines thing. It wasn't fair.

Actually, the man's name wasn't Patches
at all; it was Horvath, Peter Horvath. He
was dubbed Patches during the action in
the Philippines. Epps was there too and was
now wishing to hell that someone had taken
the bastard out while they were over there.
It was during the Marcos-Aquino elections
in February of '86. It had been a bitter
election. A shit kickin', dirty-ass fight was
what it was, and the Aquino camp was out
in force, escorting citizens to the poles and
guarding ballot boxes. Meanwhile, The
Boys (as their little group had been called
for so long) had been sent to the Philippines
with a simple task, and not one that was
new to them either. They were to get the
ballot boxes, one way or the other, and stuff
them with votes for Marcos. The good old
U.S. of A. wasn't taking any chances with
this one. So what if Marcos was a crook? At
least he was our crook.

Horvath's tactic in these situations was
generally to offer a bribe, but the Aquino
people weren't biting. The jerks were
actually honest, so Horvath decided to do
the next best thing—steal them. And that,
thought Epps, is where he ran into trouble.
Horvath was obviously an American, and
while Americans were supposed to be there

safeguarding the election, our reputation for supporting dictators was well-known.

When Horvath placed his hand on the ballot box, claiming he was going to guarantee its safe delivery to election headquarters, the Philippinos around him started ripping his clothes off. And they would have ripped him to pieces, too, if it weren't for Epps and some of the others.

I should have let them kill the bastard, Epps thought. Horvath wound up spending the rest of the day roaming around like a ragamuffin. When O'Toole and some of the others got wind of what had happened, they thought it was the funniest thing he'd ever heard. Someone started singing, "Patches, I'm dependin' on you, son . . ." They were words from an old song, and the Patches stuck.

Now Patches was heading operations in T-1, and it seemed to Epps the bastard was sticking him with every ladies' convention and fly-by-night outfit on the books. It just plain wasn't fair. Epps knew terrorism and understood terrorists better than most of The Boys. He should have been heading up T-1 instead of serving under a wise-ass know-nothing like Patches. After all, it was he who had gone to Georgetown University's Center For Strategic and International Studies, training under the world's top experts on terrorism, including Yacov Heichal himself. And not just learning about terrorism either. He learned about the kind of paranoia even the hint of terrorism could cause.

Epps recalled an example of this. It was during a high school football game where rumor spread through the crowd that the Coca Cola they were selling had been poisoned. More than a hundred students were hospitalized that day with symptoms of food poisoning, which turned out to be plain old anxiety attacks. If you translated this into one deranged mind spiking a few Tylenol capsules with rat poison, you could begin to understand the type of hold even one terrorist could easily exert over an entire nation. And do you think Patches knows that? Hell no! He knew didley about the terrorist mind, a mind not satisfied with causing a little hysteria and grabbing a few headlines. No, these were lunatic minds that wanted to kill. Like the Black September group during the '72 Olympics, who killed 17 hostages, or the Libyan backed group who bombed a Berlin discotheque. Like Rafael.

Epp's eyes hazed momentarily as he thought back to his lone encounter with the famed terrorist. He was almost mine, Epps thought. It was in early '84 when Epps helped thwart the attempted bombing of the Lincoln Memorial, nearly nabbing Rafael in the process. I should be assigned to catching pricks like that, he mused, turning still another page of the dosier. I know terrorism, all right, but does that matter to Patches? What's the use?

"Mickey Mouse," Epps continued grumbling as he stared at the words on the page. "Mickey-fucking-Mouse."

A Monday morning at the Sixth Street Elementary School was like any other, and yet this Monday morning was different.

Grant Michaels stepped from the passenger side of the station wagon and waved his mother good-bye. She knew better than to try and kiss him out here in front of the guys. Even though she was inclined to do so—he looked so cute—she waved back and pulled away from the curb.

Grant approached the school and felt the difference all around him. It surged in his chest when he inhaled and assailed the atmosphere around him when he breathed out. The kids in the yard played the same, the teachers watched the same, and the bullies, with red and blue splotches on their faces and arms, stood busily plotting their next attack as always. Everything was the same, and yet nothing was. It was as if the whole world had been turned inside out, revealing a cheap cloth lining that let you know this thing called life was really not quite what it seemed. Grant knew that today. He was almost a man, and he was supposed to know things like that.

He walked through the gate same as always, but this time it was different, and God, it felt good. There was a quickness to his step, a bounce and jauntiness in the way he carried himself, not perceptible to the naked eye—not yet—but Grant felt it and smiled.

He stopped and looked around. Bert Reynolds, his left eye swollen shut from where a bee stinger had slammed into it a few days earlier, was shoving a second grader. Jimmy and Albert stood nearby, like buzzards hovering over the kill. Grant walked over.

Bert saw him first and stiffened almost instinctively. There was terror in his eyes, as fear cut through him like shards of glass ripping his heart to shreds. He backed up a step.

"Whatcha doin'?" Grant asked with mock innocence in his voice.

Now the other two boys closed in around Bert, as if closing ranks would make a difference. Of course, if what they thought about Grant were true, nothing could protect them.

"Who wants to know?" Bert said finally, but his voice lacked conviction.

"I do." Grant stepped closer.

"Oh, yeah," said Bert. He attempted his old sing-song, but his voice wavered and cracked. Then Jimmy Buckley spoke.

"You stay away from me," he whined.

"You stay away from me or I'm gonna tell my mom on you, Grant Michaels."

"Your *mom*?" Grant asked with a smirk. He let out a soft, vicious chuckle.

"Shut up!" Bert stammered. He was facing Jimmy. "Grant Michaels is nothing but a fag . . ." The words crumbled on his lips, falling like ashes from an ancient urn. He was again looking into Grant's eyes, and something in them sent a chill whistling through him.

"You talkin' to me?" Grant asked smiling openly. It was a malevolent smile draped across his lips, a hideous welcome mat. "You leave that kid alone," he snapped. He looked at the second grader.

"I'm gonna tell my mommy," the boy squealed. "Mrs. Redmond," he called. "Mommmmy!" He began to cry.

Grant stepped closer, and now the second grader cowered by the legs of the other quaking boys. Then the school bell chimed and they all ran.

Wait, Grant wanted to call out as he watched the second grader zigzagging across the yard, bawling all the way. I'm here to save you. But the difference was on him, and he knew even the second grader felt it.

Grant stood for a moment before joining the trooping kids heading for class. He was almost a man. This knowledge made him feel powerful, but with the power came a slow realization. It slipped over him quietly like a net, and Grant knew that once you turned the corner towards adulthood there was no turning back.

Slowly Grant made his way to class, and for the first time in his life he felt alone.

Allen Michaels was a man possessed. He'd just returned from the library and was grinning like a fat rat in a cheese factory. He had every reason to grin.

That afternoon he'd gone to the office of Reeves Entertainment, the company that was producing *That's Incredible Special Edition*, and they had given him a check for $15,000, just for having Grant go on TV and predict something. At first they were only going to give him $7000, but when Allen told them his son would absolutely predict something on the show they doubled it.

It was beautiful, Allen thought. He'd met with a man named Ackelson who told him he was pleased as punch to have the boy on the show.

"How much would you give me if the boy could predict something on your show?" Allen had asked as he sat in Ackelson's plain office with a large wooden desk and a few cloth covered chairs. Scenes from previous shows adorned the walls like baubles on display at a museum.

"What do you mean?" Ackelson asked, curiosity wrinkling his brow.

"I'll have him predict something like he did on the Phil Reed show." Ackelson was obviously interested. I've got him now, Allen thought.

"How much would you ask for something like that?"

Allen didn't hesitate. "Fifteen thousand." And after a few conferences on the phone, many minutes later Allen emerged from the office $15,000 richer.

Allen chuckled to himself. He was a smooth operator. "Fifteen G's," he purred, taking the check from his pocket and admiring it. He had it all figured out.

He entered the living room still gazing at his newfound wealth, dropped the library books on the coffee table and called to his wife. "Eve!"

All afternoon he'd been thinking about the change in her. It had shaken him at first, made him feel small, but now armed with a check for fifteen G's and the books, he was about to put her back in her place.

Eve entered from the kitchen, soapy globs of dishwater spattering the floor, her face bent into a question mark. Allen displayed his smile.

"Well, if you called me in here to see your smile, thanks, but I've got work to do, so if you'll excuse me, Mr. Happy Face." Eve turned to leave.

"Wait!" She turned back. "I want to show you something." Allen proffered the check.

"Fifteen thousand smackeroonies," he said.

The furrows in Eve's forehead deepened. "For exploiting your son?"

"No. For letting him do what comes naturally."

"I'm ashamed of you," Eve said. Her eyes lashed out at him.

"Why?" Allen said, meeting her gaze. "Because I want a better life? Eve, baby, I've been thinking about what you said the other evening, and you were wrong. Yeah, sure, I'd been hitting the sauce pretty hard. You were right about that part, but wrong about everything else."

Eve eyed her husband gravely. "I wasn't wrong about stopping this. Allen, this is the last time. It's over."

Allen felt the confidence drift from his bones. What was the matter with her, anyway? Couldn't she see what she was doing to them? But of course she can't. That's why he had to show her. He forced a smile. "This talent Grant has is a natural thing. You didn't know that, did you? Well, neither did I, but these books say so." He gestured towards the books on the coffee table. "It would be wrong not to develop his talent. We'd be depriving him, and we wouldn't want to do that, would we?" Allen had finished his appeal, and now he stood, perspiration stains spreading across his shirt, a tense smile spread over his face.

"Develop it?" Eve said. She eyed her

husband incredulously. "What do you mean, develop it?"

"Just that," Allen squawked. "This thing can be controlled. He was wrong about not being able to do it again. He just doesn't know how."

"And you want that? A sideshow freak for a son?"

"I want what's best for us," Allen said.

"Allen, please, I . . ."

"I want to be rich!" Allen blurted out. "I want to be somebody! Yeah, that's right, Allen Michaels wants to be important. Is that so bad?"

Allen stood, now dripping perspiration, staring open mouthed at his wife. The words had leapt from his throat, leaving him feeling parched yet relieved, as the weight of long denial rose gently from his chest.

A slow blooming silence mushroomed between them. Eve stared back at her husband, realizing the man she'd lived with for all these years had been a stranger.

"It's over," she said. There was a finality to her voice, and the last shreds of Allen's confidence deserted him.

"Fifteen thousand dollars," he stammered.

"You can't have him," Eve said.

"We can be rich."

"You can't have him!"

"He's our son, *my son*. I'll decide what

happens. to him."

Eve's reply was a frosty stare. But Allen knew that this time he was right, and his failing confidence was soon replaced by an old and welcomed friend—anger.

Allen Michaels sat in his highback recliner thumbing through one of the books he'd gotten from the library that day: *New Soviet Psychic Discoveries* by Henry Gris and William Dick. The Soviets, Allen discovered, were very big on developing telekinetic powers, and that's what Grant had—the power to predict things.

Allen had discovered from the book that while it was rare, it wasn't unusual for someone to display some type of power occasionally. Everyone did so at one time or another, but they didn't realize it—like the phone call you got from Aunt Maggie just five minutes after you were thinking of her, or the places you visited in dreams that turned out to be the same in real life. All of us have it to some extent. Some more than others, Allen thought. Grant was among the few, one of the special ones, and he was determined to develop Grant's uniqueness.

He thought back to Grant's stubbornness about doing it again. "It's a good sign," Allen said to himself. He's becoming more like the old man everyday.

Allen knew that once he showed Grant the books and explained it all to him—that he could do it again, any time he wanted to—Grant would come around, and together they could develop Grant's gift into something that would secure all of their futures.

Allen closed the book, rose and headed towards the staircase. It was time for a talk with his son, man to man, just the two of them. In the end they'd all be rich.

With a self-satisfied grin Allen started upstairs.

While Allen was reading, Eve was packing. She'd gone upstairs straight from supper without saying a word and began throwing things into a suitcase. She didn't know where she was going or even what she would say to Grant. All she was sure of was that they could not stay in the same house with Allen, not the way things were.

She removed a few sweaters, blouses and some underwear from drawers, folding them neatly before putting them in the suitcase. She thought of how Allen had always teased her about being so neat and methodical.

"Eve, we've been married for twelve years, and for twelve years you've rolled my socks in the drawer the same way. Honey, if the body snatchers ever replaced you, I'd know." And then he would laugh. There was a time when his laughter was infectious, filling the house with a warmth that penetrated her bones—but not now. Things were different now, and she was walking out.

Eve's thoughts turned to Grant. How would he take their leaving home. She hoped he would understand.

The bag nearly filled, Eve placed the fleece-lined jacket her mother had given her on top, closed it and snapped shut the clasps. Now came the tough part. She had to go into Grant's room and explain to him what they were doing. It was going to be rough, all right, but it was something that had to be done.

Eve Michaels picked up her suitcase and walked across the room. Then taking a deep breath she opened the door and stepped out into the corridor.

CHAPTER 14

Doris Sachs got off her knees, kissed the amulet that hung from a fake gold chain around her neck, and said, "Thank you, Reverend Joe." She was feeling almost good, which was a lot better than she'd been feeling lately. I have Reverend Joe to thank for this, she thought. He was her guru, her savior, her hope.

Things had been pretty bad since Charlie died. Hell, who was she fooling? They were awful. She kept dreaming of her husband night after night, often waking calling his name. "It's a sign," she said out loud. She was more positive than ever when she met the boy who predicted the accident. My

Charlie's trying to get in touch with me. I know it.

Doris now fingered the amulet and thought of Charlie. It nagged at her, his trying to get in touch. Friends said he was gone and she should try and forget. "Pshaw," Doris said to that. Her Charlie had something he wanted to say to her, and she was not going to give up on him no matter how badly his memory pained her.

Doris was standing in her bedroom by the dresser. It was daytime, yet the drapes were drawn and the light out. She had turned her bedroom into a shrine, a place where she could seek refuge and worship Reverend Joe.

She now looked at the framed photograph of him atop her dresser. The fiftyish man with a scraggly beard and hippie haircut had a beatific smile, a smile that somehow eased her pain.

Reverend Joe's picture was surrounded by many lit candles that bathed his face in an eerie light, a reverent light, Doris thought, as she grasped the picture. Moving it to her lips she kissed it, closed her eyes and again said, "Thank you, Reverend Joe."

If things were bad when Charlie died, after she met the boy on TV they got worse. Her sanity began fading. Like the sunset in a dying western sky, it slipped steadily away. The worst part was she knew it, knew she was going crazy. She had to do something, but what? That's when she heard of Reverend Joe.

It was a miracle; it was providence. Someone had left a flier on her windshield displaying Reverend Joe's photograph and proclaiming: "Reverend Joe is all you need." It was the truth.

From the moment Doris had met Reverend Joe she knew things would be better. She'd visited his storefront on a busy section of Vermont Avenue, not far from Wilshire Boulevard. His place of devotion was small, but as Reverend Joe told her, "When you know the truth you don't need much space." He delivered his message with such conviction that a warmth came over her. It was as if she were finally home.

During the next several weeks Reverend Joe convinced Doris that she, too, needed little space. In fact, he was in the process of convincing her she didn't need much of anything, especially material things and money.

For what might seem an exorbitant amount of money to a lay person, Reverend Joe sold Doris her amulet, her photograph and brass frame of himself and all the candles that surrounded it. Of course Doris knew that money was not important. As the Reverend explained, "You must free yourself of all material attachments if you truly want to find the truth." Doris did. She wanted to know the truth about herself, the world, and of course Charlie.

Doris now looked at the windup alarm clock on her nightstand. She'd sold her wristwatch a few days earlier, the money going for what she deemed a worthy cause. She gave all she could. In return she was promised word from Charlie—maybe not today, but one day soon.

Doris noted the time, nearly 2:00 P.M. Time to go. At 3:00 each day Reverend Joe's small band of followers gathered to sing his praises, and Doris could not be late. She moved to the closet where she grabbed a light jacket for later, when the sun went down. "Soon, Charlie," she said softly. Then gathering her things together, she went out.

Ortiz zipped his trousers and looked across the room at the girl lying naked on the bed. She was a dowdy, young girl, maybe 15, in dowdy surroundings. The room was a tiny matchbox of a room with cheap plastic furnishings. The heavy odor of stale grease and frying chicken drifted in through the open window, flirting with the cloying odor of the girl's perfume.

Ortiz's brow never once wrinkled in the disgust he felt. Moving to the mirror, clouded by years of cigarette smoke, he knotted his tie and affixed a diamond stick pin to the center. Then taking out his wallet, he selected several large bills and threw them on the dresser. He again looked at the girl.

"Thanks," she said, smiling. "Come back anytime."

Ortiz didn't answer. He pulled on the jacket of his Brooks Brothers suit, donned mirrored shades and opened the door.

"Hey, could you make sure it locks," the girl called as Ortiz stepped into the corridor. "I wanna catch a quick nap."

Ortiz started down the hall, leaving the door hanging wide open.

"Lousy Mexican bastard!" the girl called after him.

Once downstairs and on the street Ortiz moved quickly. A well-dressed man like himself stuck out like a sore thumb in this neighborhood. He could ill afford to be spotted here.

It was Ortiz's passion for prostitutes that compelled him to return to the neighborhood again and again. He was a businessman, an entrepreneur whose wise decisions and investments had built his tiny business into one that grossed nearly a million dollars each year. That was a lot of money for most, but not Ortiz. His insatiable appetite for sex with women of the street was equaled only by his desire for wealth. So he continued to pick up girls in sleazy neighborhoods, his chauffeur dropping him off at the fringes. Likewise, he continued his scheming ways to acquire more wealth.

Ortiz moved through the tiny shopping area to the white limousine parked before the liquor store. His chauffeur, seeing him approach, hopped out and opened the door. He stood at stark attention as Ortiz climbed in, then closing the door behind him, he slid behind the wheel.

Ortiz gazed out the window watching the decaying neighborhood whiz by, hating it and then himself for needing to come there.

"A fine day," the driver said, rescuing him from his thoughts.

"Is it?" Ortiz snapped. He was in no mood for conversation.

"Fine and dandy," the driver added.

"You enjoy it. To me it is like many others."

"You could say that," the driver said with a chuckle. He handled the big car expertly, moving through the downtown ghetto and on into the business district. "Of course, I think today is special. You gotta look at it like that. Know what I mean?"

"Yes," Ortiz said. His reply was filled with contempt, and the driver continued on silently, leaving him to his thoughts.

Things were not good. The idiot, Sanchez, had botched the operation. The Rafael character had disappeared, and with him went their hopes and dreams. What remained was fear. His disappearing was a bad sign—very bad. Suppose he had been a blackmailer, or worse—a government agent. They would all pay dearly for that little mistake.

Ortiz brooded silently as the big car headed for the outskirts of the city. It was not a nice day at all.

"See, the way I figure it, each day is a new experience."

"Huh?" Ortiz said. His eyes snapped forward.

"You know, about each day being special and all," the driver said. "That's what makes it that way. See what I mean?"

"When will my regular driver be back?" Ortiz asked.

"Coupla days, I guess. He's got the flu. Can't tell with that old bug, though. Could be down for a week."

"When he returns I'm going to tell him to never again be ill."

"Come on, Mr. Ortiz, that's . . ."

"And if he is," Ortiz added pointedly, "I'm going to insist he find a better replacement than you. *Copish*?"

The driver stiffened for a moment. "Yes, sir," he said.

He continued on in silence, and for the first time all day Ortiz smiled.

It was night. The ghetto streets were throbbing with the sounds of music and boisterous laughter. Squealing brakes, roaring engines and trumpeting horns seemed to push into the already crowded night, like passengers cramming their way into a tiny elevator. It was an endless maze of sound that twisted and turned its way into your mind, but led to nowhere.

This is what greeted Ortiz as he exited the tiny rooming house on bustling Los Angeles Street. This was his third trip into the bowels of the city in the past two days, and the more he came, the more he hated coming. But being no fool, he knew he had no choice. He was nothing more than a victim.

He moved quickly down the street, doing his best to ignore the people around him. They were poor people, the discarded refuse of the earth, and he hated them.

"Hey, got a quarter," a derelict with rheumy eyes and a dirty red beard called. Ortiz put his head down and pretended not to hear.

The limousine was parked in front of the bus depot, as were several more of L.A.'s homeless. Upon seeing Ortiz approach, the driver hopped out and opened the door for him. Then slowly they made their escape, dodging their way through the late night traffic.

Ortiz closed his eyes to the world outside his window. He was worried. Three times in two days. Normally his desires were quenched with trips of once a week, maybe twice a month. Three times in two days. He was raging out of control.

It was the fool, Sanchez, who had done this to him. Why did they have to trust him? He tried to warn them that day at the meeting. He was against telling this Rafael character their plan, but Rodriguez had insisted.

Fools!

And then it dawned on him. It wasn't Sanchez's fault at all. Oh, no. The fault of this thing rested squarely on the shoulders of Rodriguez.

The car stopped.

Ortiz's eyes fluttered open.

"Where are we?" he asked.

The driver chuckled. "Remember what I was telling you about each day being special?"

They were on a dark street, one that seemed to be lined with old warehouses that hunkered along the sidewalk like derelicts in the dark. The lone yellow globe of an old street lamp cast an eerie light over dilapidated surroundings.

"Where the hell are we?" Ortiz barked.

"Why, we're here," the driver replied with a chuckle.

"Have you been drinking?" Ortiz demanded. "It's against the rules to drink."

The driver turned, facing him and removing the ever present shades. "I'm not drunk," he said.

That's when Ortiz got scared. Fear is a funny thing, the way it can creep up on you, like a ghost at the stroke of midnight. One minute you're fine, then . . .

Ortiz's fear started as a feathery tickle in the hollow of his gut, yet immediately it began to bloom.

"When is my driver coming back?" he asked, but he already knew the answer.

"He's not."

"Who are you? What do you want? Money?"

A wave of laughter jumped from the driver's throat. Ortiz looked into the man's eyes, like stones from the pit of hell.

The man was no longer laughing. He was staring intently at Ortiz.

The fear banged into his head, careening into his brain. "I have mo . . . mo . . . mo . . ." He fumbled for his wallet, but a viselike grip snared his wrist. He looked into the driver's face, the intense eyes, the perfect smile, and at that moment Ortiz's life flashed before his eyes. It was too short, but he knew it was over.

Suddenly, uncontrollably, Ortiz began to cry.

Grant sat on the floor of his bedroom eyeing the action figures he'd borrowed from Jimmy Buckley. Jimmy had been his best friend, his only friend, but no more. Even if Jimmy kissed his Nikes and begged him, their friendship was over. Grant didn't have friends anymore. "I don't need any, either," he mumbled to the toy figures.

In fact, Grant was thinking he didn't need toys anymore, either. Toys were for babies like Jimmy and Bert Reynolds. "Shit," he barked and tossed the toys in the direction of the waste basket. He had all that he needed; this thing that roamed around in his mind was friend enough.

"Granty." His mother's voice came from outside the door.

"Yeah?"

"Can I come in?"

"Sure, Mom."

She entered carrying the suitcase. "Hi," she said with a quick, uneasy smile.

Grant eyed the suitcase. "You goin' away, Mom?" Distress crept into his face.

"Well," she replied too cheerily, "*we* are."

"We are?" There was little boy wonder in his eyes. "Where're we goin'?"

"Please, Grant, no questions until later. Just help Mommy pack. Okay?"

"Sure." A myriad of questions flashed through his mind.

It was hard for her to stand there and look at him, her little boy, his face a panoply of wonder over the prospect of going away. But this wasn't any old trip to Grandma's, not this time. Eve's thoughts again wandered back to happier times when Grant was a baby, and the three of them would do things together on weekends. Off they would go, the proud father carrying his son, filled with tales of their future, and the proud mother absorbing it all, a happy listener.

Eve's mind drew back to the task at hand, and she went to the closet and removed a small overnight bag. "Grab some shirts and underwear, dear. Just enough for a few days."

"And then we're comin' back?" Grant asked.

"Grant, please," she snapped. Then seeing the look on his face, she softened.

It's not his fault. I allowed this to happen.

"Later, baby," she said. "I'll explain later."

"Someone goin' somewhere?" Beefy Allen Michaels stood in the doorway, a rash of anger caving in the remains of his self-satisfied grin.

Grant looked at his mommy who was staring close-mouthed at his daddy.

"What's goin' on here?" Allen barked.

Eve began throwing things into the suitcase.

"Now, see here, Eve." Allen raced over, grabbing his wife by the wrist. "I don't know what the hell you think you're doin', but if you think you're taking my son you're crazy," Allen's voice boomed, as he began applying pressure to Eve's wrist. She winced.

"Stop," she said. "You're hurting me."

"You can go if you want, but Grant stays here."

"Why?" Eve charged. "So you can put him in a cage and parade him around like a trained monkey?"

Allen's grip tightened, wringing tiny tears from his wife's eyes.

"You just don't understand, do you? You're just too damn stubborn to listen to reason."

"Allen, you're hurting me."

Grant noticed the tears forming in his mommy's eyes. He had been watching, awestruck, as his parents argued back and forth. His brain was beginning to clog, and he tried to blink the haziness away.

"Someone ought to hurt you. Maybe then you'll learn!"

"Allen, you're breaking my arm!"

He squeezed shut his eyes tightly, but the arguing wouldn't stop. There was a time when he would have gone away and drifted peacefully, miles away from the hurt they were causing him. And for a moment he started to go . . .

"Is it broken, yet? Huh? Is it?"

"Allen, please!"

. . . But things were different now, and so was he.

"Stop!" Grant screamed, the words charging from his throat like a herd of crazed stallions.

Allen let go. Was this his son? Yes, it was.

The boy was turning out to be a regular firecracker, just like him.

"Look what you've done. You've scared him," Eve said. Her arm was regaining its color, and she was again placing things in the bag.

"I'm not scared, Mommy," Grant said. There was nothing to be scared about. Mommy and Daddy were not going to argue ever again. They were both going to smile a lot and be real happy.

"See, he's not scared," Allen said. He smiled his gruesome smile at his son, but Grant did not look away. Allen turned back to his wife. "Stop that!" he said, noticing she was back to packing. "He's not going anywhere." Allen Michaels grabbed the overnighter and heaved it in the direction of the closet. "You can go, but Grant stays." The yelling was starting again.

Grant beaded on the bag moving in the direction of the closet. The thing leaped from his mind.

The overnighter seemed to be moving slowly, like a mime figure in mock slow motion. Then *Phfzzt!* It was gone.

There was a sound, huge and electrical, like a giant short circuit wiping out half the lights in the city, and what remained of the bag was now crunchy and black and smoldering and piling up on the carpet before them.

Allen and Eve stared mesmerized at the

ashes falling to the floor, mouths agape. Their eyes were doing crazy things in their heads, and Allen felt his dinner bubbling up in his stomach. Then slowly, as the couple tried to make sense of the thing, their eyes fell on Grant. He stood staring back at them steadily, and at once they both knew he was behind it.

Allen reacted first, his flesh turning all clammy and goose-pimply at the same time, while his insides felt as if any second now they would go flying off into his head.

There was something different about Grant, something weird and horrific that made Allen want to go running from the room. But he didn't. He held his shaky ground and stared back at his nine year-old son—the soft brown hair, the fiery green eyes, the solemn expression, and on the corners of the child's lips, a hint (just a hint, mind you) of a smile.

Seated at the kitchen table, Eve Michaels gulped down her third cup of coffee in less than an hour, while Allen, seated across from her, reached for the bottle of Scotch for the umpteenth time that evening. He began pouring himself a nice, healthy shot. Eve threw him a questioning glance, but Allen continued to pour—and why not? His whole world had just collapsed around him, the end coming under the guise of a terse smile and an exploding suitcase.

The shot of whiskey vanished down Allen's throat. He again reached for the bottle.

"That's not going to make things any better," Eve said.

"What is?" Allen asked. There was helplessness in his voice.

Eve couldn't think of anything worth saying, so she snatched up her coffee cup and took a huge, tasteless swallow.

There was another few minutes of silence in which Allen again reached for the bottle. He was fast becoming drunk. "Where do we go from here?" he mumbled as much to himself as to anyone. "Where do we go from here, get it?" Soft, insane laughter grumbled deep in his throat. "It's a song, get it? *Where Do We Go From Here*." He threw back his head and let out a huge, mirthless laugh. When he started babbling something his wife couldn't understand, it angered her.

"This is what you wanted," she suddenly accused. "A special talent, remember that? Well, now our son has a special talent. Only thing is, maybe he killed a man with it. Then again, maybe he's killed lots of men with it." She shot him a chastising glance. "And now poor Allen doesn't know what to do. Well, for starters you can smile, hubby dear. You got your wish."

"I just wanted our lives to be better," he muttered. "Better."

172

His thoughts drifted to a few hours earlier. The overnighter was lying on the floor, a mosaic of char and ash. He and Eve were staring horrified at their son. Allen spoke. "Son, those crashes, did you . . . ?" He couldn't ask.

"I don't know," replied Grant. Then he said, "I don't want you to yell anymore." His voice was quiet, yet there was a horrifying quality to it, a creeping evil that sent Allen's skin crawling while Eve felt an icy chill whistling down her spine. His parents gawked at him. "You hear me?" he said.

"Yes," they both replied.

"No more yelling. Okay?"

"No more," they both said.

Now Grant was upstairs sleeping. When Eve looked in on him she reported back how angelic he appeared.

"Some angel," Allen had said. "Our son takes good old U.S. government issue aircraft and turns it into confetti."

Allen and Eve drew silent again, wondering what their next move would be.

"No one must ever know," Eve finally said. "If anyone finds out they'll take him away from us." She thought better of her last statement. "If they can," she added.

Allen opened his mouth in protest, but realized it was useless. "What do we do?" he mumbled, as again he reached for the bottle.

"I don't know." His wife placed a forbidding hand firmly over his.

Allen nodded, pulled his hand off the bottle and looked his wife in the eye. "Maybe we ask him," he said.

Eve took another swallow of tasteless coffee.

CHAPTER 15

Hopper walked slowly back from the knot of men that stood around the car towards Epps. He smiled. Epps liked Hopper, a stocky black man with a bushy mustache, a wide nose and a ready, gap-toothed smile. Hopper had the sort of easy going disposition you didn't normally find in an FBI man. Epps thought it was Hopper's disposition that had carried him all the way to the job of Chief of Investigators, Los Angeles Division.

"Well, surprise of surprises," Hopper said as he approached. His smile widened.

"I could say the same thing," Epps said, showing his own teeth.

"The fellas in LAPD's missing persons must feel honored to have one of 'The Boys' come out."

"And Chief Inspector of the FBI. Didn't know a missing Mexican businessman rated so high." They shared a laugh.

"Okay, okay," Hopper said. "Enough tap dancing."

"The direct approach is always the best," countered Epps.

"I'm glad we agree. Now, what the hell are you doing here? If your department's interested in a missing person, he must be a hell of a lot more than just a missing person."

"Likewise," Epps replied.

Hopper released a chorus of throaty laughter. "Son of a biscuit eater, you guys sure are evasive. Okay. Does the name The Coalition ring a bell?"

"Bingo," said Epps.

The two chatted for the next five minutes, relinquishing what little info they had. When they were through, each had a similar, hazy picture. Jorge Ortiz, a wealthy entrepreneur and one of the men linked to the group marked for observation, had disappeared. His limousine had turned up on this abandoned side street in downtown Los Angeles. His chauffeur was missing, and both Epps and Hopper suspected foul play on the part of the chauffeur.

"Think this Ortiz disappearing has anything to do with what The Coalition is planning?" Hopper asked cautiously.

"I don't know," Epps replied. "What have they been planning?"

"You son of a biscuit eater," Hopper said. The toothy grin was back. After a little more parrying Hopper asked, "Care to have a look?"

"Thought you'd never ask."

"Or is it you thought I was trying to keep this one for myself?"

They approached the car. Epps knew Hopper pretty well, and while jealousy between departments was common, he found none of it in Hopper. Of course, the man wasn't a fountain of information either.

Epps saw a uniformed officer step away from the limousine, dropping an object into a plastic bag. The glint of the object caught both their eyes.

"Wait a minute," Hopper called as he and Epps stepped up for a closer look. "A knife," Hopper said, a cross between a statement and a question. His eyes drifted over to Epps who stood poker-faced.

"Yeah," the officer said. "We found it underneath the driver's seat."

Hopper again looked to Epps. "Well?"

"Well, what?"

"Don't well what me. Something's got

your ass, and you're not telling me what it is."

"I think all this cloak and dagger is getting to you, Hopper."

"And I think you're full of it," Hopper replied.

They checked the car over, spoke to the police and exchanged notes. All evidence seemed to indicate that the chauffeur had kidnapped Ortiz and was perhaps holding him for ransom, but Hopper wasn't satisfied.

"Son of a biscuit eater. Epps, how long have I known you?"

"Too long. Seven, maybe eight years."

"And in that time have I ever tossed you a red herring?"

"You've been square with me, Hopper. I have to admit it."

"So, fess up. Ever since we saw that knife back there your eyes've been dancing. Something's up."

Epps felt a pang of guilt. "Hopper, I'm only gonna say one thing. Check the knife—carefully."

"As if we wouldn't have," Hopper offered, again displaying the gap-toothed smile.

A few minutes later, when the men departed, Epps nearly floated back to his car. Adrenaline was pumping through him like nitro through a supercharger.

"Okay, Patches, put me on a Mickey Mouse case, and see if I don't turn it into the biggest bust of all time." Epps laughed. Then climbing into the car, he turned the radio all the way up and laughed again, long and hard. And as the sedan cruised back to HQ, Epps' thoughts drifted back many years to an evening in Washington D.C.

Julio Sanchez entered his bedroom, lowered himself slowly onto the bed, the springs singing against his weight, and sighed. Thoughts, scattered like dust bunnies in a windstorm, spiraled through his mind. Images of Angel, Rafael, Rodriguez and finally Ortiz danced through. Ortiz was missing, and The Coalition blamed him.

"It is not my fault," Sanchez barked to silent walls, but secretly he, too, blamed himself. Of course, that wasn't important now. What is? Sanchez couldn't remember, but he knew he had to do something, and he had to do it soon.

He began removing his shirt and felt perspiration waxing anew over his fleshy torso. He had been drinking and smelled of alcohol and sweat; now his own odor slowly wafted up to his nostrils, serving only to remind him that he was drunk, but not drunk enough.

Sanchez rose, feeling the weight of fresh guilt. "God, I feel old," he grumbled. He went into the kitchen where he found half a bottle of tequila and deposited himself, glass in hand, at the kitchen table.

Sanchez needed sleep to clear the cobwebs from his mind, but he knew if he was to sleep at all, it would be in a drunken stupor.

It had not been a good day. Hell, it had been a bitch of a day. Even with his thoughts scattered as they were, Sanchez knew tomorrow promised more of the same.

The Coalition was scared. A madman was on the loose, Ortiz was missing, and they recognized the connection.

"This is your fault," a bleary-eyed Rodriguez had bellowed to Sanchez earlier that day. "My poor Ginger. She is dead."

Their plan was blowing up in their collective faces, and the fool was mourning his dog.

"Now Ortiz is gone, and I blame you," Rodriguez accused.

"It is not fair."

"Did you not bring this madman into the country?"

"Yes. I made it possible for him to enter the country," Sanchez admitted, "but I did not act alone. Everyone agreed."

Sanchez's feeble words fell on deaf ears.

It was his fault, and he had trouble convincing even himself that it wasn't.

But that wasn't the worst of it. Suppose Rafael had planned for the rest of them what he had done to Ortiz—whatever that was. Of course, The Coalition could not live with suppositions. There was too much at stake for that. Something had to be done to keep chance to a bare minimum. Rafael had to be eliminated.

Sanchez had known this for some time, not consciously but in his guts. That afternoon, however, the decision to eliminate Rafael had become a reality. The Coalition was afraid, afraid for their lives and their collective wealth. Rafael was no longer a luxury they could afford. He had to go.

It would be a pleasure to eliminate him, Sanchez thought, but many had tried before him and had not lived to tell of it. Still, Sanchez had told them that afternoon that he would take care of everything. It wasn't because he had to; he made that very clear. He felt no guilt over Rafael's presence, but the man needed to die.

No one asked him how. They were all too busy breathing sighs of relief. And so there it was. A man he had hated almost from the start was now his quarry. Somehow he had to get Rafael—if Rafael didn't get him first.

Sanchez opened the bottle of tequila and discovered he didn't need a glass. He put the bottle to his lips and drank, each numbing swallow pushing him steadily toward a drunken sleep, but not one inch towards a solution.

Breakfast was strained. Allen and Eve hardly were speaking, and when they did, the fear in their voices was obvious. Grant didn't mind one bit. They were smiling. So what if they were scared, and their smiles didn't seem all that happy. It was a price worth paying. They were smiling more than they had for a long time, and, of course, there was no yelling.

"Pancakes are good, Mom," Grant said as he dumped glops of Aunt Jemina over the already syrup-soaked pancakes. "Maybe we can have pancakes everyday," he went on.

"Sure can," Allen burst in suddenly. "No more sending our boy off to school on just cereal. No way. Pancakes whenever you want 'em, son. How's that?"

"Great," Grant said. He smiled and they smiled.

"Uhh, Grant . . ." Allen stammered. "About this TV thing, I . . ." The sudden coolness in Grant's expression froze the words on his lips. "Well . . . I mean . . ."

"No more TV, Dad. Okay?"

"Uhh, sure, son. Sure." Allen grinned, his face looking like it were about to split, like an overripe melon.

"Want more?" Eve broke in, her words coming in a sugar-coated gush. She spoke through a smile so false it seemed almost pained. "You can have more if you want."

"Can't," Grant said. "We'll be late for school."

"School?" Allen said. "Do you believe this kid? What a great kid we have, honey."

"Yes, great," Eve said.

"You don't have to go to school today," Allen told Grant. "You're entitled to a day off. You know, sort of for good behavior." He forced a laugh.

"Allen, he's right," Eve said. "He has to go to school." The words had leaped from her lips, not planned, but once she'd said them she realized it was right.

"No, not today. Not if he doesn't want to," Allen said, now eyeing his wife as if she were from Mars.

"I wanna go," Grant said. "School's important, right?" Grant's eyes were on his dad.

"Well, uhh, sure." With each word Allen watched his son's expression. He was on shaky ground, and he knew it.

"Didn't you always tell me not to miss school and to study as hard as I can?"

"Well, yes, but . . ." Allen felt the wetness beginning in his armpits. A drop of cool sweat slid down his side.

"Yes," Eve said. "Get your books. I don't

want you to be late." It was the first definitive statement she'd made all morning, the first thing she'd said not to please her son, and God, it felt good.

"Yes, ma'am," Grant said and left the room.

"Are you crazy?" Allen rasped in a throaty whisper.

"Do you see the way you're acting?" Eve said. "We're his parents, for God's sake."

"Do you remember what happened here last night?"

"That doesn't change anything."

"There, Eve baby, I'm gonna have to disagree. It changes things all right. It changes things one helluva lot. Eve, we have to be together on these things. He mustn't think we're not together."

"Allen, he doesn't run this household."

"Didn't!" Allen burst in. "He didn't run this household, but now . . . now . . ." His voice faltered.

"He's a child. He can't know what's good for him. We can't permit him to rule us. It's not fair."

"Fair? So now the lady wants fair!" Allen's voice was rising again. "Is it fair that we have to give back fifteen thousand dollars when we know our kid is worth fifteen million, hell, billion?"

"I was talking about for him," Eve said, her voice rising above his. "It isn't fair for him."

"Huh? Come again? Fair for him? Are we living on the same planet, or what? The kid's a goddamned killing machine, and you're worried about what's fair for him."

Allen would have said more, lots more, but when he looked up again he realized that Grant was back in the room, staring at them and looking very displeased. So Allen did the only thing he could think to do. He looked into his son's fiery green eyes, and he smiled.

Allen was waiting when Eve returned from taking Grant to school. He was where she had left him, at the breakfast table, only now the dishes were cleared away, replaced by a fresh bottle of Scotch and a glass.

"I been thinkin'," Allen said, and at once Eve realized he was well on his way to a morning drunk. "I been thinkin' about Grant. We gotta talk to him, make him understand how important this thing is."

Tight lipped, Eve went to the sink, turned on the water and began washing the dishes. Allen trailed after her.

"I mean, he's got an obligation to us now. We gotta make him see that."

Eve spun around, rage behind her eyes, her lips pressed thin and white, her silence screaming at him.

"Hey, whatsa matter with you?"

"What do you want from him?" she barked.

"He owes us," Allen whined. "All we've done for him over the years, he owes us."

"Allen, he's only a little child."

"He's a goddamned freak," Allen said. "NASA, the FBI . . . somebody'd pay plenty for what he's got."

That's when she slapped him, her wet hand leaving a vicious red mark on his cheek, as drops of water cascaded down his chin.

"You talk as if someone had given him a gift and now he doesn't want to share it with us. Do you honestly believe he's acting ungrateful? 'Cause if you do, I pity you."

Allen's hand flew to his face. Instinctively his fingers curled into a fist as his anger began to rise. The muscles in his neck tightened into little knots. Then his hand dropped to his side.

"Eve," he said with a deep sigh, "I don't want to hit you. We've had a rough night. Maybe we should talk later. But Grant . . . he can help us. Just think about it." He turned to go.

"Allen, I don't care about me anymore. Maybe if I had cared more about me things wouldn't have gotten this bad. Who knows?" She shrugged. "But if you really love him, you'll be a father to him. He needs that now—not fame, or fortune, or TV shows or fifteen thousand dollars. He needs a father. *You* think about that."

They stared at each other for one hopeless moment, their pasts and presents fusing together and hanging on the precipice of their future. Then Allen broke the gaze, walking from the room and taking with him any chance they might have had at reconciliation. At least the worst is behind us, he thought. Later he would realize how wrong he had been.

CHAPTER 16

Epps was pouring over a stack of dog-eared pages when the buzz came. His desk, strewn with files and dossiers, was a vertible mountain of papers. His breakfast, a half-eaten doughnut and ice cold cup of coffee, lay somewhere beneath the heap.

Today was the third consecutive day that Epps had gone without a serious meal, and while he was a man who liked his food, nothing could sway him from his task.

The squawk of the intercom demanded his attention. Epps punched a button and picked up the phone.

"Yeah, Hazel?" The annoyance in his voice was obvious.

"Mr. Horvath to see you, sir," was her reply.

"Patches," Epps mumbled. "Shit"! Then into the intercom, "Send him in."

He immediately began stuffing papers into folders and was tossing them into drawers when Patches entered.

Peter Horvath didn't look like an operative. Squat and balding, his wire-rimmed glasses accented an already obtrusive nose. His appearance, mused Epps, is why he was chosen to be one of The Boys. Always wearing cheap business suits, Patches looked more like an accountant— and not a very good one, either.

"I hear you've been burning the midnight oil, Epps. What's up?"

Epps laughed. "For a chief operative you've sure got one lousy information system. Who told you that?" he asked as he dumped the last visible file into a drawer.

Patches shrugged. "When a man can't trust his own moles, who can he trust?" he said, and they both laughed.

"I just thought of something," said Epps. "This is your first time in this office, isn't it? I mean, you've worked here ten, maybe fifteen years, and I don't believe I've ever seen you in here before. Don't tell me you came for the decorations? Did someone misinform you about those, too?" He laughed again, but this time Patches didn't oblige.

"What are you working on, Epps?"

"Don't you remember? You handed me the assignment personally. The Coalition, right?"

"That's the assignment I gave you. I just wanted to make sure you remembered that."

"You know, you're the first chief I've had who took the time to remind me of what my assignment was. Thanks."

"Then you do remember?"

"What's that supposed to mean?"

"All those dossiers you've been requesting. If I didn't know better I'd swear you were up to something, which can't be the case, 'cause I haven't received report one about anything."

Epps fixed him with an expansive stare. "Well then, seems you answered your own question."

"Have I?" His eyes narrowed. "You've been here as long as I have, Epps. You know the rules. Now you might not agree with them, but before you go getting your ass in any kind of trouble let me tell you, as the new head of T-1, I'm a stickler for them. I like to know everything that's going on in my division."

"Why?" Epps said, his voice dripping contempt. "So you can get all the credit?"

"Heroes don't sit well with me," Patches said. Hard black stones peered through the slits of his eyes.

"What about the heroes that saved your ass down in Manila?" Epps said. "How soon we forget."

"Manila," Patches said softly and sighed. "Manila seems a long time ago to me. I hear some of the men now wish I'd been taken out down there. You one of 'em?"

The corners of Epps' lips twisted gently upward. "Let's put it like this. If I were you I wouldn't have anything against heroes. What do you care if someone else gets the credit?"

"It's my division, Epps. I worked hard for this."

"You don't have a monopoly on blood, sweat and tears, you know."

Patches sighed again. "Watch your ass, Epps, 'cause if you're working on something other than what you've been assigned, I'm gonna snatch your butt so fast it won't show up on the videotape replay. Comprendé?

"Yeah," Epps replied.

Patches left, but the bitter taste in Epps' mouth lingered long after, like a heavy dose of overbrewed coffee.

Epps began removing dossiers and files from drawers and placing them back atop his desk. Rafael came to mind. This time I'm gonna nail the bastard, he thought as he resumed his search for clues. And this time, come hell or high water, I'm doing it alone.

* * *

At lunchtime at the Sixth Street Elementary School, kids streamed into the yard like ants fleeing an aardvark. Sandwiches and Twinkies were quickly wolfed down, many discarded half-eaten or not eaten at all. For food was not the main attraction at this lunchtime fair. Food only was a necessary evil, something to satisfy the grumblings that invaded tiny bellies sometime after breakfast. But the star of the show, the thing that yanked kids from their desks, pushing them into the yard as the noontime bell made its daily call, was play. And playing at lunch hour was easily the high point of any school day.

Grant stepped from the building, a fresh dose of adrenaline cracking through his veins, quashing even the remotest vestige of hunger that may have arisen. Excitement spiraled wildly, as his darting eyes searched the yard. Grant was feeling good, happy, confident—and mean. There was a mischief playing in those fiery green eyes, and yes, Grant thought, the fire was there. He felt it. Then he saw Bert Reynolds.

The excitement roared into his fingers and toes. On the outside, however, he was cool. That was important when you were almost a man—being cool—and Grant definitely was.

Slowly and deliberately he started across

the yard. He was a cat, a powerful tigercat stalking his prey, the King of the Hill. The phrase entered his thoughts, and he had to smile. King of the Hill was a game he'd played once back in the third grade, back when Jimmy Buckley was still his best friend. It was actually a fourth graders game, played on a rickety red picnic table that sat in one corner of the yard. Grant had watched them, the fourth graders, hungrily for weeks, wanting to climb atop that old table and join in the fray.

The rules to the game were simple. Every boy had to try and throw every other boy off the mountain. There were many casualties, enough that the game was forbidden by the administration, but the boys played secretly, or as secretly as they could, making the spoils all the sweeter.

King of the Hill. It was the name that had attracted him. If I'm king, I'm somebody special. And so when the boy said, "Hey, wanna play?" how could he refuse? King of the Hill—now *that* was something.

The day was windy, with a late October nip in the air, and his mom had sent him to school in a jacket. But a jacket would only weigh him down and slow his progress, so the jacket was quickly discarded, atop a pile of other quickly discarded clothes. His quest began.

Grant placed one leg on the bench of the

table, about to propel himself upward, when a swarm of tumbling kids washed him along with themselves to the ground. Quickly all scrambled to their feet, ready to climb again. Grant was ready, too.

His eyes gleamed like tiny emeralds as he eyed the coveted spot, his spot, high atop the mountain. He started up, tugging at a boy in front of him until the boy fell out of the way. Grant pulled and pushed, and suddenly both feet were resting safely on the bench. Next, his left foot hit the table and . . . Oooooff! Grant again found himself on the ground, lying on his back, admiring the hazy sky.

King Of The Hill.

The phrase snapped him to his feet, and once again he was pulling, pushing, clawing. A few struggling minutes later he was again at the first level, but he'd been here before; this was nothing. The game was King of the Hill. *King.*

Grant pulled at a boy nearly ten pounds heavier than himself, throwing his balance, then easily knocking him to the ground. He placed his left foot atop the table, then his right, and now he too was on top, protecting his position.

One of the other boys on top stepped towards him. No, Grant thought, I'm not going down. The boy was about to shove when Grant did the darndest thing. He'd seen it on Saturday morning wrestling, and it worked like a charm. As the boy's hands were touching him, and all his weight was committed, Grant spun around, a perfect pirouette. The weight of the boy's misguided push glanced easily off his shoulder, and now the already off balance boy was easy prey for the others. Bye.

Hey, this feels good, Grant thought. He was holding his ground, defending his throne. That's when he made his mistake. He had just side-stepped an even bigger boy and was admiring his work when all of a sudden . . . Aaaghh! He was yanked by his shirt from behind. He heard the shirt rip, but that was all right; a slight pivot and he'd regain his balance. No problem. He was too confident and wasn't watching his flank, and when he realized it . . .

Grant felt as if a raging bull elephant had just rammed into his side. A moment later he was airborne for what seemed a full 60 seconds, then he hit the ground with two other boys on top of him. The air wooshed from his lungs, but that wasn't so bad, not really, not when you considered the knife that had slammed into his stomach.

For a minute even that wasn't so bad. It was cold, so cold. When the minute was up, his stomach caught fire.

"What's the matter with you?" one fourth grader said as he climbed off of Grant.

"That didn't hurt."

The boy was again turning his attention to the task at hand when suddenly he wheeled back around, frightened eyes pinned to Grant's stomach. Grant looked down and saw the blood staining his shirt.

Gingerly he pulled the shirt from his pants and lifted it, the stickiness, like taffy, gluing his fingers. The tip of a freshly sharpened pencil was imbedded in his belly, fresh blood crawling around the giant splinter and running down his side.

By now the game had stopped, in fact all play in the yard had stopped as attention centered on Grant. Someone pulled the pencil from his gut, as Mrs. Redmond arrived with a wet handkerchief.

Later that afternoon two workmen removed the picnic table from the yard. Grant's wound was handled by a doctor—a little peroxide, a shot, not even stitches—but his internal wound, the damage to his psyche caused by his obvious failure in front of everyone at school, lay open, seething and festering until now.

King of the Hill!

Grant understood the significance of the phrase. As he strolled across the yard his little boy's mind even saw it metaphorically. The school yard was the hill, Bert the king, and *he* was on his way to the top. And this time I'm covering my ass.

Bert was picking on Freddy Tobin, a fat freckle-faced fifth grader, the crowd around them armed with mean laughter. Freddy's eyes were busy digging a hole in the ground that he wished he could crawl into.

"Man, you're so fat you don't got an address, you got a zip code." Bert's glance at the leering crowd was rewarded with laughter.

Grant moved closer.

"I hear you fell out of bed, and it measured a ten on the rick-toe scale." Bert smirked. "You're so fat your mother..." Bert's mouth snapped shut. He'd spotted Grant and realized it was too late to get away without it being obvious he was afraid of him.

He forced a smile. "Hey, Spooky," he called. Grant pushed his way to the front of the crowd. "Where you been hidin'? In the Twilight Zone?" Albert Weinmueller and Jimmy Buckley were already backing off, while Freddy Tobin thankfully melted into the crowd.

"You're the one that's been hidin'," Grant said. "Shithead," he added.

The murmuring mass of kids grew silent. Grant stepped closer. King of the Hill. Yes. I'm almost there. "From now on when you see me on one side of the yard, make sure you're on the other," he said.

"What?" Bert squawked with obviously forced indignation.

Grant stepped closer. "The other side." As he slowly began raising his right hand, Bert Reynolds backed off a step.

King!

"You," he commanded of Bert, "over there," he said, his hand now before him, his index finger pointing across the yard. "With the second graders, where you belong." The crowd erupted.

Grant looked into Bert's face and for the first time realized he didn't look mean at all. In fact, he looked like any other fifth grader, just a plain old kid.

"Move!" Grant commanded, stepping closer still.

Bert was candy. "I'm gonna tell Mrs. Redmond on you," he said backing off. "And you better not touch me either, 'cause my father's a lawyer and he'll sue the shit out of you." They were empty threats, and everyone in the yard knew it. Bert turned and walked away.

King, Grant thought, King of the Hill. He watched as Bert moved away from the group, feeling all at once that something was wrong. I should feel good, he thought. I should feel like a king. Instead, as he watched Bert slinking away, he felt like crap, and for the life of him he couldn't figure out why.

* * *

Rafael sat cloistered in his room. He had recently checked into a cheap motel on Labrea Avenue in Hollywood, a place where as long as you paid your bill no one saw a thing.

He had been holed up in the musty smelling room for two days, only showing his face on the street well after dark. The time was drawing near, and he couldn't afford being recognized.

Rafael was thumbing through a back issue of the *Los Angeles Sunday Times* he'd found on the back seat of a stolen car when he found the article:

WONDER BOY PREDICTS
AIR DISASTERS

He read the article through quickly with interest, then slowly a second time, committing each pertinent bit of information to memory. Finished, he looked up thoughtfully.

The time is so close, he thought. Nothing must interfere. He'd come into the United States for one purpose, and no little boy could be allowed to block his task. Rafael chuckled. That was ridiculous. Most psychics were frauds, and even if he wasn't, singling out that plane would be an incredible coincidence. "No," Rafael thought out loud, "not a coincidence, an impossibility."

Turning the page Rafael once again began thumbing through the paper. His attention,

however, was now totally gone. He commanded thoughts of the boy to leave his
mind, but it was no use. Rafael was
worried. He had to know more about Grant
Michaels.

CHAPTER 17

Clad in his navy blue pajamas, Grant lay atop the covers staring at the ceiling. Though it was bedtime he hadn't turned out the light yet and maybe he just wouldn't; maybe he'd leave it on forever, and if someone came and tried to turn it out, maybe he'd zap them into the Twilight Zone. Mommy hadn't yet shown up to tuck him in, but that's okay, he told himself. I'm gettin' too big for that kinda stuff anyway. Yet he lay there, waiting.

He'd been almost a man for nearly a week now, and gosh, it was tough. He was a big shot at school; hell, he was *numero uno* and everyone knew it. Still he didn't have any friends, his prime candidate for friendship being Bert Reynolds of all people. It happened that afternoon just after school as Grant was beginning his lonely walk home.

"Hey, want some company?" he heard from behind. He turned and saw Bert Reynolds standing there alone, the dethroned king eyeing the new king. "I'll walk along with ya?" Bert said. It was phrased as a question, yet hung before them as a beaten man's plea.

"No thanks," Grant said. He looked beyond Bert, wondering if Jimmy Buckley was lurking somewhere in the background. He wasn't. "I like to walk alone," he added.

"Just thought I'd ask."

"Yeah."

"See you tomorrow." And that was it, a peace offering of sorts, but Grant wasn't interested.

As images of Bert drifted by, Mommy and Daddy entered his thoughts. They were so different now, at least Daddy was. The smiling was nice; Grant liked that. He smiled a lot and always looked happy, but of course he wasn't. He was scared.

Grant thought he didn't mind the scared looks on his parents' faces, but he knew that he did. His secret hope had been that they'd go away, that after a while the phony smiles would be replaced by real ones, and everyone would be happy. He thought he could scare them into bliss.

And it almost worked. Mommy was looking more and more confident everyday, and she was talking to him like he was a kid again and not a creature from another planet. But Daddy was different. Daddy was scared, and Grant didn't know what to do.

A light rapping at the door caught his attention.

"Yeah?"

"It's Mommy," and she came in.

"Still awake, honey?"

"Yeah." She came over and sat on the edge of the bed.

"Waiting for Mommy to tuck you in?"

"Nah," he said.

"Well, I'm going to do it anyway." She helped him under the covers, tucked him in and placed a gentle kiss on his forehead. "There," she said. "Better?"

"I guess." But his pleasure was obvious.

She looked at her son and frowned. My, how he had changed. There was a new maturity to him that showed around the mouth, a firmness to his jaw, and his eyes were the eyes of someone who had known pain and disappointment. They were his father's eyes, but he was just a baby. *Her* baby. It wasn't fair.

"Is there something you want to say to

me?" she asked.

"Like what?"

"Like anything."

"Dinner was good." She shot him a benign smile. "Pancakes for breakfast again?"

"I don't think so."

"But Daddy said . . ."

"Honey . . ." Her voice trailed off.

"Why can't Daddy be happy?" he asked. Surprise registered on her face. Maybe he shouldn't have asked, but it was too late since he already did.

"What makes you ask that?"

"He's not happy, is he?"

"No."

"Why?"

My inquisitive child, Eve thought. But this wasn't the typical "Why must we die?" or "Where is heaven?" type of question. Nothing so simple. No, the easy ones had all been asked years ago. "Is there really a Santa Claus?" The ones you could lie through and smile to yourself about were all gone, and Eve found herself left with the task of dealing with the truth. The truth was that she didn't have all the answers and definitely not the answer to this one.

"I don't know," she finally said.

"I wouldn't hurt Daddy. You know that, don't you?"

Eve nodded.

"You're happy, aren't you, Mom?" She

didn't answer, but her forced smile was answer enough.

Instead she said, "It's getting late." She kissed him again, this time on the lips, and a moment later she flicked the room into darkness and was gone.

Grant lay, eyes fixed on the ceiling. What he'd wanted was no more yelling and for everybody to smile a lot and be happy. There was a time when smiling was enough, when smiling and happy meant the same thing. But that only held true in a little boy's world, and he was almost a man.

Mommy and Daddy weren't happy, and the reason was him. Yet what really had him baffled, what really sent his thoughts crashing around inside his mind, leaving him feeling dazed and alone, was that he wasn't happy either. With all his new maturity and newfound power he still didn't know how to make things right.

He lay still for quite a while, his mind a kaleidoscope of confusion, his thoughts centering on nothing in particular. Then Daddy came. He hadn't heard the door, but he looked over and saw his father approaching.

"Hey, champ, just making sure there was nothing you needed." He smiled, and for some reason the smile reminded Grant of the grimaces he'd once seen gracing his father's face. He fought the urge to look away. "Can I talk to you a minute?" Allen said. Grant nodded.

Allen walked around the bed, sitting on the side by the window. The light flooding in played mysteriously about his face, carving deep shadows around his eyes and jawline. He looked almost skeletal.

"So how was school today?" he asked.

"Good," Grant answered.

"You don't have to go tomorrow, not if you don't want to."

Grant considered this for a moment. "I better go," he said.

"You sure?"

"Yeah," Grant said.

"You love us, son?" Allen asked suddenly.

"Huh?" Grant said, obviously surprised.

"You know. Do you love us, me and Mommy?"

"Sure, Dad," he said, and he meant it. No matter what had happened between them he still loved both his parents very much.

"Good, good," his father said. "Son, you're getting big now. You've got to have some responsibilities."

"I do. I clean my room, water the lawn . . ." He stopped when he saw his father vehemently shaking his head.

"Adult responsibilities."

"I'm not going on TV," Grant said, his voice hardening.

"No, of course not. You shouldn't do anything you don't want to, right?" The forced smile was back.

"Right," Grant said.

"Listen, son, what I mean is that maybe, and of course this only if you want to, but maybe you can tell some people what you can do."

"What people?" Grant's eyes narrowed.

"Friends," Allen said quickly. "Friends of Daddy."

"Why?"

"Uhh, it's hard to explain. But you'd be helping me and Mommy, and I absolutely guarantee you won't have to go on television ever again. You want to help me and Mommy, don't you?"

"Sure."

"That's my boy," he said, and this time his smile was genuine. His hand moved to Grant's head, stopping suddenly, the smile disintegrating. "Is it all right? I mean, can I muss your hair?"

Grant nodded, and his father mussed his hair just like he used to. Grant smiled. He's happy, he thought! Suddenly things didn't seem so bad. They didn't seem bad at all.

Eve was reading the paper when Allen came down. He looked too happy. Something had to be wrong.

"I spoke to him," he said.

She started to ask who, but realized how ridiculous that would have sounded.

"I spoke to him," he repeated. "Guess you didn't think I'd do that. Thought I was afraid, didn't you?"

"No," Eve said.

"The truth is I was. Scared my own son would turn me into something resembling chimney sweepings. Then I remembered the old Michaels' charm, and Grant being just a kid, hell, he didn't have a chance. You know the old saying about catching flies with vinegar?" He flopped down in his chair and released a wave of laughter.

"What did you say to him?" Eve demanded.

"I asked him if he wouldn't mind telling some people what he can do."

"What people?"

"Whadaya mean what people? People who'll pay hard cold cash for his talent, that's what people."

Eve jumped up. "Allen, I warned you!"

"So what are you gonna do now, leave? How many of those suitcases do you have? Hey, maybe it won't be the suitcase next time. Maybe it'll be you."

"Allen!"

"Shh, keep your voice down, dear," he said with a smirk. "You don't want to upset little Grant, now do you?"

"Allen," she said softly, the control in her voice surprising even her, "I'm going to say this once more and that's it. If, and I doubt it strongly, but *if* you feel anything for your son you'll give up this dream of yours and help him. I spoke with him tonight, too.

Allen, he's still a child. Still frightened."

"*Him?*" Allen said incredulously. "Frightened of what?"

"He's a child, regardless of what he can do."

"All right, Eve, you win. I'll help him. I'll help him good. You just tell him to listen to me and everything will be hunky-dory." He was smirking again.

Eve sat silently for a minute, then heaved a great sigh. "You poor pathetic creature," she finally said. "You poor sick thing."

The bearded man was seated in the periodicals section of the library hastily going through a stack of old newspapers. Liz Gordon, the periodicals librarian, watched him through the corner of her eye. The man would quickly read an entire newspaper, toss it on a stack of discards and grab another. He seemed to gobble up information like the locusts that had gobbled up her father's crops.

Liz wanted to tell the man that that was no way to enjoy a newspaper. Newspapers had to be read slowly, which was what she was about to do with the gossip rag that lay on the counter in front of her.

She had been warned repeatedly about reading rags such as these on the job. "No respectable librarian would be caught dead reading one of those," her boss, Miss Hawkins, had said often enough. That's all right, Liz thought, I'm not a librarian anyway. In truth Liz wasn't a librarian, she hadn't even finished high school.

She was 16, although she looked much older, and six months ago when she left the farm and drifted to Los Angeles and the big time, she read of the job on the library's bulletin board. It was only part time and paid minimum wage, but no one asked a lot of dumb questions, like "What's a kid like you doin' in a place like this?" So she took it, and lo and behold, Liz Gordon had hit the big time.

Liz was beginning to read and enjoying it thoroughly, when she heard someone clearing his throat. "Yes, can I help you?" she asked, looking up into the bearded man's face. What a gorgeous smile!

"Anymore?" Rafael asked.

"No. Two weeks worth is all we keep. Anything earlier is on microflilm downtown at our main branch."

Noticing the newspaper lying open on the desk in front of her, Rafael's eyes were snared by a headline:

AIR DISASTER WONDER BOY COMMUNICATES WITH MARS.

"Is that a recent paper?" asked Rafael.

"Yes," Liz said with an embarrassed smile. "It just came out."

Rafael donned a pair of shades and hurriedly left the building.

"Hey!" Liz called. "You have to put those

papers back." But it was too late. He was gone.

Liz sighed and secreted her gossip sheet under the desk. Oh well, she thought, this is the price one must pay for instant success. With an air of officiousness Liz moved from behind the counter to the table where she put the discarded newspapers away.

The sun was shining, the birds were singing, and Julio Sanchez felt like shit—partly because of the booze he'd been consuming of late, and partly because as each day crept miserably by he realized just how difficult handling Rafael would be. Difficult? There's optimism for you. In truth, this Rafael thing was turning out to be downright impossible.

Sanchez was in his car, driving along the Santa Monica Freeway. It was just past 5:00 so quite naturally traffic was a bitch. He'd just finished interviewing a button man over on Fourth Avenue in Santa Monica, and like everything else that had been happening to him lately, the interview was crap.

He'd rendezvoused with the man in a small and very well-kept rooming house. The man wore dark glasses and sat by the window shining a spotlight into Sanchez's face to keep visual contact to a bare minimum.

"I hear you need a little laundry done?"

the man had asked.

What is this? James Bond? Immediately Sanchez did not like the man. His voice was high and wimpish, and it's hard to like someone shining a 1000 watt light bulb in your face.

"I want someone 'handled,'" Sanchez said.

"What's the deal?" the wimpy-voiced stranger asked.

"Twenty thousand cash. Ten in advance and ten after. How you handle him is your business."

"I like it when the boss isn't picky. Got a picture?"

"No, I do not," Sanchez said.

"Either you're an amateur at this, or your target's camera shy, which means he's a pro, and I charge extra for doing pros."

Sanchez squirmed a little in his chair.

"Who is he?"

"His name is Rafael."

"Rafael what?"

"I don't know. It isn't his real name. It is a name he uses in his work."

"Rafael? You mean like in Rafael the terrorist?"

"Yes," said Sanchez.

The interview ended soon after that amidst waves of wimpish laughter.

So that's how things are going to be, he thought, as he sat amidst the stalled traffic. And all because of the arrogant, indomitable Rafael. Three days from now the ambassadors to every member nation of the World Bank would be arriving in Los Angeles. In three days their plan would have been set in motion. As things were now, within three days he had to locate someone to handle Rafael—lest he do it himself.

Sanchez spotted an opening in traffic, maneuvered the big car into the right lane, and a few minutes later was approaching the Overland exit ramp, abandoning the freeway. He'd take his chances on the street.

A half hour and several worn nerves later he was pulling up to the gate of the high security condominium complex in which he currently resided. The smiling security guard in the booth, recognizing Sanchez, waved him in. Sanchez waved and smiled back. Inside he was laughing. The security of the place was sophisticated enough for an amateur, and even the more seasoned thieves would think twice before challenging the surveillance system with its closed circuit TV and security personnel on patrol, not to mention the sophisticated alarm system. But to a pro, to someone like Rafael, this system was a piece of cake. Sanchez himself had spotted weaknesses in the system just over the six months he had resided in the complex.

Sanchez parked his car in the security

underground garage and took the short walk over neatly manicured grounds to his residence. Reaching his front door he stopped. Since this thing with Rafael, Sanchez had developed his own security system.

He eyed the front door scrupulously. There it was. The single hair he had placed between the door and doorjamb. Had the hair been moved or broken Sanchez would have been alerted to the fact that someone had entered, but it was still neatly in place.

Now Sanchez moved casually around the grounds, smelling the roses blooming about his home and admiring the daisies and geraniums. Recently Sanchez had personally repainted the trim around all of his windows, in the process painting the windows shut. Now as Sanchez surveyed the trees, admired the babbling brook, and contemplated the flowers, his eyes were on the windows. Any dirt or scuffing on the sills? Any chipped paint? Any visible cracks? No. His little fortress was secure.

Sanchez went back around the front, pressed the digital alarm code on the push button pad by the door, and entered. The price of security, he thought. When he walked into his living room Sanchez realized that whatever the price, it wasn't enough.

The computers, the closed circuit TV, the

push button alarm system, the security guards, the fresh paint and even the single hair were not enough. Sanchez realized all this when he entered his living room and heard the strange American voice say, "Welcome home." He knew it for sure when he turned and found himself staring down the barrel of a very unfriendly .44 magnum.

While Sanchez was admiring the gun, Rafael was finishing his reading. The article in the gossip rag was utterly unbelievable, yet articles he found in more respectable newspapers seemed to ally his concern. An article he read in *People* magazine described the boy predicting an air disaster while on television. This child was no fraud.

Of course, chances of the boy predicting an impending disaster on the aircraft in question were slim. He'd never predicted an air disaster before it happened. Chances were he couldn't. Still, a flurry of doubts assailed him.

His was going to be the greatest terrorist victory ever. Just the thought of it sent waves of sexual energy charging through him. He'd taken all the precautions, and not taking this one might be his downfall.

In that instant Rafael's mind was made up. Just as he must get rid of this baggage before the thing could be completed, in turn he must take care of one last little doubt that gnawed at the base of his skull. The doubt was Grant Michaels. The child had to die.

CHAPTER 18

They were arguing again, and Grant knew it. Even though they donned incredibly phony smiles whenever he entered the room, they couldn't hide the truth. There was a hatred brewing between them, percolated in the depths of their souls, bubbling up into their hearts and spilling forth in angry whispers, cutting glances and veiled threats.

Whatever had once existed between them was fast ending, and Grant felt the burden of guilt, like the weight of the world, resting squarely on his shoulders.

I'm the cause of this. Me! Sure, they argued before, and yes, he hated the yelling, but that's all it was—yelling. Not like this. This was cold and mean. This was whispers in bitter tones that reeked of the deathly stench of hate.

He'd invented going away to escape. It was his freedom from the arguing and the yelling. Yet in truth it hadn't been freedom at all. Instead it had ensnared him, a clever trap from which there was no escape.

Grant was seated in his room at his desk, attempting homework. Muted light from a dusky sky trickled in as day turned into night. He had been at it for hours, but it was no use; he just couldn't think. Angry whispers assailed tiny ears, and he couldn't think.

When he arose and opened the door, the voices were upon him. He headed downstairs.

"Oh, Grant," his father said as he reached the landing. "I didn't hear you."

Grant continued down, staring at the practiced smiles on his parents' faces.

"Everything okay, champ?" There was a nervous edge to his father's voice.

"Yeah," Grant replied. What am I saying? He had come downstairs to put his foot down, to tell his parents enough was enough, but looking at them here he felt hopeless, like the last breath of winter on an early spring day.

"Trouble with your homework, honey?" his mother asked.

"Sort of."

"Why don't you go back upstairs. As soon as Mommy's finished down here she'll be right up. Okay?"

"Okay." He turned.

"Honey, don't you have a smile for Mommy?"

Grant hadn't realized how many muscles it took to force a smile. He used every one of them.

A few seconds after he was back in his room, the arguing started anew even before he'd closed the door.

My fault! The thought burnished itself into his consciousness. My fault . . . my fault . . . my fault . . .

They may not have been happy before, but at least they weren't filled with hate. This newfound hatred was his fault, and he was going to have to do something about it. But what? It was too soon to decide, but one thing was clear. He had to do something—soon.

Eve finished helping Grant with his homework, left the room and eased the door shut behind herself. She took the short walk down the hall to her bedroom, stopped outside the door and listened. Allen was still downstairs on the phone. She went in.

She sat on the edge of the bed and stared down at the pink chenille bedspread with the puffy rose pattern. How long have we had this? Four, five years? Her thoughts drifted back to that time in her life.

Allen had recently been made regional sales manager at Zacky Farms, a chicken farming outfit that supplied most of the supermarkets in Southern California. He'd only been with the firm for two years, so this was definitely a feather in his cap. Allen had always been a good provider—she was proud of that—yet evenings when he returned home Allen espoused dreams of owning his own chicken ranch and surpassing the sales of Zacky and even the famous Frank Perdue in the east. He was never satisfied. Back then she thought his incredible ambition a good thing.

Things weren't any better between them, and it was obvious that staying had been a mistake. But when they discovered what Grant could do she was so terrified, so utterly confused. She deluded herself into believing that now Allen would be a father to his son and no longer attempt to exploit him.

She realized now that none of this was Allen's own fault. He was a sick man.

"Sick!" Allen had squawked a while earlier. "You mean, you think I'm crazy, right?"

"No, not crazy. You're just not thinking straight right now. Surely you realize most fathers would not take advantage of their children's . . . gifts."

"Surely *you* realize most children can't put luggage through a test even Samsonite couldn't pass." Suddenly Allen brightened. "Hey, Samsonite . . . that's not a bad idea. They could use Grant in one of their commercials. Picture this. They take a piece of luggage and put it through the regular paces, you know, a gorilla jumpin' all over it, fallin' out of cars, the works. Then they show Grant . . ." He stopped in mid-sentence, contemplating what he'd just said. "Nah, forget it. What Grant has is too important. The government . . ."

"Allen, no!"

"Yes, Eve, they should know. This is a matter of national security. Suppose Russia got their hands on him? You wouldn't want that, would you?"

"No one would be interested in him if no one knew."

Somehow this little fact eluded Allen. He'd made up his mind. He was going to tell someone about Grant—anyone who would listen.

So far she had the insanity thing on her side. The article in the *Enquirer* didn't hurt either. Everyone was calling Allen a crackpot, but it was only a matter of time before someone would listen, or Grant would use his power to do something hideous. Then they would take him away—forever.

She couldn't handle that. Since things with Allen had soured, Grant was all she had in the world. A world without him was no world at all. Hence her decision. She must take her son and run. She must convince him that coming with her was the right thing to do, and together they must flee.

"Take anything you want," Sanchez said. "I don't keep much cash in the house, but there are many things that you can sell."

The stranger eyed him curiously. "Come on, do I look like a crook?"

Sanchez had been too busy gawking at the gun to pay much attention to the American wielding it. He was a tall man, over six feet, with dark brown hair and pleasant features. His clean shaven face screamed of good upbringing, as did his expensive beige slacks, Bass loafers and a burgundy windbreaker. He did not look like a thief. This brought something else to Sanchez's mind. Killer!

"What is it that you want?" he asked.

"Just some talk," the man said.

"You have a strange way of engaging a man in conversation," Sanchez said, trying to hide the fact he was about to shit his pants.

Lowering the gun slightly, the man chuckled. "And *you* have a sense of humor," he said.

"I'm also tired." Sanchez eyed the sofa. "May I?" The man motioned him over, and the fat man sat. "Anything particular you wish to chat about?"

"As a matter of fact, there is." Epps now moved out of the doorway he'd been standing in since Sanchez had entered. He allowed himself a moment to take in the elegance of his surroundings. The room was exquisitely decorated in a chrome and glass motif that permeated a sense of regal sereneness. Even the *objets d'art* were all crystal. The sofa on which the fat man sat was a light blue, crushed velvet horseshoe. Epps seated himself on one of the corners. "Before I go on, let me advise you not to try anything heroic. I'm not here to kill you, but I will if I have to."

Sanchez breathed a sigh of relief. "You have my word on it."

"Good. Now I was wondering if you could tell me anything about The Coalition?"

Sanchez was cool. "Just what coalition are you refering to?"

The flicker was slight, Epps observed, but it was there, enough for the trained eye to see.

"While you're at it," Epps went on, "would you mind explaining your relationship with Rafael?"

There. The flicker was much more obvious; even Sanchez knew it.

"Rafael who?" he said.

Epps smiled. "Now that your allegiances have been established it's just a matter of time before you talk." He looked Sanchez in the eye. "And you will talk."

"Who are you?" Sanchez asked.

"Suffice to say I'm a member of a little known government agency."

A nervous laugh fell from Sanchez's lips. "It seems you have entered the wrong premises. I have nothing the government would find of interest, provided you're not with the IRS." He laughed again, now with more confidence. "By the way, how did you ever get in here?"

"I'm a professional. I've entered countries with better security than this."

"That's answer enough," Sanchez said calmly. He was once again in control. You have to wake up pretty early to trick Julio Sanchez. "I'm sure you do not wish to divulge any trade secrets. I'm terribly sorry for the inconvenience you've experienced."

Epps ignored him. "I also might add that I've interrogated better liars than you. Professional liars."

The nervous laugh was back. "Don't tell me you don't believe me? Oh, this *is* amusing."

"Fuckin'-A, I don't believe you. And amusing? You should see what I do for laughs."

Epps stuck his left hand into the pocket of his windbreaker, keeping his gun and eyes trained on Sanchez. When the hand emerged it held a cigarette lighter. He flicked it open, the pencil thin flame hopping to life.

Sanchez's heart began to race wildly. That's okay, he told himself. Any man would be nervous if an armed stranger threatened him with a cigarette lighter. This proves nothing. He laughed again. "You flick your bic for entertainment?"

"There was a guy in Managua once, a spy, a trained killer who couldn't seem to remember what had become of a shipment of arms the CIA had intended for the Contra rebel forces. The guy plain and simple wasn't a talker—till he met me." Epps displayed an expansive grin for effect. "By the time I was through the guy couldn't shut up. He not only remembered where the shipment was but remembered two caches of Soviet arms we knew nothing about."

Sanchez looked worried. His eyes were filling with horror as he watched the tiny flame grow in size. He used every molecule of strength to keep himself from appearing frightened, but inside he was falling apart.

"You need just the tinest dot of fire to light a cigarette," Epps went on. "Yet you open one of these things and you could sit it atop the Statue of Liberty. For the longest time I couldn't figure out what the hell these things were for. I mean, it's obvious they aren't for cigarettes."

By now he had adjusted the flame to maximum height. The dancing fire reflected deliciously in Sanchez's terror-filled eyes.

"You have made a mistake," Sanchez said, no longer attempting to sound flip or confident.

"No," Epps said, "I don't think so. At least, for your sake I hope I didn't, 'cause the only thing that's gonna stop us from smelling barbequed flesh is the answer to my questions. And if you don't have anything to say . . ." Epps paused. "Looks like I've got a lot of cooking to do." He rose.

"You . . . you wouldn't hurt an innocent man," Sanchez babbled.

"There are no innocent men. It's just a matter of matching the man with the crime." He took a step towards Sanchez, stopped abruptly and extinguished the flame. "You rather I just kill you?" he asked. "Not much pain in that."

"No!" Sanchez said.

The lighter disappeared back in Epps' pocket, and a pair of handcuffs appeared in his hand. "You're gonna have to put your hands behind your back."

"What is it that you want?" Sanchez asked, his voice laced with fear.

"Answers. Turn around."

"If I answer your questions, you promise you won't hurt me?"

"Hey, I'm not a freak or nothing. I don't get any pleasure from this."

Sanchez sighed. "Ask," he said.

"Put these on," Epps handed him the handcuffs and caught the distrusting look on his face. "Just in case you become forgetful."

In a minute Sanchez's hands were secured behind his back.

"I'm gonna give it to you straight," Epps said. "I want Rafael so bad I can taste it, and you're the only one who can lead me to him. As for your covert activities, give me Rafael and we'll wipe the slate clean."

At that moment the sky opened in Sanchez's mind, and rays of golden sunshine came sifting through the clouds. There it was, the answer to both their problems. "Do you know a good hit man?" Sanchez asked.

It was time to talk.

"Whadaya mean how did I get this number? I looked it up in the phone book, right under CIA."

Allen Michaels had been on the phone for over an hour with no results. "I know this is hard to believe, but at least come and check it out. What do you have to lose? Hello . . . Hello? . . ." Allen smashed the phone into the receiver. "Idiots!" he roared. "The country's being run by idiots!"

Over the past few days he had tried calling just about every agency he could think of: NASA, the FBI, the Jet Propulsion Laboratory, the State Department, the combined armed forces, the Defense Department, the FAA, the Secret Service, the CIA, even the Commission on Civil Rights, calling the latter to complain that he was being discriminated against. But even they wouldn't listen.

"What's the matter with everybody?" Allen said out loud. "The kid's a god-damned secret weapon."

After finally getting up the gumption to talk to Grant, he found himself right back at square one. No one would believe him.

Of course, if the kid had gone on *That's Incredible* the whole world would have known, and right now these same assholes would be begging him, *begging*, for a crack at his son. As it was, Grant refused to go on TV, and there was nothing he could do about it.

Maybe he could talk to him again, and convince him that TV is the way to go. "Don't you love your mom and dad?" Allen said in a practiced voice. He knew he was good, but it was no use. It had taken every ounce of nerve he had—several of those ounces coming from the Scotch bottle, thank you—to haul himself up to the kid's room the first time. There was no way he'd do it again.

On the other hand, Eve was different. She seemed to be developing a rapport with the kid. He noticed the way she mollycoddled him. Just looking out for her own ass, Allen thought, and doing a damn good job of it, too. But how do I get her to speak to him? She hardly speaks to me. She thinks I'm crazy. Well, you're the crazy one, Eve baby. The kid's worth a fortune, and no, I'm not afraid to be rich. Granted, I might have been a little nervous in the beginning, but no more. I'm ready to be rich.

Allen sat, lost in himself, the shadowy prospect of a life without success staring him in the face.

If the government wouldn't listen, the kid would have to go on television. There was no other option. It was up to Eve now. She was the only one the boy might listen to, and it was up to him to convince her—somehow.

In one last futile attempt, Allen picked up the phone and began dialing the number for the Nuclear Regulatory Commission. He had to find someone.

Yet even as he dialed someone was listening. Someone was listening to every word he said, and they were very, very interested.

CHAPTER
19

Grant was a freak. No one had said it to his face, but they didn't have to. He could tell the way his parents looked at him and the way the kids at school avoided him, fear and curiosity a ragged brush fire dancing behind their eyes. Word was out that he could do things—*"Grant Michaels can make wild dogs attack you and bite your balls off!"*—crazy things that he'd never even dreamt of. Rumors sprang up like mushrooms in a rain forest, Grant catching snatches of hushed conversation as he moved alone across the yard.

He was always alone now. He was king, and this was his domain. Yet with no loyal subjects, what good was it? No one would talk to him, and that was the worst part. Even Bert Reynolds, who once offered his hand in friendship, kept his distance. Grant was almost a man, but there was still some little kid left in him. Wasn't he supposed to have fun, at least sometimes?

It was 3:00 o'clock. Grant was standing in front of the school, as kids around him talked and played, making their ways home at the close of another day. Grant began walking silently, hating the kids around him. He hated them and then himself, for having this power that caused fear in their eyes and turned his parents into smiling fools.

"Jesus in heaven, there he is."

A woman's voice from behind had him spinning around. Wonder and joy blossomed on her face. It was Doris Sachs, the lady from the TV show.

He didn't recognize her at first; she seemed older and very, very tired. Once he knew who she was though, the first plane crash glided into his thoughts.

"Remember me?" she said. She took a step towards him, and images of her halting steps at the studio appeared.

"Stay away from me," he declared. He turned to run, but what was he running from?

"Wait!" she called. "Please!"

Grant sprinted a few steps, then stopped

and turned. He looked again into the woman's face, saw the hope in her eyes, and knew why he couldn't stay.

"Leave me alone," he called out. "I hate you!"

This time he did run. Turning off her shouted pleas, he sprinted down the block. Yet he couldn't seem to run fast enough or far enough to escape her muffled cries. It wasn't until many minutes later that he realized the plea he was listening to was coming from inside.

Doris Sachs stood in front of the Sixth Street Elementary School wondering what to do. She hadn't meant to frighten the boy, but she had to talk to him. She had even missed her worship meeting with Reverend Joe to be here today. She couldn't just go home.

Everyday since she'd met Reverend Joe she had attended services, and each day she waited for a sign, but none came. Doris didn't despair; with the strength of the Lord behind her she knew things would work out right. Then last night as she sat by candlelight reading the scriptures she was struck by a thought: The boy was sent to me by God. She hadn't thought of the boy much as of late, but now she realized it was her God-given duty to to find him.

She spent the entire morning first locating his address and then coming into the neighborhood to find his school. Even then she wasn't sure she'd find him amongst so many children, yet when she saw him it only proved what she thought all along. This was meant to be.

Doris began walking. She didn't know where she was going. What she did know was that she had to find the boy, and when she did he would give her what she wanted—a message from Charlie.

Grant Michaels reached the park and collapsed on a bench, his ragged breath coming short and fast. He was tired. He didn't know how long he'd been running aimlessly, but his legs ached and his tongue was dry.

He didn't want to hate Doris Sachs, but he couldn't help himself. Something inside blamed her for all that had happened. If her husband hadn't been in that plane maybe . . .

Grant got up and headed for the drinking fountain. The park was empty, since it wasn't a park kids often came to. There was really nothing there, just a few bushes, a patch of green, a few trees and some pigeons. It was a place where old folks could come to pass the time, nothing more.

Grant reached the fountain and was about to drink when he heard her. "Please, boy." He turned and there she was, standing before him, arms outstretched. "I just need to talk to you for a minute."

"No!" Grant screamed. Anger and hate

fused within him. "Stay back!" he warned. "I don't want to hurt you." But he did want to hurt her. He wanted to hurt her a lot.

Doris gave him an indulgent smile. "Don't be scared, boy. I don't mean you any harm, but my Charlie . . . Is there a message for me?" She advanced a step and noticed the sudden malevolence spreading across the boy's face. Looking into his eyes she saw something resembling evil dancing there. His gaze was fixed on the sky.

"What's wrong?" she asked. She followed his intense stare to the heavens but saw nothing, just clear blue stretching out into eternity. "Is it my Charlie?" She stepped closer and grasped him by the shoulders. "Is there a message for me?"

Grant didn't answer. He continued to be transfixed, his eyes vacant and dumb. What's the matter with him? Then, at once, there was a twinkling of life, not in his eyes but more about the lips. The corners turned gently upward.

Again Doris looked to the sky, but there was nothing. What is it? She was turning back to the boy when she finally saw it and turned again, squinting. A tiny speck of black was marring the canvas of perfect blue. She couldn't make it out, but whatever it was, it was moving towards them, slowly expanding to a dot and then a fist and then a hazy black cloud.

What is it? Did the boy cause this? How?

The thing was moving too quickly to be a storm, but what was it?

A dusty fear, soft like an early winter's snow, fell quietly over her. She stared on in dumb fascination as the dark thing, now huge and sinister, slowly obliterated the sky. Finally when there was nothing but blackness overhead, she realized the thing was coming down, coming down for her.

She didn't know when Grant had backed away from her. She was aware of nothing but the cloud, and God, it looked familiar.

It was back when she was a little girl, seven, she believed, on the farm in Idaho. Then too, something had blackened the sky and fell upon them with its tentacles of destruction. Seven years, she thought.

The thing was now just a hundred feet above her. Fat and black and billowy, it dropped with amazing speed.

"It's the devil's work," she called, eyeing Grant with new eyes. "The devil's work!"

And then they fell on her.

Locusts, hungry and insatiable, covered her from head to foot. Hundreds, maybe thousands, quilted themselves over her, their muddy brown skins blotting out every inch of what was Doris Sachs.

The hum of their wings was enormous. It filled the neighborhood, and the things kept coming, knocking blindly into each other, fighting to light on her, to feast on human flesh.

She screamed, but her futile cries were lost; like whispers in a windstorm they melded into nothingness admist the beat of thousands of tiny wings.

They came to eat, to devour, as they had devoured her father's crops all those many years ago. "I hear they gotta eat ten times their weight every twenty-four hours or perish," someone had once said. This thought now rocketed through what was left of Doris' mind, what little piece of her senses hadn't yet been ripped to shreds by the sheer madness of the thing.

Charlie, I'm comin', I'm comin'.

She fell to her knees and realized for the first time how heavy these locusts were, and that they were eating her alive.

I'm comin'.

Her face was now a burning mask, as powerful little pincers ripped at her flesh. She felt something sucking out her eyes, then climbing into the hollow where they had been, in search of more delicacy. Her entire being was aflame as tissue and muscle were ripped from bone. This time when she tried to scream she realized how ridiculous it was, for somehow they had gotten inside of her and were now munching their way down her throat, devouring her larynx, and continuing on into her belly, where they delighted on what food remained before eating through her stomach walls and lining.

239

The pain no longer mattered. The part of her that felt pain was gone, and what remained was a rejoicing, for she was going to meet her maker—and Charlie.

Hallelujah, Charlie, I'm comin'.

Doris was prone now, or at least what was left of her was, and the things kept coming and coming and coming . . . Then like a fog lifting over a Scottish moor, they rose sluggardly into the sky, hovered fat and stupid for a moment, and were gone.

Grant Michaels stood horrified, watching his work. In the end all that was left were rags, and teeth and the heel of a shoe and the tiny fake gold amulet she received from Reverend Joe. But there was no Doris Sachs. The woman was just plain gone.

Grant stood for a moment taking all this in. Noooo! something inside him screamed. He turned to run from the park and promptly passed out.

Grant opened his eyes and looked around. He was in a white, metallic room with a small window to his right. He glanced out the window and saw that the sun had set. He didn't know where he was or how long he'd been there.

He must be in a hospital, but why? He turned his head to his left and saw his mother asleep on a chair. Tiny wrinkles of worry crisscrossed her forehead. Then her brow furrowed, the wrinkles deepening, her eyes opened, and she smiled.

"Hi," she said softly.

"Hi."

"You gave us a scare." She moved to the bed where she rested a soothing hand on his forehead. "But you're all right now."

"What am I doing here?"

"Someone found you lying in a park this afternoon and called the paramedics. They said your heart was racing."

What was I doing in a park? Grant wondered, the incident of the afternoon totally forgotten. "What time is it?" he asked.

"Ten-thirty. When they found you the doctors gave you something to make you sleep." A sudden graveness crossed her face. "They said you had a strong emotional experience. Do you know what that means?"

"I think so."

"What happened?" she said softly, cautiously.

All Grant remembered was leaving school, and . . . Slowly the thing was returning to him—the lady at school, the park, the hate he felt towards her.

"Are you all right?" his mother asked.

The color in Grant's cheeks was slowly fading to a deathly white, and he was beginning to tremble.

"Grant, what is it?"

He didn't answer. The incident in the

park was being played back hideously before his eyes, and all he could do was watch.

Eve grasped his shaking hand and found it to be ice-cold. Then she dropped it. "I'm getting a doctor," she said and ran from the room.

Grant lay there, the blood washing from his cheeks, his eyes hazy and distant. The woman was just plain gone. He still couldn't believe that he had done it. "I'm sorry," he whispered to no one. Tiny hot tears escaped his eyes, parading down his cheeks. The woman was gone, and this too—like so many things in his recent life—was his fault.

"He's in here."

Grant heard his mother's voice from outside, then she entered with a white-coated doctor.

"He's shaking," she said.

The doctor came over and began taking his pulse. "I can give him something to hold him until morning," he said.

"Yes, please do that."

The doctor looked at Grant. "You look like you've seen a ghost. What happened?"

Grant didn't answer. He didn't know how.

"Mrs. Michaels, why don't you go home and get some sleep. I'll keep an eye on him throughout the night." He pulled out a syringe and began filling it. "After this he won't wake up for quite a while." He stuck the needle in Grant's arm, but Grant didn't flinch.

"I can't leave him. I'll sleep here," Eve said, pointing at the chair she'd slept in earlier.

"You won't rest there, and neither will he. Look, why not go down the hall to the lounge? There's a mighty comfy sofa down there." He smiled.

"Well . . ." Eve said, eyeing her son.

"That settles it. I'll chat with Grant for a minute, and then I'll join you for a cup of coffee." And without another word from her the doctor escorted her out. Returning, he said to Grant, "Well, it seems you've had some scare. I'd like to hear about it."

The doctor came back towards the bed, displaying his perfect teeth and smiling his perfect smile.

"I have a feeling you and I are going to become friends," he said, stopping by the bed. "Good friends."

CHAPTER
20

Sanchez was talking. For the past several days that's mostly what he had been doing. And Epps was listening, to names, dates, times and the incredible plan The Coalition had devised. He was especially listening to what Sanchez said about Rafael. It was quite obvious how the fat man felt about him.

"I regret ever making it possible for him to enter the country," Sanchez said.

Epps started to admit that personally he was happy but thought better of it. "Tell me more about your plan," he said instead.

Sanchez released a burst of proud laughter. "It intrigues you, eh? The kid-

napping of every ambassador of every
member nation of the World Bank. Imagine
the ransom we could have demanded."

"And you think Rafael plans to go
through with this thing without you?"

"Of course. It would be the greatest
terrorist coup of all time. Holding the most
powerful nations in the world for ransom.
They would have to pay. The potential loss
and political repercussions would be too
great."

"An awesome feat," Epps admitted, "if he
could carry it out."

"He *can* carry it out, and he *will* carry it
out unless you stop him. You must kill the
murdering dog." Sanchez was adamant.

Epps sat poised in thought. The greatest
terrorist coup of all time! It would be the
only thing that would bring Rafael out of
hiding.

"You do plan to do something?" Sanchez
asked.

"Of course I do," Epps said. "Relax. I'm
not letting Rafael get away this time. No
way."

Sanchez, who had been on the edge of his
seat, sat back. "It's simple, really. They will
only be in California one day to visit Disneyland. That little addendum to their plans
was courtesy of one of our members." He
smiled. "Señor Epps, with the right man
this could have been successful."

Epps said nothing. It could still be

successful, he thought. One wrong move and Rafael would be the victor, and his ass would be up shit's creek without a paddle.

Sánchez went on. "The ambassadors will be abducted as they board a chartered bus at their hotel. Rafael must survey the hotel several times. He will be there, but disguised."

And there it was. Rafael was handed to him on the proverbial silver platter, but he'd have to be very careful. His own plan would have to be precise and foolproof, because if he didn't wind up bagging Rafael, he could be more than dead meat. He could be a dead man.

It was 11:00 P.M. and Allen Michaels had finally arrived at the hospital. He'd just recently conjured up the nerve to visit his son, and as usual, his nerve was bolstered by alcohol.

The word they received that afternoon was that the boy had fainted. Maybe there was some type of short circuit in his brain, Allen thought. Maybe he's lost the power—for good.

That would be the worst thing that could happen. All evening and into the night Allen had pondered what this loss might mean. For one, it would mean finding a job again, going back to work. But more importantly, it would mean still another dream dashed on the shoals of adversity. Husks of wrecked dreams had been stacking up, clogging his life, and he wondered if this one were lost would he have the strength to erect another.

Suppose he can't do it again.

Allen found himself hounded by the same old thought, a nagging reminder of his own vulnerability. He hoped that his premonition was wrong. If Grant lost his power it all would be over for him.

It has to be something else, Allen thought, anything else.

Allen exited the elevator and surveyed the empty corridor. The nurses' station stood unmanned; there wasn't a soul in sight.

Allen started to get mad. There was no one watching over his son. Then he chuckled. If someone was at the station he'd be hard pressed to convince them he needed to see his son at such a late hour.

And I do need to see him. Oh God, yes, I need to see him now.

He started down the hall.

Finding the room he turned the doorknob and quietly entered. Allen started into the room then stopped. It didn't feel right. The feeling had pounced on him the moment he walked through the door. The room was quiet and still, too still. Allen had that eerie feeling you get upon entering a cemetery, or a tomb. The hairs on the nape of his neck were standing on end and ... Stop it!

You're just visiting your son in the hospital, he told himself.

Grant was lying quietly, obviously sleeping, and Allen wasn't yet ready to awaken him. In time, he thought. He sat and eyed the huddled figure lying on the bed. He's really grown. His thoughts danced back to when Grant was a baby and he was holding him for the first time.

"My son," he had whispered. "My son, my son." He displayed the smile of a proud father, and yet this fragile little creature, this important new life he was holding felt foreign to him. It felt like a stranger invading his precious little world.

Becoming a father was a scary business. It was something you wanted yet dreaded, as your heart filled with antipathy towards your newborn child. He once tried explaining this to a friend who was childless, and while he smiled and nodded, Allen knew these were feelings only a father could understand.

He sat now, staring at the outline of his son and wondering what the future held for him. With his new power the boy had a chance; they all did. If only he still had it. That was the $64,000 question. He tried not to think of it, but there it was. He had to know the answer. He wouldn't talk long. He just wanted to see how his son was doing, and then he'd let him go back to sleep.

Allen started towards the bed, but a noise in the corridor, on the other side of the door, stopped him in his tracks. The eerie feeling was back.

He faced the door and realized it was opening slowly.

"Allen!" Eve entered the room, her face a mass of confusion. "What are you doing here?"

"I was worried about Grant," Allen said.

Eve eyed her husband with disbelief. "Have you seen the doctor? He was supposed to meet me in the lounge almost an hour ago. I . . . uhh . . . fell asleep." She appeared embarrassed.

"No one was here when I came in. In fact, this hospital's deserted. My son should be in a better hospital than this one."

Eve didn't respond but started towards the bed.

"Uhh, Eve, have you spoken to him?" Allen asked.

"Yes."

"Can he . . . I mean, is he okay?"

She eyed him curiously for a moment. "I think he's going to be just fine, but we need to talk to the doctor."

"Good. If he wakes up I want you to ask him something."

"What?" Eve demanded, her voice laced with contempt.

She was standing by the bed now, leaning

over, and all of a sudden she felt it, too.
Something was wrong. Quickly she grabbed
her son's hand. It was cold in her grasp,
white and hard as stone.

"What's wrong?" Allen asked, reading
the worry on his wife's face.

Eve didn't answer. She yanked back the
covers on the bed, and that's when she
started to scream.

The lobby of the Ambassador Hotel in
Los Angeles is a monstrous affair, actually
twin monsters; the lobby has two levels.
First is the Wilshire level, with its spa,
tennis club, assorted restaurants and shops
that include a florist and a jeweler, although Epps couldn't figure for the life of
him why anyone would buy jewelry at
inflated Ambassador prices with the
jewelry mart less than a mile away. He
chalked it up to the naiveté of the rich.

On the second level, the lobby, with the
front desk and cashier, Epps and Sanchez
set up their watch. This lobby was a
monster all by itself. Huge and garish, its
floor was covered with a red and black
carpet that reminded Epps of a drunken
nightmare. Tiny chandeliers spilled from
several spots in the ceiling, and there was a
huge mural to the right of the cashier's
desk. Epps found the lobby quite stuffy,
like many of the people who stayed there.

Epps hated the rich. He also hated the fountain that sat in the middle of the lobby, replete with cherubs and stone fish all spraying their wealth into a large marble pond.

Epps stood eyeing the passers-by: guests, gawking tourists, bell men in red jckets and the maintainers in beige and brown. Rafael could be disguised as any one of them. On this level also was the world famous Coconut Grove and other banquet halls all in preparation for a party, and parties meant people, too many people.

What Epps hated most about the place was the number of avenues of entry. Earlier he had stepped through a lovely glass enclosed patio, out into the east garden. The garden was a Hollywood picture postcard dream. Assorted trees including palm, aspen and banana, well-manicured lawns and colorful beds of flowers were a treat for the eyes, but there were several walkways that led to the street. Rafael could enter through any one of them, and leave just as easily. Epps shivered at the thought that Rafael could have observed them already.

"Well?" Sanchez said. They were standing in the lobby, dressed all in white as kitchen helpers.

"Well, what?" Epps said.

"Well, what do you think?" Sanchez said.

"I don't like it." But it wasn't his to like. The liking would come later, after they had nabbed Rafael.

Epps tried not to think that he had just one day. Tomorrow the ambassadors would arrive, and if Rafael got away with the kidnapping and he hadn't alerted The Boys to stop the thing, Epps knew he'd be spending the rest of his days in jail. Today was his day. If they didn't get Rafael today, he was going to have to tell Patches.

Epps and Sanchez surveyed the lobby, watching and waiting.

The screaming awakened the hospital.

The staff came running, and when they entered they found Allen at his wife's side saying "What? What?" as Eve stood pointing at the corpse in the bed saying "There . . . there." It would have been laughable if it weren't so serious, thought Nurse Fogarty. And wasn't comedy based on tragedy? She thought one of her professors back at City College had left her with that gem of wisdom.

Someone was in trouble, and Nurse Fogarty vowed to herself it wasn't her. Granted, she was the on-duty nurse that evening, but this was all out of her realm of responsibility, although she knew damn well one of the residents would try to pin it on her. Residents were always trying to pin their own mistakes on the nurses. But not this time, Fogarty thought. No way!

She'd been a nurse for too long—ten years—to allow a know-nothing resident to get away with blaming her for something like this. Besides, she'd seen far worse than this over the years, things that would have gotten the administration kicked out on their collective butts, and they knew it. This was not going to get blamed on her. The administration would see to it.

Nurse Fogarty held Eve Michaels while the resident, Dr. Corrigan, shot her up with a sedative. And after they were all convinced that the man standing next to Eve was indeed her husband, they got down to business.

"All right, who's the joker?" Dr. Corrigan asked, looking around. No answer. "Look if this is some kind of joke, speak up. We'll have our little laugh, and I can get back to catching my forty." Still no answer, and that's when he started looking at her.

Look all you want, Fogarty thought. You can't pin this on me.

Corrigan spoke again. "All right, let's start checking the rooms and find out who's missing. I guess he just wandered in here and died. Bert, call downstairs, we're going to need an autopsy on this one. And for crying out loud, Fogarty, find the boy. You *can* do that, can't you?"

"Yes, doctor," Nurse Fogarty said. She was thinking, No way!

CHAPTER
21

"What the hell are ya lookin' at me for?" Allen Michaels squawked to his wife. They were seated in their living room, wisps of morning sun threading through the window. The police had just departed.

"I didn't say anything while they were here," Eve said. "This is a family matter." Her voice came out thin through a throat parched from crying. "But now that they're gone, I can speak freely. What did you do with him?"

"Huh? Honey, you don't mean that. You're a little spaced out 'cause our son just disappeared."

"A little spaced out!" Eve screamed.

"That's an understatement, but that's how you'd see it, isn't it? A little spaced out. What did you do with him?" she charged.

"Nothing! Eve, he's my son, too. I love him. I wouldn't do anything to him."

"You don't love anyone. Not even yourself."

"Eve!"

"He was in the room when I left. He was gone when I got back, and *you* were there."

"Listen to what you're saying. That doesn't prove anything."

"They hang men with less proof."

Allen looked at his wife. Her eyes were vacant red rivers of contempt. Her face was contorted, and when she spoke her voice was a hissing snarl. What could he say? Since Grant had vanished he'd watched the expression on her face change from agony to fear to hate, a hatred directed towards him.

The search of the hospital proved futile. Grant was gone, and the man lying in his bed was not a patient. No one knew who he was or where he came from. Eve told them of the doctor she'd spoken with, but she had no idea of what he looked like. "He was a doctor." "Young or old?" "He was a doctor." "Hair color?" "He was a doctor." And so it went.

When the police began questioning them at home that morning, Allen assumed the hatred scrawled across his wife's face was directed towards them. Now he knew better.

"Eve, I don't know what to say. I'll do anything to help them find him. Really!"

"There's one more thing you can do—leave!" The words knifed into him.

"Honey, you don't mean that."

"I should have left before. I should have known it would come to this. It's too late to save him now, but there's one thing I'm not going to try and save—this relationship. I hate you." Her words were soft and cruel, slipping into his gut like an icicle and silently ripping his insides to shreds.

"We need each other now," he said.

"All I need is my son," stated Eve. "Bring him back to me."

"Honey, I . . . I can't."

"Bring him back to me, Allen." Her eyes were hazy. "Bring him back to me, Allen, or I'll kill you."

A few seconds later Eve Michaels passed out.

"Where are we going?" Grant asked.

"For a ride. A long, long ride."

They were traveling in a green 1975 Olds Cutlass that Rafael had purchased for cash (no questions asked) earlier in the day. Grant looked alternately at Rafael and out of the window. "You're not a doctor, are you?" he asked.

"No, I'm not," Rafael said.

"I didn't think so."

"Oh?"

"You look like a doctor, and when you spoke to my mom you sounded like a doctor, but I knew you weren't."

"You are very perceptive for a . . . How old are you?"

"Almost ten," Grant said quickly. "Almost a . . ."

"Yes?"

"Nothing," Grant said.

"Well, Master Michaels, you're a very intelligent young man."

"What's your name?" Grant asked. His green eyes, reflecting city lights, twinkled in the darkness.

"They call me Rafael."

"They call me Grant." He gazed farther out the window. They were approaching the entrance ramp of a freeway, and he wanted to see what street they were on. They passed the sign too quickly for him to read it and he sat back. "You don't want me to go on TV, do you?" he said suddenly. His voice was stern.

"No," Rafael said.

"I won't go," Grant said. "Ever again."

"I don't want you to go on TV, Grant. I promise that." He smiled his perfect smile.

Grant was looking out the window again. The bright lights lessened, and he realized they were heading out of the city. "Is my daddy meeting us?"

"Huh?" Rafael's face spun momentarily towards him.

"My daddy. He sent you, right?"

"Yes," Rafael said. "He is meeting us."

"He told me about you. He said he wanted me to meet some friends and talk to them about what I can do." The statement triggered unwelcome thoughts—Doris Sachs, his parents yelling, no one to talk to at school. He really didn't want to think about what it was he could do.

He was silent for longer than he had been since the trip began. Rafael glanced over, thinking he'd fallen asleep, and noticed him staring forlornly at the endless pavement. "You look like you haven't a friend in the world," he said.

Grant remained silent.

"Do not despair, Grant Michaels. I will be your friend." Reaching over with his right hand, he mussed the boy's hair. Grant looked up at him, and Rafael knew the smile blossoming across the boy's face was genuine.

Eve Michaels opened her eyes, and the first thought to penetrate her consciousness was: It was a dream, a horrible nightmare. Quickly she felt her left arm, her fingers passing over the tiny Band-Aid Dr. Corrigan had placed there when he gave her the shot. Her hopes declined. It was real. Grant was gone.

She was lying on the sofa, alone in the living room, the silence pressing in on her. Is Allen behind this? was the next thought to come crashing through her waking consciousness. She wanted to think so. It was easier to believe her husband had arranged this, rather than believe the worst.

She remembered watching two TV movies and a special on the subject of child kidnapping, but they had been so careful with Grant. He was constantly reminded never to talk to strangers. He could not accept rides from anyone without their permission. She drove him to school every morning and had picked him up until he requested her not to. "I wanna walk home with Jimmy," he had said, and while she didn't want to, she knew it was time. He was growing up; it was time to start letting go.

His first few days on his own she had followed him, feeling guilty but wanting to make sure he was following her instructions. He was. They had done everything to ensure his safety. They had been so careful, and still he was gone.

Is Allen behind this? She didn't want to blame him, but blaming him made the ache in her heart easier to stand. So she blamed him and hated him and cursed the day he was born.

Eve suddenly realized she did not want to

spend another day in his house. She sat up and looked around her. The things of their collective pasts stared back. She was sure Grant would be back, but it would be just the two of them, no matter what. She was going to get a divorce and raise Grant on her own.

Eve felt a little better knowing she'd made a decision, finally taken a stand. This act of her life was over, and the curtain had come crashing down.

They had gotten on the Harbor Freeway, riding it into the Santa Monica, then transferring to Route 405 where they headed south.

After some brief conversation the boy had curled up by the window and fallen asleep. It was a fitful sleep, in which he cried out twice before settling back into his black web of dreams. He seemed to have a lot on his mind for one so young.

Rafael wondered if what the boy's father had said was really true. He had not intended to snatch the child. Carrying extra baggage around was something of which he did not approve. When he tapped into the Michaels' phone lines, however, he saw the potential in the child—if any of it were really true. He had to find out. He could not kill the child until he was sure.

"Locusts!" the boy cried out. Rafael gazed over at him. His eyes flapped upward like a busted window shade. He looked hurriedly around the car, taking in his surroundings. Then seemingly satisfied, the panic faded from his face, his eyes rolled shut, and he was asleep again.

Time is of the essence, Rafael thought. I cannot afford to play nursemaid for too long. He would have to win the child over quickly and put him to the test. The ambassadors were arriving in Los Angeles tomorrow, and then they would be on their way. He would have to know tomorrow. One way or the other he would have to make a decision about the boy.

He drove past towns named Inglewood and Carson and Long Beach, names that meant nothing to him, yet soon his name would be on the lips of people even in these hamlets.

"I'm gettin' hungry." Rafael looked over, and the boy's eyes were wide upon him.

"What would you like? McDonald's?" Rafael asked.

"Sure," the boy said.

They pulled off in Garden Grove, but the McDonald's wasn't open so they settled on a diner. After a few hearty bites Grant toyed with his burger. Rafael waited a while before speaking. "Finished?" he asked.

"When are we meetin' my dad?"

"Not until tomorrow."

"Oh?"

"Is that all right?"

"Sure," Grant said.

"He wanted me to talk to you first."

"Okay," Grant said. "Talk."

"Not tonight. I'm getting tired. We should be looking for a place to stay. Tomorrow we will talk." He displayed his perfect teeth. "Have you ever been to Sea World?"

"No." Grant's eyes were questioning. "Where are we going? How will my dad know where to meet us?"

"You trust me, don't you?"

Grant stared at him, weighing his question. "Yes."

"Good. I will take good care of you, Grant Michaels. Your father gave me special orders to do so. Now, about Sea World, have you ever been? It's not far from here." His smile widened. "I think you would like it."

"You think we could go? I hear they have a killer whale."

"Yes, I think we can go."

"Can my parents go, too?"

"No, just you and me. We can talk at Sea World. That would be fun, yes?"

"Yeah," Grant said. He smiled at the stranger, then frowned. "I'm almost a man, you know?"

"No, I'm afraid I hadn't realized that." He gazed at the boy with a discerning eye. "Men enjoy Sea World, too—with their friends." He extended his hand. "Friends?"

Grant squeezed it, noticing how calloused

it was. "Friends," he said. They both smiled.

Later they checked into a small motel off Route 55. Already dawn was rising in the east, as Rafael helped Grant into bed. This part is risky, he thought. He had to make sure no one saw them. By now an alert for the boy must have gone out, and a man of Hispanic descent with an American child might stick out in someone's mind.

Going to Sea World was the biggest risk. He hated public places, where he was most noticeable, but there was nothing he could do. He was gaining the child's confidence. By tomorrow night he would know for sure if the boy could serve him. After that . . .

Rafael glanced over at Grant before shutting his eyes to sleep. The boy was fidgeting again, unable to find peace in sleep.

A moment later they both were the victims of horrid dreams, as sleep carried Rafael far into the past . . .

His mother was dead. He was in the groves working, quiet tears spilling down his cheeks. He looked to the skies and prayed for rain, so no one would notice his tears. His twelfth birthday was coming in three weeks and his mother was dead.

Two weeks before his father had gone to the foreman begging for a loan. "It is for medicine," he had said, but the foreman just snarled. "I am not begging for a handout. Just an advance on next week's work."

The foreman laughed. "If I pay you for next week today, you will be gone in the morning."

"I am a man of my word. My wife, she is dying. Please!" His words fell on ears of stone.

Rafael wiped the bitter tears on his sleeve. He squeezed an orange, wishing it were the foreman's throat. He promised himself he would squeeze oranges every-day, strenghtening his grip, so when he had his chance at the foreman he would not fail.

Rafael wanted to kill the foreman, but for the man who owned the grove the punishment would be more severe. He would destroy the man and allow him to live out his life in utter poverty.

Rafael's mother was dead, and they were going to pay . . .

He awakened to sunlight pouring through the window, as the nightmare was again tucked away—until darkness came. Today the thing would begin, and when it was over the name Rafael would be etched into the annals of history.

CHAPTER 22

It was 8:00 A.M. and already Epps was seated behind his desk. The file for The Coalition lay open before him, but his thoughts were miles away.

He lingered in the lobby of the grand hotel most of the night, hoping to catch a glimpse of Rafael, but no such luck. He wasn't sure if Rafael had come earlier or if he wasn't coming at all. What he was sure of was that his time had run out. The ambassadors were arriving this morning and heading for Disneyland this afternoon. He couldn't get proper coverage of the thing without going through proper channels. Patches would have to be told.

He picked up the phone and pushed a button on the intercom. "Hazel, I need to talk with Horvath as soon as he gets in. Priority."

"Yes, sir," Hazel replied.

"Shit," Epps muttered as he dropped the phone on the cradle. "Shit, fuck!" There was no way he could tell Patches about The Coalition's plans without mentioning Rafael, then quite naturally the bastard would take over the entire operation. And he knows didley about terrorists!

Suppose Rafael had abandoned the kidnapping idea, he thought. Then I'll be telling Patches for nothing. But he had to take that chance. If Rafael did kidnap the ambassadors and he did nothing to stop it, he could never forgive himself.

"No sense worrying about it anymore. In a few minutes the whole thing will be out of my hands," Epps said eyeing the intercom which was buzzing. He pushed the button and picked up the phone. "Is Patches waiting to talk to me?" he squawked, dropping decorum and calling his boss by his nickname.

"Excuse me?" Hazel said.

"Nothing."

"Mr. Hopper would like to speak to you."

Hopper? Something sparked in Epps' mind, igniting thoughts of hope. "I'll take it."

"Son of a biscuit eater, ain't you the early

bird," Hopper said. "Tried you at home, thought maybe you were out gettin' laid."

"No such luck," Epps responded.

"Listen, remember that guy Ortiz, disappeared from his limo a few weeks ago?"

"Yeah."

"Found him this morning in the strangest place. A little kid's hospital bed. The kid's gone and Ortiz is in his bed—dead."

"How?"

"Strangled. And don't ask if I'm sure it's him. It is."

"What about the kid?" Epps' mind was racing.

"Hold your horses, buddy. I'm not lettin' out anymore info until you spill," Hopper said at length. "We ran that blade through everything and turned up squat. What am I looking for, pal?"

Epps smiled. "I could kiss you. Hopper buddy, you and I need to get together. I'm on to something that's big enough for us to share."

"Our departments never work together. I think it's sacrilege."

"Not our departments, Hopper. Us. Freelance."

"What you've got must really be big."

"Do bears bear? Do bees bee?" They shared a laugh. "Can we get together in an hour, my place?"

"Can do."

"By the way, who's the kid?" Epps asked.

"Uh-uh. My mother didn't raise no dummies. We'll compare notes when we're together."

"Same old Hopper," Epps chortled and signed off.

"Patches will speak to you now, sir," came Hazel's less than reserved voice.

"I love ya, Hazel," Epps said with a chuckle. "Put him through."

A moment later Horvath's voice scratched through. "What's happening, Epps?"

"Happy birthday to you, happy birthday to you, happy birthday dear Peter, happy birthday to you. So, how does it feel to be one year older?"

"Cut the shit, Epps. You know good and well it ain't my birthday."

"Huh? You're kidding. I have it right here on my calendar."

"You come in early and place a priority call just to wish me happy birthday?"

"You *are* the boss."

"Fuck off," Horvath said, and the connection was broken.

"Correction," Epps said to the dead phone. "You *were* the boss." Then he laughed like hell.

Grant took in all there was to enjoy at Sea World, yet showed little reaction. Once during the Shamu the killer whale show he uttered a soft "wow." Aside from that and an occasional smile, the child displayed little reaction. There was something dark and brooding about him. Some secret thing possessed his mind and would not let it be. Dolphins dancing on their tails and a man surfing on the backs of two whales should have garnered more of a reaction.

After the Kooky Castle show Rafael took Grant for a walk. They rested on a bench in a lovely tropical garden, and as the sun began its descent they chatted.

"I hope you are enjoying your day, friend," Rafael said.

"You really are my friend, aren't you?" Grant asked. His eyes danced merrily over the prospect.

"Of course," Rafael replied.

"I like you," Grant said.

Rafael sighed. "Well, Grant, it is time to talk." The boy's eyes turned instantly distant, and Rafael saw him reliving some unspeakable horror. "It can wait if you'd like," Rafael said.

"You mean, I don't have to talk if I don't want to?"

"Correct."

Grant smiled. "Thanks." He paused a minute, laboring over a decision. "I'll talk," he finally said.

"Why was your father so anxious for me to meet you? Do you know?"

"Yeah," Grant said softly. Again Rafael could see the horror within him turning its ugly head.

"Tell me. Please?" Rafael prodded.

"The power." Sitting as still as stone Grant told of the first two disasters and what he could do. He left out the incident with Doris Sachs.

When he was finished Rafael regarded him for a long moment. "This is a wonderful talent you have. There must be ways you can help people with it."

"There isn't," Grant said flatly.

Rafael looked at the child and wondered. "Can you show me?"

"My father said just talk."

Rafael sensed the change in him and decided not to press—not yet. If the boy could do what he claimed, knocking a single airliner from the sky would be child's play. "Your father was correct. Thanks for the chat."

"Is that it?" Grant asked.

"That's it." His perfect teeth were showing.

"When will my father get here?"

"Soon," Rafael replied. "Say, how about seeing the dolphin show again, friend?"

Grant nodded, and Rafael mussed his hair.

"My name is Epps, and this is Mr. Hopper."

Allen looked from the white to the black man standing in his doorway. They looked like policemen. "You've found Grant?"

"No, Mr. Michaels, we haven't. Can we come in?"

Allen led the two men into the living room. Epps noticed the dark circles under his eyes. "Is Mrs. Michaels in," Epps asked.

Allen glanced in the direction of the stairs. "She's not feeling too good."

"I understand. Mr. Michaels, have you ever heard of a government agency known as The Boys?"

"What's this all about?" Allen asked. "Does this have anything to do with those phone calls I been making?"

"In a way," Epps said.

"I knew it." Allen chortled and again glanced in the direction of the stairs. "You guys' phone number isn't even listed. How'd you find out about me?" He moved closer to the men, talking in guarded tones as he occasionally glanced towards the stairs.

"You've called several other agencies. We're all interconnected in one way or another. When one receives calls of this nature, quite naturally they notify the others."

"Hey! Whadaya mean 'calls of this nature?' I'm no crackpot! The kid's a fuckin' secret weapon!"

Hopper spoke up. "We're not here to argue with you, Mr. Michaels. You want your son back, and we think we can get him.

Would you mind telling us just exactly
what it is he does?"

Finally, Allen thought, someone had
listened. At that moment he thought of his
lifelong dream.

"How much?" he asked.

"Huh?"

"How much will you pay for Grant's
talent?"

The two agents glanced at one another.
Epps finally spoke. "Mr. Michaels, we're
here to help you get your son back."

A sheepish smile spread across Allen's
face. "Yeah, that's right. Guess I forgot."

He told them the entire story, from the
beginning right up to the exploding suitcase. When the two agents finally left, their
faces were noncommital, but Allen knew
that they would be back.

When Epps and Hopper got back to the
car, Sanchez was waiting for them. "I
should have known," Epps said. "Kidnapping and ransom don't interest Rafael.
They interest you." He eyed Sanchez with
contempt.

"What do you mean?" Sanchez asked.

"He wants to kill them," Epps said. "Sure
as shit he wants them dead."

"A bomb?" Hopper suggested.

"Probably," said Epps. "Does anyone
know where the ambassadors are headed
when they leave California?"

"Mexico," replied Sanchez.

Epps hadn't heard. He was deep in thought. The child sounded dangerous; even Rafael seemed to think so. If the boy could do all his father had claimed, the government would indeed be interested. Of course, their interest would be far from what Allen Michaels thought. If Grant were truly a secret weapon the government could not afford him falling in the wrong hands.

Plain and simple, if—and it was a big "if"—but if the boy could do what his father had claimed, then he would have to die.

BOOK
THREE

CHAPTER 23

Grant was thinking about when Doris Sachs disappeared . . . *She didn't just disappear, Grant.* All right, when Doris Sachs died . . . *Died? She more than just died, Grant. You killed her, remember?* Grant did remember. She was set upon by dark ugly locusts, and then the woman was just plain gone.

Grant was thinking about all this and wondering. For the past few days he did not think of it, but now he willed it into his mind. Like a curator examining the work of a great master, he eyed the deed, turning it over and over in his mind and examining it from all angles. Something's wrong here.

He thought back to the thing with the bees. He felt powerful then, calling them up and sicking them on the boys, but this was different. He'd never thought of locusts before. Oh, he knew what they were. He'd seen them wiping out crops in an old movie on TV, coming like a plague and destroying an entire farm, but locusts were not on his mind that day in the park. All Grant wanted then was not to be there, to be away from Doris Sachs.

Then they came.

I didn't call them, Grant thought. I couldn't have. Then he thought something else. The thing did it. The dark thing that lives in my mind did it.

It was both a horror and a relief.

Grant was lying in bed, in a dingy motel room in downtown San Diego. The room was shrouded in darkness, while bright slivers of white light from the street stabbed into the black. His father would be coming in the morning. Rafael had spoken to his father on the phone and told Grant he would be coming. Then Grant would go home, and maybe sometime Rafael could come and visit. He hoped so. It had been so long since he'd had a friend.

What if the thing doesn't want me to have friends? What if the thing wants to hurt my parents?

Grant jerked upright in bed, and Rafael,

lying on the bed across from him, looked up.

"What is it?"

"I was just thinkin; that's all."

"About the power?"

"Yeah," Grant said.

"Sleep," Rafael told him, and rolled over.

Grant lay back down, trying to hold the bad thoughts at bay, but they tumbled into his consciousness, filling his mind with unanswerable questions.

The thing had grown in him. Like a toddler first learning to walk, the thing had gained confidence and now seemed ready to roam around on its own. It first materialized under the guise of going away. Gradually it matured until now, like Grant, it too was almost fully grown.

I'm going to make this thing go away, Grant told himself. No matter what, I'm never going to use it again. Never! First, he had to remember not to get mad anymore. That's when the thing was strongest. If he never got mad again, maybe the thing would shrivel up inside him and die. Then maybe Mommy and Daddy wouldn't be scared anymore, and the hate would be gone. They don't hate each other; they hate the thing. And I hate it, too.

I hate you, and I'll never use you again.

Grant shut his eyes, willing sleep to come. He felt the thing, dark and secretive, roll over in his mind. It was resting now, gathering its strength. Grant would need his strength, too. He was going to kill the thing, just like the thing had killed the lady in the park. Before it got too big and hurt somebody else, he was going to kill it.

When Allen got upstairs, Eve was packed and sitting on the edge of the bed, scowling at the bank statement of her personal account.

"I'll be at the Hyatt on Wilshire for the next few days," she told him, looking into his small hurt eyes. "I don't know where I'm going after that. The police will know where to find me." She stuffed the statement into her handbag and began placing the last of her cosmetics into a carrying case.

"Eve . . ." Allen started to say, but she held up both hands and shook her head.

"Enough talk," she said. "It's time I did something. I'll wait until Grant gets back before I file for divorce." She snapped shut the overnight case, and with the snapping came a finality, as if the final page in a book had been turned. Allen felt it. "I won't press any kind of charges," Eve went on, "but I want him back—soon." She rose, hoisted the bags and headed for the door. Allen stepped aside, allowing her to pass.

In the living room she called for a cab. Allen trailed her downstairs and stood silently watching as she hung up the phone.

"We need each other now." When he moved towards her, she stood up, stiff, like a pillar of salt. "Eve, I had nothing to do with it. At least hear me out."

"I have heard you out." She headed for the door.

"Listen!" Allen called, stalling her progress. She turned and looked at him, seeing for the first time all the little boy that was left in him. She wondered what she ever saw in the man. "I'm still your husband. Shouldn't you hear what I have to say? I won't try to stop you, but at least listen."

"I can't," Eve said, the words coming as if from some faraway place. "If I listen you might convince me to stay. "I'm vulnerable now, and part of me really wants to stay. I need some time. We can talk in a few weeks . . . after Grant gets back." She eyed him ruefully.

"How long do you think you can last on what you have in the bank?" he charged, a mean chuckle slipping from his lips. "You'll be back."

"Just for my son," she said.

Outside a horn sounded.

"That's my cab." She picked up her bags again.

"I'm sorry. I didn't mean that. It's just . . ."

"Don't!" she said.

She opened the door, threw a fleeting glance back at her husband, the stranger she'd lived with all these years, and walked out.

Five minutes after Eve had left, Allen resolved within himself never to take her back.

"Epps. So glad you could make it."

Peter Horvath (also known as Patches) welcomed Epps into his cluttered office and pointed to a timeworn chair alongside his desk. Epps sat.

"Everything okay?" Patches asked, as he fiddled with a report that lay open before him.

"Yeah, sure. Why do you ask?"

"You've been a busy man lately, and I haven't seen any paperwork to support it. I'd hate for you to fall too far behind."

The two men eyed each other, poker-faced.

"Guess Hazel's fallen a bit behind on her typing. I'll talk to her about it. Thanks for letting me know."

"My pleasure," Horvath said. "I'd be interested in seeing what you've been up to."

Epps rose. "I'll have something on your desk first thing. Is that all, sir?"

"Relax," Horvath said. He closed the report and pushed it aside. "We haven't spent enough time getting to know each other. That's the reason for this bad blood, you know, and it's my fault. I'll take the blame."

Epps didn't know how to respond. He stared cautiously at his superior.

"I mean, you try like hell, Epps. You really do, and I know I can be a bastard." A curious smile appeared on his lips. "You even tried wishing me a happy birthday. By the way, my birthday is June 22nd."

"I'll try and remember that," Epps said.

"Write it down."

"I will."

"Now!"

The command snapped Epps into action, and he scrawled the date in a small notebook he kept in his breast pocket.

"Enough about me," Horvath went on. "I'd really like to know more about you. Like what's your relationship with the FBI?"

Epps exploded. "If you have a problem with the way I do things, let me hear it outright, otherwise fuck off!"

"I could have you suspended for that remark, Epps, but I won't."

"Thank heaven for small favors."

"You were going to tell me something the other morning. That's why you came in so early, trying to bring yourself to say it. Then you get a call, and bingo, it's happy birthday."

"You've got some imagination," Epps

said, but he was getting nervous.

"I decided to check the calls that came into the building that morning. There was one from the FBI." He eyed Epps with contempt. "What do you have, Epps? This is your last chance. After this I'm on your ass."

The two men stared daggers at one another.

"My report will be on your desk first thing." Epps started for the door.

"I'm not finished!" Horvath bellowed.

"You will be, shortly." Epps strode from the office, banging the door shut behind himself.

"Shit!" Horvath screamed after him. "The bastard had his chance. Now, his ass is mine."

It was simple, really. The greatest terrorist victory of all time, and oh, so simple. There was poetry to the thing, a bit of poetic justice at work, Rafael thought.

In a short time the victory would be his, and no one could stop him. The risk involved was slim. There was really no chance of his getting caught. He would never have to go near the plane. He would just point the boy in the right direction and poof! History.

It was cause enough to laugh out loud, but Rafael didn't. The boy was asleep on the bed across from his, and he didn't want to wake him. Get your rest, Grant Michaels. You will need it.

In the morning, Rafael would get some aerial maps. He had to be able to identify the correct aircraft. He would need maps and a short wave radio to pick up the control tower. He also needed to devise a test, proof positive that the child was all he claimed to be. It was his way of covering all the bases. After that there would be nothing left to do but wait.

Rafael glanced over at the boy. Again he was having a restless sleep. He wondered what nightmares existed in the boy's mind. Were they like his own? I mustn't think about it, Rafael told himself, and tried to force his attention back to the task at hand. He was beginning to win the boy over, but in so doing he was beginning to like him. That was a luxury he could ill afford. There was no room in his life for emotion. The boy knew him, had seen his face, and there was only one way to deal with those who had seen him. The boy could be no exception.

CHAPTER
24

When Grant opened his eyes, the first thing he noticed was that he wasn't in his room. Quickly his gaze richocheted from object to object—the bed, the chair in the corner, the TV chained to the wall—until finally it dawned on him. He was in a motel room in downtown San Diego.

The bed across from his was empty, and he wondered if Rafael had gone to meet his father. He hoped so. He missed home. Maybe his mommy would come with his daddy, and he could tell them both about Sea World.

He had to pee. He got up and padded into the bathroom where he relieved his tiny bladder. He looked into the mirror over the sink, fingers running gingerly over his face as if it were covered with overnight stubble. His fingers glided easily over soft baby flesh, yet to him they dragged slowly over the makings of a beard, and he knew he'd be shaving before long.

He wanted to brush his teeth, but he didn't have a toothbrush, so he used his finger and a bit of dry soap—and boy, was that yucky—but when he was through rinsing, his mouth felt refreshed.

Grant looked into his eyes and noticed that the left had turned into a sea of bright red. It felt normal, but it looked like he'd been on the wrong end of a swinging fist. At that moment he thought of Bert Reynolds, but not for long. He continued staring in the mirror, and it was as if he weren't looking at himself at all but staring at a picture of another boy with one red eye and one normal one. Then, bored with the whole thing, he went back into the bedroom.

A few minutes later Grant was dressed and sitting before the TV set. He wore the same thing he had on yesterday and the day before. He had one other change of clothing that his mother had brought to the hospital for him to wear home, but he was glad there was no one around to make him change.

Where's Rafael?

Not only did Grant hope his parents would be with Rafael when he returned, he also hoped Rafael would bring him something to eat. He was starving.

He lay back on the bed watching Inspector Gadget, but not really paying attention. His mind was on Rafael. Whatever he brought him to eat would be good. Rafael seemed to know what boys liked. He knew this without being told, as if being a man hadn't changed him the way it did most grownups, who knew nothing of what kids liked but only thought they did.

Yesterday for breakfast Rafael had brought burritos and french fries, and for dinner Big Macs, with several delicious snacks at Sea World. Rafael wasn't like most grownups, he was almost like a kid, and he was Grant's friend.

Grant recalled the night Rafael had taken him from the hospital. He had started not to go with the stranger.

"Come," the man dressed as a doctor said. "Get dressed."

"Why?"

"You are to come with me. Hurry. We have little time." There was an urgency to his voice that made Grant spring into action. He got out of bed and began climbing into his clothes. "Where are we going?"

"Hurry," Rafael said, now helping him into his things. "We must go now."

Grant stopped. There was something wrong. He looked at the man dressed as a doctor, and the man smiled. It was a wonderful smile, a smile you could get lost in.

"What is wrong?" the smiling Rafael said.

"Nothin'." Grant followed the stranger from the room.

"Wait here," Rafael told him once they arrived at the car. "I will be right back." And Grant nodded.

Now Grant sat, still wondering why he'd gone along, but the rumbling in his belly brought him back to the present.

Where's Rafael?

He got up, punched the TV to black and opened the door. Already the sun had crept over the mountains far to the east, sending splotches of dancing white light spilling through the trees, spreading tiny shadows over the parking lot.

A young Hispanic family exited their room, the happy father carrying his toddling son to the car.

"We're going to the zoo today, Davy. We're going to see the lions," the mother said to the child as she walked alongside.

The father let out a playful growl, which prompted a burst of cheery laughter from young Davy's lips. Grant remembered when he was small—before the yelling started—but that seemed so long ago now.

The father fastened Davy into his car seat, and the three of them drove off to the zoo. Grant looked around the lot. Their car, the Oldsmobile, was gone.

He went back inside, where the air conditioning was keeping things reasonably cool. Passing the dressing mirror, he glanced at his reflection, then stopped and moved closer. Now his right eye was beginning to cloud up. Already it was a hazy pink, but he felt fine. *I hope I'm not getting sick or coming down with something,* as his mother called it.

Grant went back to watching his cartoons. He wasn't going to worry about his eyes. Once Daddy got there he'd know what to do.

Rafael entered the small room wearing shades, two days growth of beard, and carrying a white bag that read McDonald's.

"Breakfast," he said, shaking the bag.

"What?" Grant asked.

"Guess."

"Hamburgers?"

"Hotcakes and sausage," Rafael said, licking his lips in mock delight. Grant smiled. Rafael really knew how to treat a kid.

"Where's my dad?" Grant asked as he spilled syrup over the hotcakes and the sausage.

Rafael sighed.

Grant stopped what he was doing and looked up. "He *is* coming?" he asked.

"I'm afraid not. Not today."

"Why not?"

"I told him about our talk," Rafael said, as he poured syrup over his own hotcakes.

"And what happened?" Grant asked impatiently.

"I had to be honest with him, Grant. I told him what you told me was hard to believe." He looked at the boy. "It's not that I don't believe you. I guess I just need a little convincing."

"I really can do it," Grant said. "Did you ask him?"

"I asked him."

"And?"

"I guess I need to see it for myself."

"When is my dad coming for me?" Grant demanded.

"That's up to you. I need proof." He smiled a sheepish smile. "Sorry."

Grant was off the bed now. "Why?" he demanded. "My dad said talk, just talk. I'm not doin' no more." He plopped back on the bed and folded his arms across his chest.

Rafael sensed fear in the boy and wondered if, indeed, he had been lying. He caught the determination on the boy's face and knew there was more to this than the boy being caught in a lie. The child was filled with the fear of consequence.

"Your father was right. Talk is all we're supposed to do." He sighed again. "Listen, Grant, I need your help. We're friends, right?"

Grant nodded, but suddenly their friendship was shrouded in questions.

"I need this information for a book, and quite frankly, who is going to believe you can do these things if I say I haven't seen it for myself?"

"That's how you're going to help my father? With a book?"

"Yes."

"Then tell them you saw it," Grant said, "Tell them I gave you a demonstration."

"That would be a lie," Rafael said solemnly.

"Yeah" Grant replied. He was staring at the floor.

"You don't want me to lie, do you?"

Grant shook his head.

"Eat," Rafael said. "We will work this out later." His hand glided through the boy's hair, and Grant thought there would be no later, but he couldn't tell him.

Grant looked at the meal before him and realized he wasn't hungry anymore.

"Eat," Rafael said, as he shoveled in forkfuls of his own. "It's good."

Grant lifted a forkful of hotcake, placed it in his mouth, chewed and swallowed. He tasted nothing, but he continued working at the breakfast until it was gone.

In 63 years, Ed Holden had never learned to mind his own business, and maybe that was good. Sure, most folks called him an old fartin' busybodied so-and-so, but there were a select few who came to appreciate Holden's abundant curiosity. Take Lem Bivens. Ed Holden just happened to be looking out his window the morning a moving van pulled into the Bivens driveway across the street. Of course, several of Lem's neighbors saw or heard the truck, but Lem was no gem of a neighbor, no siree, not with women coming and going all hours of the night, and loud music, and even (some suspected) drugs. So when the van pulled into the Bivens driveway that morning, most breathed a sigh of relief and went back to their morning coffee, but not Ed.

He couldn't seem to get it off his mind that young Bivens had not too long ago left for work. He'd seen him himself, just 20 minutes earlier, pulling out of the driveway. So wasn't it strange that now a moving van would show up? This was more than a curiosity; this was news. Ed started calling the neighbors.

"Strange to see a moving truck in Lem's driveway, isn't it? Especially on a weekday."

"Good riddance to bad rubbish" is what most of them replied.

Ed peeked out again and saw the movers carrying out Lem Bivens' brand new stereo color TV. It was three weeks old, Ed remembered as they loaded it on the truck.

Then the alarm in Ed's head went off—burglars!

It took a few minutes to get the police to come out and take a look (they'd heard from Ed Holden before), but when Lem Bivens got his call at work he seemed mighty interested. Those "movers" are doin' time now. Old Ed Holden had helped bust up a burglary ring, and not because he was a busybody, either. Uh-uh. Ed Holden was a concerned citizen, plain and simple.

As night manager of the New Oasis Motel, Ed's job was to check in weary travelers and make sure when they checked out they hadn't helped themselves to half the linen. On the side, he peeked out the window from behind his desk and watched the comings and goings of all. He was just a concerned citizen.

Ed was peeking out the window watching the Garcia couple from Huntington Park climb into their spanking new Honda Civic. What the hell does he do to make that kind of money? Then he thought if he had the money he'd buy a new Chevrolet. Now there was a car, as American as apple pie.

Ed watched the couple with a discerning eye, making sure their luggage didn't seem any fatter than it had when they arrived. He saw the boy, a strange kid rooming with the young man driving the green Oldsmobile. And where the hell was the car? Did that idiot leave the kid alone? Some parent, Ed thought. Then he thought the dark haired man didn't look much like a parent, especially this kid's parent. The boy looked around for a while, and as the Garcia family drove off he went back into the room.

Normally Ed would have gone back to his morning paper, but that alarm was going off in his head again. That man and that kid just didn't belong together. Kidnapping popped into his head. He hadn't seen the kid's picture on any milk cartons or anything; of course, he didn't drink much milk. So maybe the kid's picture *was* on a milk carton, and maybe it was up to a concerned citizen to notify the police about this.

Ed Holden picked up the phone and commenced to dial, and not because he was a busybody either. Ed Holden was a concerned citizen, and he was just doing his job.

Allen Michaels was lying on his bed thinking. He was alone, had been for most of the day, and was now wondering what Eve was doing and if she were thinking of him.

Too bad, if she was. She had her chance and she blew it. Now it was just him. But it wasn't supposed to be just him, was it? No, it was supposed to be him and Grant.

Allen wondered what had happened to his son, and suddenly, for a moment, the enormity of the thing finally hit him. This was more than just a lost opportunity or a lost meal ticket. His son was gone, and he might never see him again.

Allen Michaels almost shed a tear.

"Patches knows. He doesn't know what, not yet, but he's on to something, so we are going to have to tread very softly."

Epps was seated in Hopper's car in the parking lot of the West Hollywood County Library.

"Hence all the cloak and dagger," Hopper said.

Epps nodded. The two men were in the midst of a hurried lunch. Epps was having turkey on a kaiser roll, and Hopper a corned beef on rye. Both men were drinking coffee.

"What's our next move?" Hopper asked.

"Right now the ambassadors are meeting in Mexico. In two days they fly back to Washington and then home from there."

"So tell me something I don't already know."

"My guess is the plane. He's going to try and get them all in one fell swoop."

"You think he'll use the kid?" Surreptitiously he eyed Epps as he bit into his sandwich.

Epps shot him a benign smile. "You mean, do I think the kid can do it?"

"Okay, you got me. Do you?"

Epps weighed the question for a moment. "I don't know. His father sure does. I don't think it matters. The kid can lead us to Rafael, and that's what's important."

"I gotta be square with you," Hopper said, taking a sip of coffee. "I'm taking a lot of time away from other assigned cases. We're going to need some results soon, before I start catching heat."

"You pulling out?"

"No. But we'd better get cracking."

Epps' eyes took on a hazy faraway look for a minute, as his thoughts wandered back to the time in Washington when Rafael had slipped right through his fingers. Not this time, buddy, not this time.

"What about you?" he finally said. "You think the kid can do it?"

"I hope not. If he can he'll have to be sanctioned."

"I know," Epps said flatly.

Hopper's beeper went off, and he picked up the car phone.

"What's up? . . . You don't say." The beginnings of a smile were brightening Hopper's face, and Epps could sense that something was about to happen. "Okay, thanks," Hopper said and hung up.

"Well?" Epps said.

"Son of a biscuit eater." Hopper chortled. "Some concerned citizen down in San Diego called the local police about a boy rooming with a dark haired man. They fit the description."

Every nerve in Epps' body stood on end. "How fast can we get there?"

"Half hour by helicopter."

"We'll need back up. I can't go to my department about this."

"Neither can I," Hopper admitted. "We'll just have to use the locals."

Epps was too happy to care one way or the other. The locals would do just fine. The bottom line would still be the same. Rafael was going to be his.

The car lurched into traffic.

Epps rushed off the elevator towards his office. He had just enough time to cover his trail before meeting Hopper.

"Hazel, I'll be gone for the rest of the day," he said, dashing by. "If anyone asks, tell them I'm out infiltrating The Coalition." Soft laughter drifted from his lips.

"Sir, Mr. Horvath would like to . . ."

"Screw Horvath!" Epps said. "And you can tell him I said that." Still laughing Epps charged into his office.

"Is that any way to speak of a superior?"

Peter Horvath was sitting behind Epp's desk. His legs were propped up, and his hands rested comfortably behind his head. Across from him sat Sanchez, kneading nervous fingers into his lap.

"Come on in," Horvath said with a smile. "Time to fess up."

Epps entered and closed the door.

CHAPTER 25

Eve Michaels lay on a strange bed in a strange room, staring at a strange ceiling and waiting for today to turn into tomorrow.

The room at the Hyatt was fine for her purpose. It was neat and dust free; even the toilet seat had been sanitized. It was just what she needed.

She lay back, attempting to contemplate her next move, yet her mind, like an auto stuck in reverse, sent her thoughts wheeling into the past. She wanted to consider what she should do next, but instead she considered her past.

There was Grant's fifth birthday party,

where Helen Buckley from around the corner brought her son Jimmy, and the boys became fast friends.

When Grant was eight Allen had broken down and took him to Dodger Stadium for the first time, and when he returned, Grant sang the praises of Dodger blue and swore when he grew up he'd be a baseball player.

On her fifth wedding anniversary, symbolized by wood, Allen had given her a hand carved heart of solid oak and said he looked forward to giving her gold.

Gone. All of it was gone, sealed neatly in a red ribboned box called memories and stored in the attic of her mind, to be pulled out at times like these.

Twelve years of my life, she thought, and now suddenly back at square one.

Go to jail, go directly to jail, do not pass go, do not collect 200 dollars.

But I'm not at square one, she thought. Penalized yes, but I still have something. I still have Grant.

But suppose Allen isn't lying? Suppose he really has nothing to do with it?

She pushed the unwelcome thought from her mind and yanked up another handful of memories.

Allen had to be behind it. That's all there was to it, because if he wasn't behind it . . .

She wondered what her husband was doing now, and a secret part of her hoped he was as miserable as she was. She considered the new life he had forced upon her and wondered if she had been too hasty. Perhaps she should have stayed, at least until Grant was back.

She checked her watch. Grant usually would be on his way home from school now. His afternoon snack would already be on the table, and she would be in the kichen starting supper. A roast, she thought. There was one in the back of the freezer, and they hadn't had roast in a long time. Diced carrots, mashed potatoes and gravy could round out the meal.

Eve sighed. They wouldn't be having roast together ever again. Twelve years of habits down the old tubes, she thought. Back at square one.

Her vacant eyes stared over at the night table, making sure the phone was on the hook. She picked it up, making sure it was working, but of course it was. She'd used it not too long ago when she called the police.

There was a hollowness to the dial tone she'd never noticed before, an emptiness that resounded in her ear, echoing the emptiness in her heart.

Eve placed the phone back in its cradle. Then lying back on the bed, she again guided her eyes to the ceiling and lost herself in her thoughts—wanting a future, living a past, staring herself into tomorrow.

Grant had been moping around the room

since breakfast, not saying much of anything yet obviously disturbed over the fact that his parents were not coming.

It was just past noon, the sun flinging afternoon shadows across the walls, and Rafael sensed it was time to move on.

He spoke gently to the boy. "We have to go," he said, snaring Grant's wandering attention.

"Where?" Grant asked. "Home?"

"No. Not yet."

"Then where?" the boy prodded, and Rafael felt a pang of annoyance.

"We can't stay here," he said.

"Then how will my father know where we are?"

"I will call him."

Grant focused on Rafael, his green eyes no longer trusting. "He *is* coming, isn't he?"

"Yes. Now get ready."

Brief uncertainty crossed Grant's face, and at that moment if he had plopped down and thrown a little boy's tantrum, Rafael would not have known what to do.

Instead, Grant grabbed the brown paper bag holding his one change of clothing and the few souvenirs he'd brought back from Sea World. "Ready," he said. Rafael adjusted his shades as they went out.

Outside the sun was high overhead, filtering through the trees and casting long arcs of lemon yellow over the cars that had gathered in the lot.

They were almost to the car when Rafael started to tingle. He stopped.

"What is it?" Grant asked, squinting up at him.

Rafael didn't answer. Quickly he gazed around the lot, wondering what it was that had set him off. Instinctively his right hand went into his pocket, caressing the reassuring weight of the knife.

Too many cars, Rafael thought. There were more cars than he'd previously seen in the lot at this time of day. A man was approaching, wearing business attire and mirrored shades. He, too, seemed wrong.

Rafael suddenly became a live nerve ending, every muscle in him meshing together, every sinew and tendon becoming one. His hand shot out and grasped the boy's shoulder.

"You all right?" Grant said.

"Fine."

He looked through the plate glass into the office and saw too many tourists. His eyes fell back on the man, who stopped about 50 feet from them. It was Patches.

"Howdy," he said, with a slight Texas drawl.

Rafael nodded.

"Mighty nice lookin' boy you got there. He yours?" A down home smile appeared on the man's face.

Suddenly there was movement in the lot. Three men, all in suits and mirrored shades, were running towards them.

"Get in the car," Rafael said softly. He jerked the boy forward, keeping his hand on his shoulder.

"Hold it!" Patches said. His hand was going inside his jacket, but too late. The stiletto was already out and poised at the boy's throat.

"Wait!" Rafael screamed. Movement in the lot screeched to a halt.

"Who are they?" Grant whispered.

"They want to hurt me," Rafael said, and Grant saw the venom drain into his eyes.

"Why?"

No answer.

"Are you going to hurt *me*?"

"No, but I want them to think I will." He looked briefly at the boy and donned his perfect smile. "We are still friends, yes?"

Grant nodded. The grip on his shoulder tightened.

Patches pointed his .38 caliber police special at Rafael. "Let the boy go and you won't be hurt," he said.

"You mean, let the boy go and you *will* hurt me."

"Hear that?" Grant whispered.

There was something, a sound filling the air, a distant hum getting stronger.

"Let us go," Rafael said to the man.

" 'Fraid I can't do that. Guess we have ourselves what you boys call a Mexican stand-off," Patches said. There was an air of smug self-confidence about him. He glanced towards the three agents standing several feet behind, all with weapons drawn. Then he looked to the sky.

A helicopter appeared just above the tree-tops. A man next to the pilot had a riot gun trained on the lot.

"Grant!" Rafael said. He shook the boy, and the chill of the blade danced goose bumps along Grant's throat. "Do something!"

Grant looked into his eyes and saw terror lurking. His vision began to cloud.

Epps was in the motel office, watching the whole thing through the plate glass window. Patches was standing there, gun drawn, like old MacArthur leading his troops to victory. And like MacArthur, Patches was going to get all the glory. The bastard!

Even Hopper was allowed to participate. As Patches had put it, "This will be a joint department effort." And you can bet he was taking credit for that, too.

Patches made sure he'd come along, but only as a spectator. The bastard was going to rub his face in it, and what could he do?

Then he saw it. Something was happening out there. Something more than the troops piling up against Rafael. Something strange. Birds! The trees were filling with them. All kinds and all colors were swarming in like the swallows to Capistrano.

Epps stared wide-eyed as the branches of the trees slumped from the weight of them. And still they came by the hundreds, the sound of their tiny wings drowning out that of the helicopter. Epps found himself wondering (and not for the first time) if all that malarkey about the boy was really on the level.

Rafael was staring steely-eyed at the man not 50 feet in front of him. There was something different about the man's face. The smugness was gone, and now the man appeared worried.

"What the fuck is happening here?" one of the men behind Patches said.

That's when Rafael noticed the sound of birds, billing and cooing and flapping their wings. He glanced quickly into the trees and saw they were overflowing with birds, all sitting and awaiting some invisible command.

"Let the boy go," Patches said half-heartedly.

Rafael glanced down at Grant. There was a little boy's lost look in his eyes.

It's true! Rafael thought. All of it is true!

"Let us go!" he said to the man. "For your own sake, let us go!"

Patches was laughing. His confidence had edged back, and now he was laughing at what Rafael had said.

So what if the trees are filled with birds.

Granted, that's an oddball sight. But standing before me is the greatest terrorist of all time—and he's mine.

He looked again to the sky and smiled as he saw the helicopter, circling the lot, keeping the entire party under observation.

"I'm going to get in my car," Rafael said, inching Grant along in front of him and eyeing his destination, ten feet away.

"We can't let you go," Patches told him. "No matter what the sacrifice, we can't let you go."

"I'll kill him!" Rafael threatened. He hefted Grant off the ground with his right hand, the stiletto dimpling the flesh of the boy's neck. "Now back off!"

Patches raised his gun and took a step forward.

Rafael started to speak, but something stopped him. A feeling charged the air around him with static electricity. Something's going to happen, he thought, something big.

"I'm warning you!" he cried.

"We'd like to take you alive," Patches said, "but if you don't release the boy . . ."

The trees emptied.

Angry birds, all with one intent, came diving for the men, clawing with their feet and poking with their bills.

The air turned gray with dust kicked up from the flapping wings, and the helicopter, lost in a thick cloud, went spinning into a tree. It whirled into the branches, then the blades caught solid and broke off, sending the carriage crashing to the ground. Upon impact the craft erupted in a spray of molten cinder and shrapnel.

A huge chunk of the fuselage dislodged and went hurtling through the air, turning a 90 degree angle before slamming into Patches' chest. He went tumbling to the ground like a knockdown doll at a county fair, arms and legs flailing wildly, because the birds kept coming. He was crying out and swinging madly, yet the birds kept at it.

By now Rafael had released Grant and was gaping at the boy, who stood in a trance, his tiny eyes dancing, his face all mystery and wonder.

Everyone in the lot was fighting off the birds, except them.

"Let's get in the car," Rafael said, but Grant didn't budge. Dazedly he stared on, orchestrating his work.

More men rushed into the lot and were instantly put upon by the birds. The fire that wracked the helicopter finally reached its gas tank, and the whole thing exploded with a tremendous flash of pure white.

When Rafael's eyes adjusted from the explosion he realized two of the men were on fire, rolling on the ground, their blood curdling cries covered by the thunder of flapping wings.

"Get in the car!" he commanded, but the

boy still didn't move. His lips twisted into a gnarled grin. "Grant!" Rafael screamed. "Get in the car!" He shoved the boy forward, and suddenly those eyes, filled with hate were on him.

Silently Epps watched the melee in the parking lot. It was bedlam out there, 20 agents, maybe more, all under siege. The three agents that had shared the office with him had rushed out when things started getting out of control. Two of them had been hit by fireballs and were now charred masses lying on the blacktop.

Patches was down, as was Hopper. But Epps hadn't moved, hadn't lifted a finger to anyone's aid.

"Heroes don't sit well with me."

His superior's words sang out in his mind.

Through the smoke and dust he saw Rafael pushing the boy into a green Oldsmobile. A minute later they were weaving their way out of the lot, and all Epps could think was that he still had a chance.

CHAPTER 26

Rafael drove, eyeing in the rearview mirror the mayhem and destruction receding down the street behind him. The distant scream of fire engines could be heard approaching. The street was alive with activity, people running out of their homes or shops to view the dark cloud now hanging over the New Oasis Motel.

It was a major event, and the sleepy city had been awakened by it. Everyone wanted to see, but not Rafael. He had seen enough.

He glanced over at the boy whose eyes, now devil red, seemed millions of miles away.

He can do it, Rafael thought. He can

really do it.

Any doubts he'd held about the boy had been erased—obliterated was more like it. The boy could do his part in the plan, but it was up to Rafael to give him the chance.

The proximity of the event showered him in euphoria. He felt a slight stirring in his groin but thought it away. He had to be careful. Many men had seen his face. He was most fortunate to have escaped. He could not afford to be careless—not now.

He got on the freeway and headed south, out of the city, towards Mexico. There were many ways of getting into the country especially after dark, but not in an Oldsmobile. They needed another car, a car that could travel over rough terrain and unlike anything seen in the parking lot of the New Oasis Motel.

They would need to get rid of the Oldsmobile soon, before an alert went out. He again looked over at the boy.

"Grant, are you okay?"

The boy looked in his direction, his gaze passing through him, like water through a sieve. He wondered if the boy was going to be all right.

Not only were his eyes a deep crimson, but his skin had turned a spongy white. His lips were chaffed and pale, and a dried chalklike substance had caked in the corners of his mouth. His eyes darted upward, and he started to speak, but a soft hollow sound is all that he made. Then his mouth snapped shut, his head lolled back, and again he stared vacantly out of the window.

"Grant," Rafael repeated.

Nothing.

"Grant!"

A low clicking sound drifted from his lips, and Rafael realized the boy was shivering. He pulled over.

"Grant!" he cried, but the boy continued staring dumbly out the window.

Rafael grabbed him, and it was like holding a corpse. The boy was all ice and stone. Quickly he ran to the trunk where he grabbed an old army blanket he'd seen earlier. He returned and wrapped the boy in it. Then he embraced him and rocked him slowly, hoping his own body warmth coupled with the movement would have some effect.

He's going into shock, he thought. Not now, Grant! Don't quit on me now!

After a while the shivering subsided. Rafael looked down at him. Color was returning to his cheeks, but the eyes looked awful, like something from a horror movie.

"Hang on, young friend," Rafael whispered.

He propped up Grant by the window and drove. Getting off the freeway, he found a nearby diner where he purchased a container of chicken soup.

Then he drove again, until he found an old backwoods road. He took the road for half a mile, then pulled over to the side and force fed the boy, the soup at first spilling from his lips, but little by little he got most of it down.

Hours past, and Rafael clung to the child. Shadows of evening were beginning to grow around them. The boy was calm now, eyes shut. Rafael again propped him by the window and waited.

Another hour dragged by, and now the tiny road was almost engulfed in shadow. Finally the boy began to stir. Rafael had been sitting silently behind the wheel, staring at him. When his eyes suddenly popped open Rafael burst into a wide grin.

"You had me worried," he said.

A wan smile touched the boy's lips.

"Feeling better?"

Grant nodded.

"Good. We will go somewhere where you can lie down and rest."

"I want my mommy."

It was practically an inaudible plea, but Rafael heard it all the same.

"Not today," he said, almost regretfully.

"Why?"

"We are in trouble now, Grant. You hurt a lot of men back there."

"They were going to hurt you."

Rafael sighed. "I know," he said. A

sudden sadness had engulfed him, like the evening shadows that swallowed them whole. Again he had to remind himself not to become attached to the boy.

"I want my mommy," Grant said again.

"Me, too," Rafael said softly. Then he started the car, put it in gear, and drove away.

Allen Michaels sat quietly in his highback recliner as Epps recounted the horror in the parking lot. Twice Epps thought he saw a smile forming on Allen's lips, but it vanished too quickly for him to be sure. He wondered what was going through Allen's mind.

"We lost two fine agents out there," Epps said.

Allen shook his head sadly, but Epps could tell there was no remorse in the man.

"Several men are in the hospital, including my superior and the man who was with me the other day."

"How come I didn't hear about any of this on the news?" Allen asked.

"Too sensitive. The news reported a helicopter crash and a fire. What did you expect?"

"The truth."

"That is the truth—at least part of it."

Epps was tired. His entire afternoon was spent supervising the mop up. Then he had to fly back and explain to Hopper's wife why her husband was in the hospital, while here he was, safe and sound.

Heroes don't sit well with me.

He knew from the start, from the moment he'd seen the birds gathering in the trees, that there was nothing he could do—nothing but wait. From the way Hopper's wife had looked at him, she didn't agree.

"Now, see here, Epps," Allen was saying. "My son should have been mentioned somewhere."

"Perhaps," said Epps, too exhausted to disagree.

"So now my son's with this Rafael character, and what are you doing to get him back?"

"That's why I'm here, Mr. Michaels. I thought maybe you would come back to San Diego with me. I'm sure we can find them again, but we need someone who can talk to him."

Horror flashed across Allen's face. "Why me?" he asked.

"You're his father."

"But it's *your* job," Allen said. Suddenly he brightened. "Have you thought about after my son is returned?"

"No," Epps lied.

"Well, think about it. The boy's a goddamned secret weapon. I'm sure someone would pay plenty for his talents."

"I'm sure," Epps said.

Allen jumped up. "Of course I'll go. I mean, he's my son and all . . . but you're going to have to make it worth my while."

"Mr. Michaels, there's a good chance we may not be able to get your son back alive."

Allen laughed. "Yeah, and there's an even better chance he might wipe out all of San Diego. Come on, Epps, no one's gonna hurt the kid. He already showed you he's not gonna let that happen. Besides, he's too valuable."

Wonder and curiosity appeared behind Epps' eyes. "Let me get this straight, Mr. Michaels. You want to be paid to assist us in getting your son back."

"I wouldn't put it like that," Allen said. He moved to the credenza where he picked up a bottle of Scotch and a glass and proceeded to pour himself a healthy drink. "Scotch?" he said, proferring the bottle.

"No thanks."

"You've got to see my side, Mr. Epps. We've already invested a lot in Grant, and we could use the money."

"Mrs. Michaels agrees with you?"

"Of course, she agrees," Allen said.

"Can I speak with her?"

Allen took a long draw on his drink had began pacing nervously. "We don't need her for this. All we need is you and me."

"Where is she, Mr. Michaels?"

"You play ball, and we can have this whole thing worked out." He finished his drink.

"Where is she?"

Allen stopped. "She's not here. Listen, Epps, I'm the head of this family, and if you're gonna deal with us you'll have to talk to me." His eyes lashed out at the man across from him.

"You've asked us to play ball, Mr. Michaels. I'm not saying we won't, but first I'll have to speak with your wife."

The two men eyed each other for a moment. Finally Allen fell back in his chair. He heaved a great sigh, and at that moment Epps noticed the man was sad and broken.

"When will she be back, Mr. Michaels?"

"I don't know," Allen said, sighing again. "Maybe never." He looked up at Epps, and there was a plea scrawled across his face. "She's got nothing to do with this. Really!"

Epps didn't reply. Instead he stared silently at the man seated across from him.

It was evening, and Eve had completed her major accomplishment of the day—she'd gotten through it. Next came tomorrow and more of the same.

All afternoon she'd waited for the phone to ring, and when it didn't, she called the police station, making sure they had her correct number. They did.

Now at 9:30 she was thinking of sleep, but wondering how she was going to get there.

The phone rang.

Eve dove across the bed and snatched up the receiver. "Yes," she said.

"This is the desk, Mrs. Michaels. There's a Mr. Epps here to see you."

"Is he with the police?"

"One moment, ma'am. I'll check." The voice went away for a time, and a myriad of questions fired through Eve's mind.

Epps? She'd never heard of the man. He was not one of the detectives who had interviewed her.

The voice came back. "No, ma'am, he says he isn't."

If he's not with the police, then how does he know I'm here?

"Shall I send him up, ma'am?" There was slight annoyance in the voice.

"Yes, yes, send him up."

Through the long minutes of waiting one thought stayed at the forefront of her mind. It must be about Grant. Then came the knock.

Eve yanked open the door. "Is this about Grant?" she blurted.

"Yes, it is."

"Thank God. Have you found him?"

"We have a good idea of where he is, but we're going to need your help to get him back."

Silent tears washed down Eve's face. "Come in," she said.

It was an old wooden shanty in a

dilapidated part of town. Babies could be heard crying at all hours, and loud conversations in Spanish filled the air, as did the pungent odor of alcohol, sweat and despair. But there was a bed and clean linen, so Rafael had settled on the rundown rooming house to spend the night.

"Get some rest," he told Grant, as he helped him into bed. "I'm going out for a little while."

"Where?" Grant said.

"It is not important. Just rest."

A few minutes later he was gone, leaving Grant alone to deal with the darkness, the fear and the memories.

He was scared. The dark thing had again tested its muscle, and again people had died.

I didn't do it, Grant thought. The dark thing did it. He could almost feel the thing resting safely in his mind, laughing at him.

When Rafael had snatched him up back there in the parking lot, Grant had been frightened, yes, but he hadn't wanted to hurt the men. This power of his was getting out of control. He wondered how long it would be before he hurt someone he liked.

It was with these thoughts that Grant was swallowed up by sleep and black dreams.

CHAPTER 27

Epps was ushered by a tall muscular agent into Patches' hospital room. The man lying before him looked frail and feeble, and not like the head of division T-1.

A long tube snaked from his nose, disappearing into a pouch hanging beside the bed. Another stretched from his right arm and emptied into a bottle filled with white liquid. His chest was heavily bandaged, where a chunk of the helicopter had slammed into him. He greeted Epps with a thin smile, and signaled to the agent to wait outside.

"How are you?" Epps said, breaking the ice.

"Better," replied Patches. His voice was a squeaking whisper, and Epps moved in closer.

"Sorry about all this," he said.

"You didn't tell me about the boy," Patches whispered.

"I know," Epps said. "I didn't think it was true. I mean . . . I'm sorry."

Patches nodded. "At least *you* came out of it all right." Epps remained silent. "You think I was wrong to go after Rafael, don't you?" Patches asked. He lay there wheezing softly, and it was hard for Epps not to feel sorry for him.

"Yes," Epps said flatly. By now he had moved closer and was sitting on the edge of the bed, straining to hear. "It's no secret we don't like each other, but I never wanted this."

"I know. I know," Patches sighed. "What you wanted was Rafael, and I was going to take that away from you." He attempted to raise his hand, and it fell with a soft thud back onto the bed. "I was wrong," he said. "Everybody needs a little glory. But that doesn't change anything. If I follow regulations I can have you thrown out of the service. Even put in jail."

"And if you don't follow regulations?"

A smile pressed across his lips. "I'm sure you're already arranging to go after him again, aren't you?"

"No," Epps replied.

"The truth, please. The least you can do is be honest with a dying man."

"You're too nasty to die."

Patches smiled again.

"Yes," Epps said, "I am going after him. Whatever he's planning to do will happen tomorrow. If I don't get him then, he may disappear forever."

"And you *will* get him," Patches said. "You're a good man."

Epps eyed him oddly.

"That sounds strange coming from me, doesn't it?"

"I have to admit, sir, it does."

"Well, I mean it," he said. "Listen, Epps, the reason I sent for you was to make a deal. Good man or not, you've broken regulation, and you're going to have to answer for it. I don't want to see you off the force. You deserve your glory, but I deserve mine, too.

"Now the way I see it, you want Rafael. You've been after him for years, and you want him so bad you can taste it. I can understand that, and to my way of thinking you can have Rafael."

He paused, and Epps wondered what the bastard was up to.

"What's in it for you, sir?" he asked.

"The boy. You get Rafael and all the credit, but bring me the boy. Then both of us can have our glory." A look of sheer self-satisfaction crossed his face, and Epps realized he was still the same lousy bastard he'd always been.

"What do you want with him?"

"No questions," Patches replied. "You're not in the position to ask questions. Now do we have a deal, or do I ask Richardson out there to take you into custody?"

"Looks like I don't have much of a choice."

Patches didn't answer.

Epps got up and stretched from the room.

"Epps! Don't fuck up. If you don't bring me the boy, you're through."

"Yes, sir," he said, and this time it was his turn to smile. "As long as I've got Rafael," he said, "you can have the moon."

Epps turned and exited.

The men were on fire . . .

He awoke mired in sweat, his eyes jumping open, wide and frightened. He sat up with a start and felt the clinging damp sheets as they tore away from him. On this morning Grant Michaels knew exactly where he was, and why he was there.

The men were on fire.

I didn't do it, God! He lifted his eyes skyward. It was the dark thing. The dark thing did it! The thought brought to mind the time he and Jimmy Buckley were playing in the living room and broke his mother's favorite vase. When asked who had done it both boys pointed at one another. This time, though, there was no one to point a finger at. The thing that had done the damage lived inside of him, and he'd have to stand the blame alone.

"Buenos dias, my young friend," came Rafael's cheerful voice from across the room. Grant looked over. Rafael was seated on a wooden chair, beside a grimy window, sipping coffee from a container. "It is a beautiful day outside, a beautiful day. We should be getting out. How do you feel this morning?"

"Fine."

"I must be honest with you. Your eyes are quite red. Do you perhaps suffer from an allergy?"

"No, I don't think so."

Grant rose and moved to the dressing table. He paused before the mirror, clouded from ages of smoke. Ruby eyes peered out at him from deep hollows in his face. Today the eyes were both the same, dark and lifeless. His fingers groped at the sockets and found them to be numb. The area around his eyes was dead, as dead as the eyes that peered out at him.

"I must be comin' down with something'," Grant said. "I want my dad."

His gaze moved to Rafael who stared back nonplused. "I promised you your father when I saw what you can do, and I saw it. Right?"

Grant nodded.

"I spoke with him this morning," Rafael went on. "He will rendezvous with us tonight."

"Why not now?"

"You are in trouble, Grant Michaels. He is trying to straighten things out."

"You're in trouble, too. Those men were after you."

Rafael sighed. "That is true."

"What did you do?" A new distrust was rising in Grant. "What do you want from me?"

Rafael looked solemnly at the boy. "I need your help. Those are bad men. They hurt my family, killed my mother, and now they want to kill me."

Grant looked into the eyes of the man sitting across from him and saw a softness not visible before. There was tenderness as well as pain in those eyes.

"Those men killed and then took what belonged to my people. Now they want more, and I want to stop them."

Grant nodded as if he understood, but it was all too confusing for him. "Is that why they were after you?"

"Yes. I know about their plan to ship weapons to kill more people—good people." He brought out a map. "This is a map of the sky. At 5:30 this evening a plane filled with weapons will pass over the desert not far from here. Originally I had wanted to stop the plane before it took off, but it's too late for that now. All I can do is keep it from landing." There was a knowing look in his eyes. "But I need your help." The eyes were suddenly hard and obsidian. "My parents did not deserve to die."

"No," Grant said. He could feel the odd prickling of intuition stabbing at his skull. He knew what was coming.

"I want you to stop the plane," Rafael said.

"No," Grant said, the words drifting from his lips like an arctic breeze. "Someone on that plane would die."

"They killed my parents!" Rafael charged.

"I won't do it!"

"You must!"

"No!" His vision was beginning to clog.

"Just look at the maps." Rafael opened a map and waved it before him. "Just have a look."

"I won't do it," Grant said softly, but already he was moving across the room. There was an undeniable excitement mounting within him. A side of him wanted nothing to do with what the man was asking, but a secret side, a dark side, wondered if he could.

It was just past noon when he got to the hotel. She was standing in front waiting for him when he pulled up. She was a plain woman, her hair pulled back in a neat, crisp bun and not a drop of makeup on her face. Still there was something there, and he wondered if he would think she was attractive when she was all fixed up.

"Hi," she said when she got in the car, then she fixed her gaze straight ahead, not waiting for a reply.

Epps pulled into traffic. So this was it. Sometime later today he would come face to face with Rafael, and no one was going to stand in the way.

"How long will it take to get there?" Eve asked.

"Three, maybe four hours."

There was a long period of silence, and he recalled the expression on her face the night before, when he told her what Grant had done. "But is he okay?" she had asked. "Yes," he had said and knew he wanted to take her with him.

At 12:30 they turned onto the 405 freeway and headed south.

"What will happen to Grant?" she asked.

"What do you mean?" Epps said, and he could feel the lie forming in the back of his mouth.

"They know about him now—and his power. When we get him back I suppose they'll want to take him somewhere and stick him full of needles. They'll want to know how it happens, won't they, Mr. Epps?"

"I suppose they will."

"And what do you want?"

"It's a job, ma'am."

She nodded and again fixed her eyes on the windshield. "It's my fault, you know. The whole thing is my fault."

There was nothing for him to say. He just drove. They sat in silence again until just after Culver City.

"Will they give him back to me?" she asked suddenly.

"He's your son, Mrs. Michaels. Of course they will." He glanced over at her and caught the tight smile forming on her lips.

"I love him," she said. "No matter what he's done or what he can do, I'll always love him."

She stared dreamly out the window, that silly little smile sitting on her lips, and he knew she was thinking about the boy.

"He must be a good kid," he said.

"He is. Do you have any children, Mr. Epps?"

"Nope. Haven't had time to think about getting married. I plan to, though . . . some-day."

"I bet you'll love them," she said.

He thought of Allen Michaels. "I hope so."

After a few minutes she settled back, that smile still playing on her lips, lost in her thoughts. He drove on, thinking of what a rotten world this really was, but knowing that stopping Rafael would make it a little more palatable.

There was a storm brewing.

Already the winds were kicking up. Grant tasted the swirling grit in the air as he and Rafael exited the rooming house and climbed into the four-wheel-drive vehicle Rafael had gotten for them. Grant didn't ask any questions. He climbed into the passenger seat of the jeep, buckled up and looked straight ahead.

He didn't want to talk about it. He had tried to explain to Rafael that he didn't think he could do it, but Rafael wasn't listening.

"There are men out there," Rafael had said, "bad men, who feed on poor people. These men would loan money to nations that can't even pay it back. But do you think they would loan money to a hard working family man?"

Rafael's eyes had been filled with venom. There was a tone to his voice that frightened Grant. "There are nations that owe billions of dollars, and still they can borrow money—but let a migrant farmhand ask?" His eyes flooded momentarily. "They killed my mother. We cannot let these men continue." His eyes hazed over. He was trapped in his memories and couldn't find his way out.

Grant couldn't—wouldn't do what he asked. Already people had been hurt. He couldn't take the chance of it happening again. He wanted to see his mother and father. Now more than anything, he wanted to be home. He thought of Jimmy Buckley and Bert Reynolds. It all seemed so long ago. He wished he could be back in the school yard and didn't care who was king. All he wanted was to be a boy again, just plain old Grant Michaels, a little kid who got his ass kicked at school. Now that he thought of it, that didn't sound bad at all.

"Well, my friend, are you ready?" Rafael asked. The perfect teeth were showing.

"Yes."

Grant had lied. While he was looking at the maps, he had devised a plan. He would tell Rafael that he would try, but he really wouldn't try. He would only pretend, and when Rafael saw that he couldn't do it, he would be unhappy. Grant would say he was sorry, and that would be the end of it. Then he could go home, and they would still be friends (if they really were friends, and Grant was beginning to more than wonder), and the dark thing would shrivel up, and everything would be all right.

The jeep pulled out. Already a thin patina of dust covered the windshield, and Rafael had to turn on the wipers so he could see. But the storm was getting angry, as tiny twisters of leaves and dust were tossed against the car and into the open carriage.

"It looks like we are in for a little blow,"

Rafael said. Grant hoped that the storm would be so bad he wouldn't be able to see the airplane. Then he wouldn't have to lie.

The winds began gusting up to 20 miles an hour, making travel over the gravel-covered road slow and laborious. Grant found himself touching the area around his eyes and noticed that the numbness was spreading to his cheeks and forehead.

What's happening to me?

He felt fine, but something was wrong. And as quickly as the thought had hit him came the answer, striking him suddenly like a bolt of lightning.

It was the dark thing!

There was no doubt about it. The dark thing was causing this. He didn't know why, but the dark thing was out to ruin him.

The Jeep wound along a narrow desert road, and the winds blew, yanking loose small bushes and sending them sprawling in their path. They continued on.

"We are in luck," Rafael said. "We should be able to cross in a few minutes. This storm will serve as a fine cover for us, young friend."

Rafael reached a hand over and raked it through Grant's hair, and Grant realized that his scalp, too, was getting numb.

Rafael drove on, his vision clouded with anger, his thoughts returning to the past . . .

Rafael began lacing his shoes carefully,

making sure the strings were good and tight. He would be running in the darkness and did not need a loose shoelace betraying him.

As he pulled tight the lace on his left shoe it snapped off in his hand. He eyed the frayed spot in the lace and then his shoes. Both laces were worn. The shoes were old, and while a recent gift from his father, they still needed a fresh piece of cardboard each day.

Tonight I will not wear shoes. Tonight I will be as silent as a cat.

He removed the shoes and flexed his toes, feeling a rush of excitement move through him, starting in his toes and coursing upward, until it sang sweetly in his brain. Tonight was special. Tonight he would get things right.

He grabbed an orange and wrapped his fingers around it in one final test. Slowly he continued the pressure until *woosh!* It burst open, pulp and juice oozing to the floor. Rafael smiled.

"Where are you going?" his father asked, as he headed towards the door.

"I need some air."

"Are you meeting Seraphina tonight?" he asked with a knowing smile. "Be careful," his father advised. "You are still too young to be a man."

Rafael nodded and headed out the door. I am a man, he thought, stealing away into the night.

Cautiously he approached the old wooden house. Through the darkness and the moonlight it looked down on him because he was a peasant, but after tonight it would look down on him no more.

The house was dark and foreboding, and though fear tugged at Rafael's shirttails, he didn't budge. The foreman and his family were asleep. He pressed on.

Quietly he mounted the porch stairs. Squeak!

He stopped, his heart racing in his ears. The porch complains, he thought, and again contemplated turning back but didn't. Images of his dead mother prodded him on.

He moved across the porch and tried the door. It opened easily, and he entered. For several minutes he held his ground, waiting for his eyes to adjust to the dark. Then slowly the surroundings became visible, and he also became aware of breathing. The foreman's eldest son lay sleeping on the sofa.

I must be careful not to wake him. He moved towards the rear. There were two bedroom doors, both shut. Rafael paused at the first. The sound of many young breaths could be heard from the foreman's daughters and his youngest son. Rafael moved on. He turned the knob of the second door.

There in the bed, illuminated by the

moonlight, lay the foreman and his wife. Panic rose in Rafael, as perspiration spilled from his forehead.

Rafael slipped silently across the room and stopped beside the bed. Now he could see the foreman more clearly. He had thrown back the covers and now lay exposed, breathing heavily, his ugly black mustache fluttering with every breath. A hatred bubbled up inside Rafael. He had dreamt of killing the man for so long.

He smiled. It was going to be easy, easier than he ever could have imagined. The man's throat was already visible to him. He reached down for the soft white flesh and found his wrist ensnared in a vise.

"So, my little friend, you not only wish to rob Santos, you wish to kill him, too."

The foreman had ensnared Rafael's wrist, and no amount of effort could free him.

"I am not a thief," Rafael cried. "You killed my mother!"

Now the foreman's son was in the room with a lamp shining in the boy's eyes.

"I have caught another thief," the foreman said. "Do you recognize him?"

"Don't *you*?" Rafael demanded.

The foreman scrutinized him slowly. "No," he said.

He doesn't even know me!

"Yes," the son said. "I recognize him."

"Good," the foreman said, and Rafael

could hear the satisfaction in the man's voice. "His family will not work in the groves again."

Soon after Rafael's father smuggled his children into the United States, and six months later he was dead . . .

A bitter tear fell from his eye. Rafael ignored the tear, letting it slip below the rim of his glasses and vanish against the dust and wind. After today there would be no more tears—and no more nightmares.

Presently the jeep crossed a dried and sand-filled river bed. When they reached the other side they stopped.

"Well, my friend, we are in Mexico," Rafael said above the cry of the storm. "Soon we will arrive at our destination. Thank you for your help. You are indeed my friend."

The storm was kicking up more now, the wind howling into the jeep. Grant looked over at Rafael. There was chaos in his eyes.

CHAPTER 28

"Where are we going?" Eve asked.

"I don't know," replied Epps. "I've looked over the aerial maps and figure the plane will be passing over this general area around five." He pointed to the map open on her lap.

"And you really think Grant..." She couldn't say what was lodged in the back of her throat. It was all too hideous and too hard to believe that her son had done what Epps had said. Then she thought back to the suitcase smoldering on the bedroom floor, and she knew it was all possible.

The winds whipped up as they headed into a storm. Epps switched on the radio.

The weather service was calling it a freak with winds of 30 to 40 miles per hour predicted. He looked at his watch. They were just outside of San Diego and it was a quarter of four. He pushed down on the accelerator.

They were on the desert. Giant sheets of white sand buffeted against the jeep as Rafael drove on. As the storm churned up waves of sand, turning the desert into an angry sea of white, Rafael's stubbornness became confusion.

He stopped and looked around. The truth was he didn't know where he was or where he was going. They could go no further.

No, something within him shrieked. I must avenge the deaths of my parents.

The greatest terrorist victory of all time did not seem scheduled for today. Once again came the realization that Rafael must disappear into the fabric of the earth itself—and wait. His time would come, but one thing was certain—it would not be today.

He looked to the boy. "We cannot go on."

"Maybe we should go back." There was hope in Grant's voice.

Rafael displayed a bitter smile. He couldn't go back. "Yes. In a while," he said. "When the storm has died down."

"I'm sorry about the plane."

"Yes," Rafael said absently. "Me, too."

Through the swirling haze Grant noticed his smile widening. "But you have been a good friend, Grant Michaels. The best."

"What should we do now?"

The smile vanished, and Rafael's eyes were sad pools of emptiness. "My friend, there is only one thing left to do."

CHAPTER 29

He was running.

He didn't know for how long or how far, but he ran into the storm. Angry winds slapped at his face as he ran. Sand and grit stung his eyes. Slow tears washed down his cheeks, and still he ran. Night shadows crept up around him, and a distant voice called, "Grant Michaels, where are you?" But he didn't answer; he just ran.

His breath heaved hot and raspy from a throat charred raw by the storm. He was nearly blinded by the whipping and and could only see a few feet ahead. He stopped, falling into a soft sand dune that invited him down for a long, long rest—maybe forever. His ragged breath sounded in his ears. The tears on his cheeks had caked to mud, and he was frightened.

"Grant Michaels."

The voice was nearer now.

"Where are you?"

Tiredly he dragged himself to his feet. He had to get away.

Rafael wasn't his friend. Rafael had lied. Rafael wanted to kill him.

Back at the jeep he had heard the soft click and stiffened almost instinctively. It sounded like . . . yes, it sounded like a knife, and something inside of him told him to run. Had he sat there a minute longer, surely he would now be dead. Instead, without warning, Grant jumped from the jeep. He saw the gleaming arc of the knife as it moved through the air, but Rafael was too late. He was running.

"Come back here!" Rafael screamed. But this wasn't the same Rafael, the one that was his friend. This was a monster.

"Grant Michaels, it is time to go back."

Grant ran. His legs were lead weights chained to anchors. His burning lungs felt as if they would burst. Yet slowly he edged away from the voice.

Minutes stretched into hours. This time Grant collapsed face first, knowing it was over. He could run no farther. He had run and run, but could not escape the call.

"Grant Michaels."

He was sobbing in long heaving gasps, wishing he'd never gone with the stranger. He wished he were at home, doing his homework or playing with the action figures he'd borrowed from Jimmy Buckley. He closed his eyes tight and wished real hard.

"Grant Michaels."

The voice was getting closer. He would not have his wish tonight.

The storm was beginning to subside, and he knew before long, the man would find him and kill him.

It was the dark thing's fault, and all because he went away. But maybe he and the dark thing were one and the same.

Grant began thinking real hard, as hard as he'd ever thought. He thought of storms, and locusts and bees and birds and airplanes falling to the ground.

Suddenly it dawned on him that maybe the dark thing was his secret desire, and maybe he could control it.

The winds were dying now. As the confusion in Grant's mind slowly faded away, the storm gradually subsided.

He sat up, looked around, and stared into Rafael's smiling face.

"So there you are."

Grant stood, turned to run, but knew it was hopeless. The powerful Rafael easily corralled him. He had no strength to fight.

"Do not fear, Grant Michaels. We are two

of a kind." Rafael clutched him tightly, as he had when Grant had the chill. "It is difficult being different. That is why we are friends."

"Are we?" Grant asked.

"Of course," Rafael said. "We will always be friends."

"Then you're not going to hurt me."

"No."

Slowly Grant relaxed.

It was as if someone had slowly slipped an iceberg into his back, and now he could feel it melting, dripping slowly away. But Grant knew that the warmth that oozed against his back was his own blood. He also knew that the man had needed for him to relax, and he had given in easily.

It didn't hurt, not really. He felt tired, so tired and so at peace. And he could actually feel his own life slowly mixing with the earth.

Rafael lay him down and looked sadly into his eyes. The last thing Grant remembered was that the smile wasn't perfect at all—nothing ever is. He felt the weight of the man pressing against him. And then he was no more.

Allen Michaels had been on the phone all morning, and something was wrong.

He'd just finished calling the Hyatt on Wilshire and was told that his wife had never stayed there. When he phoned the police they told him they never heard of him, and that there was no report filed on his missing son. When he called the hospital, of course they'd never heard of Grant Michaels. The FBI had never heard of Hopper, and he was sure if he could reach The Boys they would tell him that the agent named Epps did not exist.

His wife and son were gone, wiped from the face of the earth. And with them went his dreams.

"I'm sorry," Epps said. "I was too late."

He was seated in a stuffy meeting room, before a special conduct committee. A thin and feeble Peter Horvath led the proceedings.

"What became of Rafael?"

Three weeks prior to the hearing his nightmare had begun. When he returned from Mexico he was taken into custody. After several days of living in a cell, Patches came. The padding under his shirt told Epps his chest was still bandaged. He walked slowly.

"Do I get my glory?" he asked.

"No," Epps said, "I'm sorry."

And Patches went away.

"Mr. Epps, what became of Rafael?" Horvath's voice jarred Epps back to the present.

"I don't know. When I reached the body of the boy he was already gone." He eyed

Patches sorrowfully. "The body was badly mutilated. He is a sick man." At that moment revenge crossed his mind.

"You were denied your glory, too," Patches said.

"Yes."

O'Toole spoke up. "The members of The Coalition are all in custody now, but Rafael is gone, and we lost the boy. He was the real prize. Your own foolish pride kept you from seeing that."

"But how was I to know? It was his father's word alone."

"You should have asked for orders. You should not have acted on your own."

Patches spoke. "Epps, your actions have cost us a valuable catch. I'm afraid I must recommend that you be immediately removed from service, with no severence pay and loss of pension."

Epps stared stonily into his eyes. There would be no glory. "I'm sorry you see it that way, sir."

Ten minutes later the committee voted. The decision was unanimous.

EPILOGUE

He opened his eyes and saw her as he'd seen her before, sitting in a chair across from him, tiny wrinkles crisscrossing her brow. A steady smile was blossoming on her face; like a sliver of early morning sun, it brightened the room. And through her smile Grant saw that she was more than happy; she was grateful.

"Welcome back," she said softly. Tears were piling up on her cheeks.

Grant opened his mouth to speak, but nothing came. Then he noticed the tube snaking through his nose and down his throat. There were tubes and bandages everywhere.

"Don't, don't!" she said.

"Okay," he tried to say, but again he came up empty. And so he just stared at her, and she at him, until he drifted off to sleep.

A day, an hour or an eternity later his eyes opened again. This time the tubes were gone, as were most of the bandages, but his mother was still there.

"Hi," she said.

He tried to speak, but still nothing came. She placed a glass to his lips and several drops of water passed through the desert that was his throat.

"Thanks," he said, and this time he heard himself, but just barely. "Where am I?"

"Hospital," she said. "You were lucky. A man named Epps saved your life."

Again he saw the tears cascading down her cheeks.

"Thought I was dead."

"Close," she said.

"Rafael?"

She didn't answer, but her silence told the story, and Grant remembered the dead weight of the man falling on top of him.

"Well, Mrs. McCarthy, I see you've revived our little patient."

A green clad doctor had entered the room. He picked up Grant's chart from the foot of the bed.

"Well, Jason, how are you?" he asked.

Grant looked to his mother. There was caution in her eyes. "Fine," he rasped.

"Good. Good. Well, let's not overdo it."

A few minutes later the doctor was gone.

"Your name is Jason now—Jason Mc-Carthy—and we live here in Iowa City. We've always lived here." His face twisted into a question mark. "It's to protect us."

"Mr. Epps again?"

She nodded. "It's a long story. I'll explain later. Right now you should rest."

"What about Daddy?"

Her eyes clouded with memory, and in them Grant saw their pasts drifting away. "We'll talk about that later, too." She smiled again. "Sleep."

"Okay," Grant said. He was feeling tired anyway.

He lay still, slowly allowing his heavy lids to flutter shut, and he felt himself drifting steadily away. But this time he was just going to sleep.

HORROR TO MAKE YOUR BLOOD RUN COLD—
IN THE TERRIFYING LEISURE TRADITION.

STRANDS by James Kisner. He had raped and killed a young girl. They didn't need a jury to tell them that—just as they didn't need a judge to sentence him to death. After they hanged him, each of the ten executioners took a piece of the rope to remind them that justice had been done. Ten strands of rope were the only connection between the vigilantes and their victims—a connection that would come back to terrorize their souls.

____2614-7 $3.95US/$4.95CAN

THE FEEDING by Leigh Clark. Something evil inhabited the gloomy caverns beneath the Brenner's house, something incredibly ancient and insatiably hungry. It lusted for the bodies of their children; it thirsted for their blood; it craved their flesh. It would not be denied.

____2604-X $3.95US/$4.95CAN

DEAD SEASON by J. Bradley Owen. The people in the quiet town of Springriver always sensed the evil lurking under the depths of the deserted Haskell House, but their silent suspicions became screams of terror when young Tommy claimed the house for his own. His madness was the lifeblood that woke the house, his violence the catalyst that drove it to kill.

____2592-2 $3.95US/$4.95CAN

LEISURE BOOKS
ATTN: Customer Service Dept.
276 5th Avenue, New York, NY 10001

Please send me the book(s) checked above. I have enclosed $_____
Add $1.25 for shipping and handling for the first book; $ .30 for each book thereafter. No cash, stamps, or C.O.D.s. All orders shipped within 6 weeks. Canadian orders please add $1.00 extra postage.

Name _____

Address _____

City_____State_____Zip_____

Canadian orders must be paid in U.S. dollars payable through a New York banking facility.   ☐ Please send a free catalogue.

PETRIFYING TALES OF TERROR
BY DANA REED

DEMON WITHIN. It stalked the hallways of the old apartment building in search of human flesh—the food that fortified it and kept it strong. No one was willing to accept its existence, save for one innocent young woman.

____2579-5 $3.95US/$4.95CAN

SISTER SATAN. Lonely Lauren had three younger brothers, but desperately yearned for a sister. She called upon supernatural forces for help, and they delivered Rachel—a demon from the pits of Hell, an evil being who unleashed a firestorm of havoc and destruction.

____2472-1 $3.95US/$4.95CAN

DEATHBRINGER. East Cove was a charming little hamlet until the brutal killings began. One being had imposed his will on the town's living and undead alike—but who?

____2562-0 $3.95US/$4.95CAN

THE GATEKEEPER. There was something wrong with the dark, foreboding house that Erica Walsh and her kids moved into. Something unseen was watching her with vacant eyes, arousing her with probing hands. It lay waiting for Erica, calling her name in the night.

____2500-0 $3.95US/$4.95CAN

LEISURE BOOKS
ATTN: Customer Service Dept.
276 5th Avenue, New York, NY 10001

Please send me the book(s) checked above. I have enclosed $_____
Add $1.25 for shipping and handling for the first book; $ .30 for each book thereafter. No cash, stamps, or C.O.D.s. All orders shipped within 6 weeks. Canadian orders please add $1.00 extra postage.

Name _____

Address _____

City_____State_____Zip_____

Canadian orders must be paid in U.S. dollars payable through a New York banking facility.   ☐ Please send a free catalogue.

OBELISK
AN ANCIENT TERROR TO CHILL THE MARROW OF YOUR BONES
by Ehren M. Ehly

Trapped in the hot, fetid darkness of an ancient Egyptian tomb, Steve Harrison was suddenly assaulted by bizarre and horrific images of a past he had never known. Even when he returned to New York, he found himself driven by strange cravings and erotic desires he couldn't explain; his girl friend suddenly feared for her life and that of her unborn child. Steve Harrison only had one chance to restore his deteriorating body and cleanse his diseased mind—a final confrontation with incredible forces of evil, this time in Central Park, this time in the shadow of the forbidding. . .

OBELISK

____2612-0 $3.95US/$4.95CAN

LEISURE BOOKS
ATTN: Customer Service Dept.
276 5th Avenue, New York, NY 10001

Please send me the book(s) checked above. I have enclosed $_____
Add $1.25 for shipping and handling for the first book; $ .30 for each book thereafter. No cash, stamps, or C.O.D.s. All orders shipped within 6 weeks. Canadian orders please add $1.00 extra postage.

Name _____

Address _____

City_____State_____Zip_____

Canadian orders must be paid in U.S. dollars payable through a New York banking facility.   ☐ Please send a free catalogue.

BONE-CHILLING HORROR
FROM EDMUND PLANTE

SEED OF EVIL. A savage union with a strange man left Patty, a divorced mother of two, with a child she couldn't bring herself to abort—or love. He looked like a normal boy, but when "accidents" began to happen—murderous, violent occurrences—Patty knew that this child was nothing less than the spawn of the devil.

_____2581-7 $3.95US/$4.95CAN

TRANSFORMATION. Sally Martin was changing. Her body had become pale and bloated, her lustrous hair had fallen out, her jaundiced eyes were no longer able to bear sunlight. Meanwhile, ripening inside her, a hideous pulsing organism was waiting to burst upon an unsuspecting world, infecting all it touched.

_____2490-X $3.95US/$4.95CAN

LEISURE BOOKS
ATTN: Customer Service Dept.
276 5th Avenue, New York, NY 10001

Please send me the book(s) checked above. I have enclosed $_____
Add $1.25 for shipping and handling for the first book; $ .30 for each book thereafter. No cash, stamps, or C.O.D.s. All orders shipped within 6 weeks. Canadian orders please add $1.00 extra postage.

Name _____

Address _____

City_____State_____Zip_____

Canadian orders must be paid in U.S. dollars payable through a New York banking facility.   ☐ Please send a free catalogue.

HOWLING HORROR,
TIMELESS TERROR . . .

CROSSBEARERS by Marc Brellen. One by one, the venomous scum that plagued the streets of New York were dying . . . one by one, they were brutalized, poisoned, incinerated. Innocent and guilty alike had been slaughtered in the name of righteousness . . . in the name of God, their executioners had to be stopped.

____2572-8 $3.95US/$4.95CAN

WHITE SPIDER by Joyce Wolf. Once, it had been a man. Now the evil had taken a loathsome new form, with an overwhelming desire for sweet young flesh. Its pursuit was silent, its bite was deadly, its embrace was forever.

____2513-2 $3.95US/$4.95CAN

THE FORCE by J. Edward Ames. Six-year-old Matt had known the pure stark terror of an ancient dream. The Force had twisted his young mind with sickening nightmare images. Yet he was the key to a shattering evil that would make the blazing pits of hell seem like paradise.

____2480-2 $3.95US/$4.95CAN

LEISURE BOOKS
ATTN: Customer Service Dept.
276 5th Avenue, New York, NY 10001

Please send me the book(s) checked above. I have enclosed $_____
Add $1.25 for shipping and handling for the first book; $ .30 for each book thereafter. No cash, stamps, or C.O.D.s. All orders shipped within 6 weeks. Canadian orders please add $1.00 extra postage.

Name _____

Address _____

City_____State_____Zip_____

Canadian orders must be paid in U.S. dollars payable through a New York banking facility.   ☐ Please send a free catalogue